Robert G. Barrett was raised in Bondi where he worked mainly as a butcher. After thirty years he moved to Terrigal on the Central Coast of New South Wales. Robert has appeared in a number of films and TV commercials but prefers to concentrate on a career as a writer. He is the author of *You Wouldn't Be Dead For Quids, The Real Thing, The Boys From Binjiwunyawunya, The Godson, Between the Devlin and the Deep Blue Seas, Davo's Little Something, White Shoes, White Lines and Blackie, And De Fun Don't Done, Mele Kalikimaka Mr Walker, The Day of the Gecko, Rider on the Storm, Guns 'N' Rosé* and *So What Do You Reckon?*

MUD CRAB BOOGIE

BOOGIE

ROBERT G. BARRETT

HarperCollins*Publishers*

HarperCollins*Publishers*

First published in Australia in 1998
Reprinted in 1998
by HarperCollins*Publishers* Pty Limited
ACN 009 913 517
A member of the HarperCollins*Publishers* (Australia) Pty Limited Group
http://www.harpercollins.com.au

HarperCollins*Publishers*
25 Ryde Road, Pymble, Sydney, NSW 2073, Australia
31 View Road, Glenfield, Auckland 10, New Zealand
77-85 Fulham Palace Road, London W6 8JB, United Kingdom
Hazelton Lanes, 55 Avenue Road, Suite 2900, Toronto, Ontario M5R 3L2
and 1995 Markham Road, Scarborough, Ontario M1B 5M8, Canada
10 East 53rd Street, New York NY 10032, USA

National Library of Australia Cataloguing-in-Publication data:

Barrett, Robert G.
Mud crab boogie.
ISBN 0 7322 5843 X.
I. Title.
A823.3

Cover Illustration by Brad Quinn
Typeset in 10/13 Sabon by Midland Typesetters, Maryborough
Printed in Australia by Griffin Press Pty Ltd on 50gsm Ensobulky

9 8 7 6 5 4 3 2   98 99 00 01

A MESSAGE FROM THE AUTHOR

Everybody wants to know why I'm so late with the new Les Norton. They generally hit the bookshops around October. Well, I like to write them in winter, and I have to say the winter of 1997 was a pretty ordinary one for yours truly. I had an operation on my right shoulder for torn tendons and with my arm immobilised I couldn't type. I was in that much pain and misery, I thought, being over fifty, I may as well get the secret men's business fixed while I'm at it and be completely miserable. This went sensational. Except I thought I was twenty-one again, overdid it, haemorrhaged and nearly went back to the big typewriter in the sky. But, thanks to the staff at Gosford hospital and the fantastic nurses at St Vincents, I bounced back. Only, as well as a stuffed shoulder, I wasn't allowed to sit down and type even if I wanted to. So I sat around for three months eating takeaway food, looking like Elvis before he tossed tails. It was horrible. In the meantime, I brought out the book of my old PEOPLE columns, *So What Do You Reckon?*, to try and keep the team happy. And I'm glad I did because everybody liked it and it put a rocket up a few dates. You'll notice I have also changed publishers. I can't say much at this time except shizen happens. But it's definitely turned out for the best because the people at HarperCollins couldn't be kinder and I think I'll be there for a long time. Anyway, here it is. *Mud Crab Boogie*. It was a hard one to write but I think it's right up there with *The Godson* as one of the best ones I've done. I'm sure you'll like it and I did my best. Or in my case, my worst. To all the people who came along to the book signings and that for *So What Do You Reckon?* a big thanks. Even if my right hand was almost wrecked from shaking everybody else's and signing books,

T-shirts, posters and everything else put in front of me. You were great and I'd do it again anytime. I also have to offer a big apology to all those people kind enough to write to me. There's a crate of fabulous letters in my office that have to be answered and they will be. It just takes a lot of time though and now and again some letters go astray. But you should all get a reply eventually and my sincere thanks again to everyone kind enough to write. Some of those letters are a hoot.

The possum lady also says thanks for buying the T-shirts and caps. She got the surgical boot and now she goes dancing on Saturday nights. She now hopes to get the calcium deposits burnt off her knees from when she used to scrub floors so she can start twisting again. She also said there are 3 new T-shirts available at Team Norton – *Mud Crab Boogie*, *Between the Devlin and the Deep Blue Seas* and *The Godson*. The other T-shirts available include: *Rider on the Storm, Guns 'N' Rosé, White Shoes, White Lines and Blackie, Davo's Little Something, Mele Kalikimaka*

Mr Walker, Boys From Binjiwunyawunya, The Day of the Gecko and *You Wouldn't Be Dead For Quids.* Team Norton caps are also available in green or black at the usual address: Psycho Possum Productions, P.O. Box 3348, Tamarama N.S.W. 2026 (T-shirts $32.00, sizes available M, L, XL, caps $28.00, postage included). As for me? I'm off to attack the next Les Norton adventure where I think Les might head up to far north Queensland.

Visit Bob's official web site
and the home of Team Norton at:
http://www.robertgbarrett.com.au

ACKNOWLEDGMENTS

The author would like to thank the following people for their help in the writing of this book.

Ian Saxon. Care of Lithgow Correctional Centre NSW.

Bain Stewart. My big Koori minder and driver for getting me to Wagga Wagga safe and sound.

Wayne Flood. My equally as big Maori minder and driver for doing the same thing and more.

The staff and management at Romano's Hotel in Wagga Wagga and all the nice people I met in that beautiful town on the Murrumbidgee River.

The staff at Homebush Aquatic Centre Sydney.

This book is dedicated to Pauline Hanson. Because I love stirrers. Especially red-headed Queenslanders.

The author is donating a percentage from the royalties of this book to Debbie Breen and Greg Mulder at the Wombat Rescue and Research Project, 5 Palm Valley Road, Tumbi Umbi NSW 2261. Any other donations would be gratefully accepted.

To Les everything seemed to be somehow happening too fast. Time, events, places, people. Everything. Like he was locked into some weird satellite of life zooming round the world. Close your eyes, sit back for a few minutes and you woke up in Florida, Jamaica, Hawaii, Melbourne, Terrigal. Go to new places, meet new people; then either watch the people get killed or the places get blown up. Most of it thanks to boss, friend and mentor Price Galese.

Les had again escaped a life-threatening situation by the skin of his teeth, this time on the Central Coast. George and Eddie had gone back to the house at Terrigal where they picked up Jimmy's belongings. Then, after leaving the old motorbike somewhere for the rightful owner to collect and squaring things off with the prison authorities, they'd laid poor Jimmy Rosewater to rest. Les didn't go to the funeral. Apart from George and Eddie, the only ones there were a young couple from Empire Bay and the Shamash hoping there might have been a wake. Bad luck. George was a bit down for a few days then, like all the other incidents and events that revolved around the Kelly Club, it was more or less forgotten and life went on as usual. The only thing unusual at the

1

moment was that the club had closed and Les, along with everyone else, had a week off.

Price had been forced to make renovations because of the punters smoking their heads off upstairs. It was punishing. Some nights you could barely see your hand in front of your face and you'd think somebody had lobbed a tear gas grenade through the window. Billy Dunne swore he saw a rat in the kitchen with its head tilted back dropping Murine in its eyes. Not that the smoke worried Price. The punters could smoke ten cigarettes at a time if they wanted to – pipes, cigars, old army blankets, anything – just as long as they kept gambling and he got his whack. But with the new health regulations and insurance exemptions, if some employee went off with emphysema or asbestosis Price would have to wear it. So he decided to close the club for a week, put in new blowers, carpets and air-conditioning, and take a holiday. Which suited Norton admirably. He wanted to get in a few early nights, do some work round the house and keep an eye on Warren. AKA Croden the Fugitive. Time and events may have been slipping past Norton, but he was convinced he'd retained most of his sanity. Warren definitely appeared to be losing increasing amounts of his.

Warren's latest squeeze or craze was Debbie, a homely blonde hairdresser who owned a trendy salon at Coogee, drove a purple, Ford Mustang convertible and was a full-on trekkie. Norton was a bit of a Star Trek fan and liked to watch the New Generation when he got the chance and joke about it. But Warren's girl was the triple-A rated, industrial strength version. Though her real name was Debbie, she'd convinced Warren she was Zanna, an Eymorg from Sigma Draconis VI. A class M planet where the men live underground and the technologically advanced women live on top. Debbie, or Zanna, had her own third season, Star Trek duty uniform, communicator pin, phaser and tricorder. She even got Warren fitted for a first season, duty uniform and had managed to convince him that he was secretly Croden, a humanoid fugitive from Rakhar in the Gamma Quadrant. Though Les was more of a mind that with all the home-grown pot Warren had been smoking lately and all the Vodka he'd been tipping down his throat, it wouldn't have been hard to convince Warren he was John the Baptist back from the desert. At one time Debbie ran her tricorder over Norton, gave him an anapestic-tetrameter reading and tried to tell him he was secretly Kahless the Unforgettable, a great warrior who united the Klingon Empire fifteen hundred years ago. Les shook his head and tactfully told her that because of the odd hours he worked and his comings and goings he was just a plain, garden variety ELF. Extra-dimensional life form.

The reason Norton went along with all this craziness was because even if Debbie did have a few rungs missing off her ladder, she had a cheeky sense of humour and she used to cut Norton's hair for him at home, and for an Eyborg Zanna was a pretty good barber. Also she could cook. Baked dinners, casseroles, fish mornay; give Zanna a bit of butter, flour and cocoa and she could whip up a mean Tavokian pound cake in a nanosecond. Plus she was kind enough to give the boys her old answering service from the hairdressing salon and install it for them.

Thank you for ringing Earth Colony seven. Our hailing frequencies are shut down at the moment as we are performing routine dilithium vector calibrations. If you care to leave a message it will be locked into our isolinear adaptive interface link and our interconnecting sensor subsystem will reconnect with you as soon as possible.

It was Monday night, star date whatever, half way through Autumn at Planet Norton or Earth Colony Seven and the three of them were sitting in the lounge waiting for a sports show to start on TV. Les was sitting back in a pair of shorts and a T-shirt sipping a Eumundi Lager, a sports magazine open on his lap. Warren and Debbie were on the lounge dressed much the same, pulling cones from a bong on the coffee table while they tore into about a gallon of vodka and Ruby's Red grapefruit juice. Working most nights and preferring to relax and listen to a good CD, Les didn't get to watch a great deal of television. But they had the giant screen with the sound pumping out of the speakers on the stereo, and when he did he liked to kick right back and get into it. Only this time Les couldn't quite relax. He just stared at the magazine Warren had handed him earlier and tried to remember something Warren had been telling him. It seemed that as well as time and just about everything else going over Norton's head, the potential for a nice little earner had too. He stared at the magazine on his lap, shook his head for the umpteenth time then stared at Warren who was just about to pull another cone.

'What are we watching again, Woz?'

Debbie answered for him. 'The semi-final between the Sydney Sea Snakes and the Gilgandra Gillmen.'

'Yeah. But the semi-final of what?'

'Extreme Polo.' Warren pointed to the magazine in Norton's lap. 'It's all in there and that's the bloke behind it. Tonight's winner plays the Murrumbidgee Mud Crabs in the grand final next Sunday night. I've been watching it on cable at Debbie's and telling you about it for months. But like everything else, it's all gone straight over your big boofhead.'

'Christ! You're not wrong.'

'We might be just a couple of spaced-out trekkies,' chimed in Debbie. 'But we're light years in front of you, Les. Your molecular phase inverter's blocked up. You better get into warp drive boy.'

'But I know this bloke, Woz.'

'Nizegy Nev. Of course you do. He gave you your one big claim to fame.'

'I don't believe it.'

Norton continued to stare at the magazine spread open on his lap. There was a four page article on water polo and it looked like a page had been torn out. Standing in front of one team was a smiling man about forty, with lidded eyes, a pointy chin and neat, sandy hair going a bit thin on top. His standout feature though was his smile. It was one of those warm, genuine ones that seemed to radiate from his eyes and light up everything around him. He was wearing a blue suit and standing in front of a water polo team. But instead of Speedos the men around him were wearing full-length, black lycra body suits with red, blue and dark green scales all over them.

Their faces were partially hidden by the thick, black rubber caps on their heads with a number on top, snakes eyes on the sides and venomous, yellow fangs in front. They were all holding webbs and jet fins, called themselves the Sydney Sea Snakes and as well as looking lean, mean and menacing were equal favourites to win the coming grand final.

'Extreme Polo: The Wildest Game On Water', was the heading and spread amongst the article were action photos of players surging through a swimming pool throwing around something that looked like a chunky, white, gridiron ball. Each team wore the same wild-looking, multi-coloured, lycra outfit that matched their name. The Murrurundi Manta Rays, the West Wyalong Water Rats, the Tumbarumba Tiger Sharks. The full colour, action photos of the players in these outfits were truly spectacular. They were flipping in and out of the water like performing dolphins, crashing and tackling into each other, sending waves and great sprays of water splashing everywhere. Where normally you might happen to see a photo of a water polo player kicking out of the water up to his waist to take a shot at goal, the extreme version had them out up to their ankles or slithering up another player's back, spinning the ball through the air like an American quarterback. 'See the big men fly' might have been the slogan for Australian Rules. For Extreme Polo it was 'See men walk on water'. The game had developed a huge cult following on cable and regional TV. Now it was going national and Les had to admit it looked pretty good on paper. But it wasn't the game so much that was bugging Norton. It was the man in the blue suit. Neville

Nixon. He was a rock 'n' roll promoter from around the Eastern suburbs and one of those unobtrusive, low-key people who were always helping others out or doing them favours. A real nice guy. Which was how he got the nickname Nice guy Neville. Or just plain Nizegy. Oddly enough, Nizegy was always convinced he owed Les a big favour, while as far as Les was concerned it was more the other way around. But Norton being Norton he let Nizegy think whatever he wanted and even used to play on it a little.

Les had first met Neville Nixon outside the Bronte R.S.L. Club where he was promoting some black, American blues singer. It was a miserable, cold, Wednesday night in the middle of winter and Les had gone to Bronte to take a girl out for dinner who he'd given his phone number to when he was drunk and had got mixed up with someone else. He'd been crook all day from something he'd eaten earlier, didn't feel like going out at all let alone having another meal; and when he got there, Hebe was a complete hump and uglier than a hat full of arseholes. They were driving up McPherson Street when Hebe told Les to pull up, as she wanted to get a packet of cigarettes. Les parked up near the R.S.L. and Hebe walked over to a shop across the road, taking her time to stop for a chat with the owner. While Les was waiting patiently in the car and wishing to Christ he was somewhere else, he noticed a man walk past in a stylish, black leather jacket taking a joint from the back pocket of his jeans. Although there weren't many cars or people around he didn't notice Les and he didn't notice three stocky men, one taller than the others, in jeans, jackets and Doc Martens walking towards him; through Norton's windscreen they looked like English soccer hooligans. The bloke bumped them, then stepped back, smiled and apologised and got shoved around by one for his trouble. Another one grabbed him by the collar of his leather jacket and the third hood came round with his fist back to king hit him in the back of the head while he wasn't looking. Les jammed his fist onto the car horn and gave it a blast. The tall hood dropped his fist and the one next to him swore something then kicked Norton's car. So Les decided to get out. When he walked to the front of his car he couldn't believe it: they were pommies. Possibly off a ship or just washed up around Bondi with all the rest of the smelly Eurotrash.

One came charging towards him. 'Oi! This is got nuffin' to fuckin' do wiv you, cunt. So keep art of it.'

'Yeah, sure mate,' replied Les.

When he got within range Les dipped, threw a merciless left hook, and the pom walked straight into it, lifting him off his feet and smashing out most of his front teeth. He crashed back between his two mates and hit the footpath out cold, his eyes still wide open in pure shock. Then he began shaking – like he was throwing a fit or trying to swallow his tongue – as blood started pouring out of his mouth. While his mates were watching Les slammed another left hook into the face of the hood on his right, mashing his nose across his cheekbones; he howled with pain, brought his hands up to his face and half-turned away, so Les dropped with him with a short right to the kidneys. As he fell to his knees, Les went into a crouch and came round to find the tall hood had shaped up to try and have some sort of a go. Les charged up underneath him and slammed his head into the hood's stomach; he then grabbed him behind the knees, straightened up, and shoot-slammed him down onto the footpath. Unfortunately the poor fellow either didn't have the time or the nous to break his fall and his head split open like a rockmelon sending blood oozing out over the cold, hard concrete.

While he was engaged in all the fisticuffs, Les didn't hear a woman screaming in the background, or notice the bloke in the leather jacket standing there with a sort of bemused smile on his face still holding the joint in one hand and a lighter in the other. All Les noticed was that two of the hoods were gone but the one in the middle holding his nose didn't quite look sick enough. So Norton stepped over and sank the toe of his R.M. Williams into his mouth, kicking out nearly all his front teeth.

'You animal! You kicked him! You animal!' It was Hebe still screaming her head off at all the blood and prone bodies. 'Take me home. I wouldn't go out with you. I never want to see you again. You're an animal.'

Norton looked at her for a moment then ran the back of his hand over his face. 'Grrrgghh!'

'Oh God! Take me home.' Sobbing and screaming Hebe got in the ute and tried to bury her head between her knees.

Norton turned to the bloke. 'You're all right, aren't you?'

'Yeah sure. Hey thanks mate.'

'That's okay. Don't worry about it.'

The bloke looked over Les at Hebe still shaking

and sobbing in the car. 'Shit! I'm sorry about your girlfriend. She's gone battle happy.'

'Don't worry about it.' Les looked at the bovver boys laying all over the footpath and tried not to laugh. 'You might have stuffed up my night mate. But better me than you I suppose.' He went to his car and opened the door.

'Hey I know you,' said the bloke. 'You're Les. You work up the game.' Les nodded. 'I owe you one Les.'

'Don't worry about it.'

Les winked, started the car and sped off; glad to be out of there and glad to be getting rid of Hebe.

'And how dare you. How dare you beep your horn at me when I'm talking to somebody. Take me straight home, you filthy, low animal.'

Twenty minutes later Les was back home in front of the TV with a mug of Ovaltine. As far as he was concerned the fight was a bit of a hoot and the bloke in the leather jacket had done him a favour.

The following night the bloke came up to the game and introduced himself. He didn't go in, just thanked Les again for what he did and apologised for ruining his night and cruelling things between Les and his girl. Les repeated that it was okay; he'd get over it and find a new girl somehow. Neville left saying he owed Les a favour. A few days later he bumped into Les down the beach and gave him a bag of big, juicy, heads. Les smoked some, gave some to Warren and some to the girls at work, telling them he'd found it. Apart from the team at the Kelly Club Les didn't tell anyone what happened outside the R.S.L – and Neville, knowing Norton's situation, didn't say much either. After that, if they bumped into each other they'd always have a yarn or a bit of a joke. Les found Neville to be one of those friendly, easy-going blokes you couldn't help but like; quick thinking and alert but very genuine too. Nizegy still insisted he owed Les a favour and Les always said he still missed Hebe. Yet Nizegy couldn't help feeling Les was pulling his leg, because what he remembered of Hebe, she was that big a dog if you took her out anywhere you'd have to drive her around in an RSPCA wagon. Whatever Nizegy's thoughts he did Norton another favour not long after.

Les was home one afternoon early in the week when Neville rang to say if Les wasn't doing anything that night he had a girl for him and he'd shout dinner and drinks. The girl wasn't in town for long, but Les should like her; she was at least as nice as, maybe even a little better than, Hebe. Les had the night off, was doing nothing, and for a free feed and drinks he'd go out with Elle McFeast – so long as he didn't have to kiss her goodnight. Neville called round at about seven-thirty in a BMW hire car and they drove over to Milsons Point, parking outside North Sydney pool just down from Luna Park.

Around them some film or TV crew was packing up, and through the windows on the street Les noticed part of the pool was roped off and a small crowd of people were watching a game of water polo in progress. Water polo never interested Les. Swimming up and down indoor pools was not Norton's idea of a good time. However, from some players he'd met and people he'd spoken to Les knew it to be one of the most demanding sports going. As well as being super fit you needed the endurance of a champion fighter because it was virtually non-stop and players swam up to three kilometres or more during a match; a lot of it in sprints. You also had to be mentally alert to follow the ball and the plays and, although the game might look a little slow at times, there was plenty of physical contact involved. It was definitely no game for slouches. But Les had never seen a game, apart from a bit of one down Bondi baths before they got blown up and the numbered caps bobbing up and down in the pool below. Some sports didn't interest Norton. Grand Prix, golf and water polo were three of them.

'You ever play water polo, Les?' asked Neville.

Les shook his head. 'No.'

'I used to play it at school when I was young and fit. It's a bloody tough sport.'

'So I'm led to believe.'

'You should give it a go. You're pretty fit and you like swimming.'

Norton gave Nizegy a smile. 'Give me my webbs and jet fins and I'd jump in there with them.'

Nizegy looked at Norton for a moment. 'Give you your what?'

'My webbs and fins. You know . . .' Les started making abbreviated swimming motions with his hands.

He was about to say more when what had to be the most beautiful woman Les had ever seen in his life came walking down the street towards them. She was quite tall with cafe latte skin and a body equally as good as Elle McPherson's. A shock of honey-blonde hair crowned a flawless face and two flashing brown eyes that were matched only by the beauty of her smile. Somehow she'd managed to pour herself into a pair of pink jeans and a tight, maroon top that showed you a dainty navel pierced with a gold ring sitting on a firm, flat tummy. Several thin, gold chains sat round her neck and two shorter ones hung from her ears. She was with another good style of a woman, blonde and a little older, wearing denim jeans and a Bermuda jacket over a white T-shirt. Neville saw the look on Norton's face and began to turn round as the woman in the jacket called out.

'Neville my treasure. There you are.'

'Sadie. You little devil. How was the shoot?'

The two women walked up to Nizegy and the one in the Bermuda jacket threw her arms round him. Nizegy gave her a cuddle and a peck or two on the lips then turned to Norton.

'Les. This is Sadie Davies.'

'Hullo Sadie. Nice to meet you,' said Norton, giving her hand a gentle squeeze.

'And Les,' continued Nizegy. 'This is Miss Brazil.'

Norton couldn't believe it. Nizegy Neville had somehow lined him up for the night with Miss Brazil. No wonder she was so gorgeous. By the time Les said hello and came back down to earth they were in the BMW and heading for a restaurant to meet up with some film director and his Brazilian wife. It turned out Sadie was an old friend of Neville's, and Miss Brazil's publicist and minder while she was in Australia. They'd just been doing a photo shoot at Luna Park, then they were off to Melbourne the following day to open some new department store and on to Broome after that to catch up with Elle McPherson for more photos. No matter how tempting, any ideas of porking Miss Brazil appeared out of the question. Sadie was keeping a close eye on her, she had a millionaire boyfriend back home, and she also didn't particularly fancy getting full of drink then thrown up in the air and arriving at a photo shoot the next day with a neck full of love bites, a sore fanny and her eyes hanging out of her head. She just wanted to kick back and have a nice seafood dinner with some friends or whatever away from all the cameras and makeup – she especially liked the easy-going atmosphere in Australia where you didn't have to get around all the time surrounded by a phalanx of bodyguards. Les didn't mind one bit. It was just a huge buzz to be out in the company of such a stunning-looking woman who was a complete charmer as well. She loved to smile and had a lilting, Spanish accent that sent shivers up and down Norton's spine. From the word go it was a sensational night. They met up with the film director, had a delicious meal in a top restaurant, danced, sang, and Miss Brazil was all Norton's way even laughing at his corny jokes. They finished up at Redwoods in Bondi drinking margaritas and Les was home by around twelve-thirty. The high spot of the night was when Nizegy dropped Les off, and Miss Brazil put her arms around Norton's neck, gave him a kiss good night and discreetly slipped the tongue in.

Naturally if the night had a high spot there had to be a low spot. Some sleazy paparazzi just happened upon the restaurant and took a truly sensational photo of them all looking like a million dollars flashing their showbiz smiles, and Miss Brazil with her arms around Les kissing him on the cheek. It was a great photo; except that when it came out in the paper on Sunday all their names were right but Miss Brazil's partner was in there as Jack Norton. It took George Brennan about two minutes and the rest, including Warren, about three to start singing 'Hit the road Jack' as soon as they saw Les. The running gag was: how did Les go with Miss Brazil? She told him, hit the road Jack; etc, etc. Which was pretty hilarious the first four hundred times Les heard it. But it had still been a sensational night. However, apart from Neville having rung Les the next day to say hello, Les couldn't remember seeing him again. Now here he was on prime time TV running some strange new sport.

'I can't bloody believe it.' Norton stared into the magazine again.

'Neville Nizegy? Yeah, you can believe it, Les.' Warren gave Les a concentrating, stoned look over his drink as if he was about to come up with some momentous statement. 'Hey. I still remember when you both had your photo in the paper. How did the song go again? Hit the road Jack. And don't you come back no more, you goose, you goose, you goose.'

'You know what you should do Croden,' replied Les, folding the magazine. 'Grease your arse and slip into the next solar system. You're too good for this one.' The ads finished and next thing it was showtime.

Extreme Polo was more than just the game. It was the full-on, all singing, all dancing, rock 'n' roll, multi-coloured, glitter, glamour, hyped-up showbiz, raza-matazz, extravaganza held at Homebush Aquatic Centre. Norton had never been there, but from what he could see on the box it looked pretty good, what with the holograms and laser lights sparkling over the crystal clear water and the crowd cheering from the stands. First out of the change room to their side of the pool were the Sydney Sea Snakes in their lycra outfits carrying their webbs and fins. They entered through a cheer squad of six girls in denim shorts and snake skin vests boogeying and shaking to Eric Clapton's 'They're Tearing Us Apart'. Except the words came out as 'I'll tell you from the start. The Snakes will tear your heart apart.'

Next out were the Gilgandra Gillmen. Seven players all dressed up like the creature from the black lagoon running through a cheer squad of girls dressed in skin tight, little creaturette from the black lagoon outfits. Each team in the comp appeared to have its own song. The Gilgandra Gillmens's was Chuck Berry's 'Tulane Johnny' – only the words went: 'Go go Gillmen. Gilgandra Gillmen. Go go Gillmen. Gilgandra Gillmen.'

The lights and lasers flashed, while the cheer squads danced and shimmied; the teams looked mean and glared at each other from across opposite sides of the pool as the fans clapped and sang in the stands. Two referees in all white with red baseball caps came and stood in front of the teams as the players put on their webbs and fins. While all this was going on in the background, the TV commentators tried to explain the rules to the viewers.

The head commentator was Neil Brooks, and who better for the job? Ex-olympic swimmer, part of the dreaded Mean Machine and probably the best sports commentator in Australia. Brooksie didn't have a great deal of explaining to do. Extreme Polo was pretty much like the normal game only much faster and with a bit of Rugby League, Aussie Rules and Gridiron thrown in. Seven a side; three forwards, two backs, a lock and a goalkeeper. The goalmouth was three metres wide in one metre sections and a metre and a half high. A goal in the middle was a splashdown for three points, the outer goals were a zip and worth one point. There were two replacements allowed and instead of halves the game was played in three, twenty-five minute thirds with a ten minute break in between and you didn't change ends. The players wore identical jet fins and webbs; the webbs weren't joined at the thumb for a better grip on the ball. The ball, or grenade, was solid white rubber, something like a gridiron ball only chunkier with spiral mouldings, so if you threw a wet pass, the ball could spin out again from where it hit the water instead of mainly stopping dead. You could take the ball underwater for two metres, push off the bottom, climb up your team mate or an opponent's back to pass or shoot for goal, and shove your opponent's head underwater from any angle in a tackle.

Brooksie was about to explain the tackling and fouls and limited offside play from dry passes when a siren sounded and the players hit the water. One official blew his whistle as the other lobbed the grenade in the middle and it was on.

Swimming in water polo is quite different from normal swimming where you put your face down in the water and move your head to the side in rhythm, while bowling your arms over your head to stroke through the water. In water polo, you look mainly straight ahead, keep your face and shoulders out of the water, then chop at the water in short rapid strokes and flutter kick; something like paddling a boogie board. In Extreme Polo, the players used webbs and fins and surged through the pool as if they were jet propelled; back arched, head and shoulders out of the water up to their waists. Thrashing around in their crazy outfits and swimming four times faster than normal the players looked like fourteen monster, dragon lizards. They surged through the water, arms flailing in front of them, or swam sidestroke, backstroke, breaststroke or just kicked backwards with their fins while they either tackled their opponents, passed to their team mates or tried to slam the grenade at the goalmouth for either a splashdown or zip. The goalkeepers wore extra padded helmets with kevlar grills in front something like ice hockey, because in a lot of shots for a splashdown the goalie often copped a grenade straight in the face.

They had aqua-cam, top-cam, goal-cam and deep-cam. Deep-cam was set under the water and picked up the players plunging to the bottom in a great cocoon of white bubbles; then, when pushing and kicking up off the tiles completely out of the water, the top-cam would catch them either passing to a team mate or slithering up some players back to slam the grenade at the net for a splashdown or zip. Goal-cam was set behind the net at water level and it looked truly awesome, almost frightening, to see a team of lizard-like figures churning towards the camera at a rate of knots, while another team of lizard figures tried to stop them as the water boiled and waves splashed from one side of the pool to the other. Neville Nixon had taken water polo into the new millenium, added colour speed and rock 'n' roll and turned it into something like WWF on water. Norton was more than impressed. Before he knew it the first third was over with the Sea Snakes leading the Gillmen 11–7. Brooksie cut for a commercial break and Les turned to the others, his mouth slightly open.

'Well what do you think of Extreme Polo, Les?' asked Warren.

'What do I think? Bloody sensational. What about all the slow-mos of those blokes in them nutty outfits flipping up in the air then sommersaulting back down into the water? Ker-splooshka! And what about goal-cam? Shit! I thought at one stage those creatures from the black lagoon were going to come straight through the net and out the TV screen. Bloody hell!'

'Who do you reckon will win? asked Debbie.

Les thought for a second. 'It's only early. But I'd say the Sea Snakes. They're a slippery-looking bunch.'

'Yeah. It looks that way,' agreed Debbie.

'But get your money on the Mud Crabs next week,' said Warren.

'Too right,' nodded Debbie.

'Who are they?' asked Les, pointing to the magazine. 'There's not a real lot in here about them.'

'I tore their photo out and put it up in the salon,' answered Debbie.

'So you're a very heavy, mud crab groupie Zanna.'

'Oogie, oogie, oogie. Do the mud crab boogie, daddyo.'

'Sounds good to me.'

By the time Les got another beer, plus a slice of the pizza they'd been pigging out on earlier, and Warren and Debbie pulled a few more Ken Dones, it was time for the second third.

The second third was even better than the first if maybe a little rougher. There were more fouls and the Gillmen's goalkeeper almost got flattened from a side shot at a splashdown. But after they swam him to the side of the pool and the zambuck hit him with the smelling salts he was in there again. A Sea Snake forward got his nose broken from a stiff arm and there was blood in the water. This was sucked up by an attendant with a water-vac, the forward got replaced, and after a brief stoppage the game continued. By the time the final third was half over Norton had figured out some of the rules and surmised the game's general strategy. The first third you didn't go in too hard and sorted out your plays. The second third the biffo went in and each team tried to sort the other one out and separate the men from the boys. The final third everyone knew where everyone else was coming from, so the players went flat out but relying mainly on skill and speed more than aggression. Finally it was over with the Sydney Sea Snakes running or swimming out winners 26–16. Six splashdowns and eight zips to three splashdowns and seven zips. Brooksie interviewed the two team captains and the player of the match then, after a few brief words from Neville Nixon, it was all systems go for the grand final the following Sunday. The Sydney Sea Snakes vs the Murrumbidgee Mud Crabs. Between the game, the camera angles, the hype and the rock 'n' roll, Norton said he'd definitely be watching next Sunday; and even though he hadn't seen them, he'd be barracking for the Mud Crabs along with the others. In fact, why not make it a Mud Crab grand final party? Bunting, streamers, coloured punch; the works. Debbie was enthusiastic. She'd even wear her full-dress Star Trek officer's uniform complete with Star Fleet Command medals and citations and Ferengi Alliance Symbol. Warren would wear his too.

'What are you going to wear to the Mud Crab party Les?' asked Warren.

'I don't know,' mused Norton, looking towards his room. 'I'll have to see what I've got in there.'

'You wouldn't have to wear anything, Les. Just come as you are,' said Debbie. 'You're a big enough crab as it is.'

Warren clicked off the TV set. He was stuffed and close to home and ready for the sack with plenty on at work tomorrow. Debbie was off home too. She was tired and like Warren had a big day on at the salon the next day; one of the girls who worked there was out Bondi way that night and going to give her a lift home. Norton didn't have to work. But he'd been up early training with Billy Dunne, then had spent most of the day snorkelling around North Bondi with some blokes from the surf club. After a day in the sun and a few beers he was tired and keen for an early night. Plus he had to get up early the next day for some more training and to get some work done round the house. A horn tooted out the front, Les said goodnight to Debbie and then, after she and Warren locked in passionate embrace on the front steps and she jumped in the space pod and blasted off back to Sigma Draconis VI or Coogee or wherever, Les was left alone with the boarder.

'So have you made your mind up what you're doing for the rest of the week yet?' yawned Warren.

'No. Not really,' replied Les. 'I might go away for

a couple of days. But I want to finish that thing off out the back.'

'Fair enough,' Warren yawned again.

'Fucked if I know what I'm gonna do about those tiles though,' Les yawned too.

Next thing, Norton had cleaned his teeth and was curled up in bed half-asleep. He still couldn't quite get over what he'd just seen on TV and he was almost certain Nizegy had got the idea off him from those few brief words he'd had with him outside North Sydney swimming pool. It was one of the best nights Les had ever had and he clearly remembered everything he said and did that night. I always figured Nizegy was quick, thought Les. But how quick is that? Or am I just slow? Norton yawned again. Buggered if I know. I'm buggered if I do.

Warren was still in bed snoring when Les ambled into the kitchen around six the next morning wearing an old, blue tracksuit. It wasn't quite Norton's idea to get up that early, but Billy Dunne was an early riser and Les had agreed to meet him down North Bondi at six-thirty for a workout. It was the best time of the day to train though and Bondi generally always looked the goods first thing in the morning with the sun coming up over the ocean and not many people around. After some cereal, coffee and a quick clean up, Les went outside and piled into the mighty Datty. Norton had a new car now; an old, black Datsun 1200 he'd bought off some desperate for two hundred dollars. It wasn't much bigger than a go-kart, looked like an absolute shithouse and mechanically would have been flat out pulling a French letter off a slack dick. But it had five months registration on it and would do till Les found something decent; if anybody wanted to steal this one in the meantime they were welcome. Les was a little disappointed to find the wind had increased and it was already starting to grey over when he pulled up in a small cloud of smoke next to Billy who was leaning against the door of his wife's red Laser.

'Not much of a day William,' said Les, getting out and kicking the door closed behind him without bothering to lock it.

'No. That southerly's come up out of nowhere. Still, you know what they say Les.' Billy feinted a perfect left hook at Norton's jaw. 'A bad day at the beach is always better than a good day at work.'

'You're pretty right there.' They picked up their bags and started walking towards the surf club. 'Anyway. What do you fancy doing?'

'Just our usual Claudia Schiffer workout I suppose,' shrugged Billy.

Billy had bought a couple of goat boats, or old-style, wave skis at a garage sale, one for himself and one for Les, which they left at the surf club. Billy suggested they jog around to Bronte and back, paddle four laps of Bondi, do a few rounds on the heavy bag, then finish with some ab-work and practice some choker holds and unarmed combat moves with their rubber knife – the usual things people do first thing in the morning before they leave for the office or wherever. This took roughly about two hours; then when they were finished, cleaned up and walking back to the cars, Billy suggested that if it was still blowing a southerly tomorrow they'd take the skis down Rose Bay and go for a paddle in the harbour where it would be sheltered. Les agreed and said he'd ring that night and let Billy know what he was doing. Next thing Les was in the mighty Datty and home. Warren was seated in the kitchen wearing a pair of designer jeans with a grey, denim shirt sipping a cup of coffee. Considering the amount of booze and substance abuse he and Debbie had got into the night before, he hadn't brushed up too bad. Les tossed his sweaty gear in the laundry then took a bottle of mineral water from the fridge and found a glass.

'So what's happening, Croden? What part of the galaxy are you flogging your low advertising in this time?'

'The Gamma Quadrant,' replied Warren.

'The Gamma Quadrant,' repeated Norton. 'It's always the fuckin, Gamma Quadrant. Why can't you trekkies go somewhere else for a change? Like the Epsilon Pulsar Cluster or something.'

'Actually,' said Warren. 'I'm beaming down to deepest, darkest Cremorne for a casting. Twenty vibrant young chaps and we need one to play a hairdresser in an ad for hair conditioner.'

Norton took another mouthful of mineral water. 'These . . . vibrant young chaps Warren. All . . . gay I imagine.'

'Let's just say Les, the ones that aren't are that fuckin' jolly it doesn't fuckin' matter.'

A tiny smile flickered in the corners of Norton's eyes. 'Was it some bloke who said that advertising is the rattling of a stick inside a bucket of swill?'

'Possibly,' replied Warren. 'Though you could have

24

him mixed up with the bloke who described advertising as the science of arresting the human intelligence long enough to get money from it.'

'Oh.'

'Or: you can fool all of the people all of the time if the advertising is right and the budget big enough.'

'Yes,' nodded Les. 'To an advertising agency, an intellectual is anyone that can turn on a TV set or switch on a radio.'

'Or read a newspaper.' Warren finished his coffee and stood up. 'Anyway. I have to get going,' he said, putting his cup in the sink. 'What's your play today landlord?'

Les nodded to the backyard. 'Try and get the pool of fuckin' remembrance sorted out.'

'You and your bloody rock pool. Why don't you just blow the fuckin' thing up and be done with it. It's giving everyone the shits.'

'I think I will,' replied Les. 'And me and the house with it.'

'Well, whatever you do,' said Warren. 'Just remember two things, Les.'

'Like what, Woz?'

'Never step on a Klingon's blue suede shoes. And always obey the Prime Directive.'

Norton made the Vulcan sign with one hand. 'Live long and prosper Croden.' The front door closed, a car started and Warren was gone. Les had another glass of water then, after deciding to put breakfast off for the time being, went out the back to try and solve a small problem that had been annoying him.

Like most of the other houses in the street, Norton's backyard wasn't all that big. But it was neat, caught the sun most of the day, and there were a few flowers and vines growing along the fence and the side of the toolshed where Warren grew his ganja. Les decided to put in a small rock pool, tile it, place a few of those realistic-looking, stone frogs and lizards around it and install a couple of solar-powered water pumps. Then kick back and watch the water bubble away gently and peacefully courtesy of mother nature. He got a builder in to excavate the rock pool, cement it and waterproof it; and he did an excellent job. When Les said how he intended tiling it, the builder said he could tip Les into the absolute grouse and guarantee he finished up with the classiest, one-upmanship to the max, little rock pool in the Eastern suburbs. The builder knew an Irish carpenter who'd been helping to demolish an old house in Maroubra where he'd found a wooden box of antique tiles in the basement that were well worth a look. Norton said righto, bring them over.

The Irishman brought them around the next day and Les was rapt the moment he saw them. They were a deep, cherry red with a delicate, bronze, flower pattern running through them. They came in two lots. One lot stacked in the box were about the same size as a small bar of chocolate with a semi circle cut out of the sides. The other lot were wrapped in old oilskin and were about the same size as a twenty cent coin with a bronze flower in the centre. These slotted neatly into the other tiles, locking them together to make a unique and lovely pattern. They even had the name of the original tile company, Kandos Grand Tile Co., written on the side of the wooden box and you could sort of make out the same name written across

26

the folds of the oilskin. Warren made a phone call and evidently there had been an old tile company in Kandos NSW that closed down just after the first world war. More than pleased with what he'd got, Les paid the Irishman and they put the tiles out in Norton's shed. The one thing that surprised Les was the weight when they were carrying them out; for their size, the antique tiles felt like they were made of lead. Naturally there had to be a hiccup.

Les got a tiler in who got half the pool done then told Les he was about sixty of the little tiles short to finish the job. So Norton got in touch with the Irishman through the builder, who apologised and said, yes, there was another bundle of the smaller tiles. They'd just slipped his mind when he was moving them. But Les could have them for sure. The only other thing was he'd been having a drink at the time and couldn't remember where he'd put them. They were either somewhere in his house, at a friend's place, or a garage in either Maroubra, Coogee or Marrickville. However, not to worry, as soon as he remembered where they were he'd bring them straight over. Which was why Les nicknamed the rock pool the Pool of Remembrance, after the ANZAC memorial in Hyde Park. Because every time he rang the Irishman he always sounded hungover and still couldn't remember where they were; and this had been going on for months. Subsequently, Norton was now well and truly pissed off looking at a half-tiled hole full of dirt and leaves in his backyard that done properly would have looked unique. It was a pain in the arse.

Les was staring at the pool looking for an answer

when the phone rang. Shit! he thought, I'd better get the phone before that stupid message cuts in and whoever it is thinks we're all a bunch of ratbags. He hurried to the flyscreen door, went inside and picked up the phone.

'Yeah hello.'

'Is that you, Les?'

'Yeah.'

'Mate. It's Neville Nixon.'

'Nizegy.' Norton's eyebrows rose. 'Well I'll be buggered. How are you?'

'I'm good, Les. What about yourself?'

'Can't complain, mate. Can't complain.'

'That's good. Did you happen to be watching TV at all last night Les?'

'Are you asking me, Neville, did I happen to see the Sydney Sea Snakes sneak in against the Gilgandra Gillmen? Yes I did. And you didn't brush up too bad on the box yourself, old fellah.'

Nizegy cracked up over the phone. 'You're a legend, Les. So what did you think?'

'I thought it was pretty good, Nev. Where did you come up with an idea like that?'

Nizegy gave a bit of a chuckle. 'Let's just say these things come to me, Les.'

Yeah I'll bet, thought Norton. 'You're a dead set genius, Nizegy.'

'Not quite, mate. Not quite. Listen Les, what are you doing?'

Norton glanced towards the backyard. 'Not much. As a matter of fact I've got the week off from work.' Les gave Neville a brief run down on what was happening at the club, then wondered why he bothered. Next thing it was like the phone lit up in his hand with warmth.

'You've got a week off. This is unbelievable. Les, what about having a bit of lunch with me today?'

Les looked at the phone as more warmth seemed to seep through. 'Yeah all right,' he shrugged.

'Okay. You know the CYC at Rushcutters Bay. How about I meet you in the bar there at twelve-thirty?'

'Righto. Sounds good to me.'

'Ohh mate, this is unreal. And I still owe you a favour you know.'

'If you say so, Neville. So who's it going to be this time?'

'No one. Just you and me. But I'm going to tip you into something.'

'All right, Neville. You can tell me about it over lunch.'

'I will. I'll see you down there, Les.'

Norton put the phone down and stared at it for a moment. Well I'll be. Bloody Nizegy ringing me out of the blue. And he says he wants to do me another favour. Shit! If it's half as good as the last one I'll be happy. But what a bloody good bloke. All this time and he still remembered me. In a better frame of mind Les went back outside and continued trying to nut out what to do with the rock pool.

After gazing at it for a while his only alternative was to get the tiler back in, do as much as he could with the antique tiles then match one end up with dark red ones or something. If he waited for the Irish carpenter to remember where he'd left the original ones, he'd finish up with a beard down to his knees.

Possibly he was being a bit of a perfectionist because you mightn't notice it so much once the pool was full of water. But it would have been nice to have had it done properly with all those lovely, interlocking, old tiles with their unique, gold flower pattern. Oh well. He gave a last shrug and went back inside. After pottering around in the kitchen for a while and cleaning the house up a bit, Les climbed into a clean pair of jeans and a green polo shirt, revved up the mighty Datty and thundered off to the Cruising Yacht Club of Australia.

Being mid-week, he was able to find a parking spot almost opposite beneath an elegant, old white house; one like a lot of other elegant, old white houses built side by side along the leafy rise where Darling Point faces the harbour before it spreads itself up towards Edgecliff and Double Bay. He kicked the door shut and stopped for a moment to view the sandstone wall that circled Rushcutters Bay Park where the harbour laps Elizabeth Bay and Potts Point. Yes, this sure is a nice part of town, mused Les as he stepped across New Beach Road. There was no missing the tan brick, low-rise of the CYC, with the palm trees, red bouganvillea and big white anchor set at an angle out the front. The two old cannon in the foyer would look good around my rock pool, Les chuckled to himself as he stepped down off the footpath and checked his watch. It was a little after midday. I'm five minutes late, that's nothing, he thought. Then Les stopped. No I'm not – I'm twenty-five fuckin' minutes early. Neville said twelve-thirty. That's what he got from thinking about that silly bloody rock pool. It was still cloudy, but sheltered from the southerly in the harbour, so rather than stand around like a stale bottle of pee for nearly half an hour Les thought he'd take a stroll and check out some of the yachts and the sights.

He left the CYC, walked past a small food shop then a ships's chandler – whatever that was – finally coming to a marina with a yacht brokerage, a restaurant and cluster of shops that formed a bit of a mall before it ran out into the harbour. He walked through the open air restaurant, down a wooden ramp and onto a concrete jetty almost jammed with million dollar yachts and cruisers rocking gently at their moorings in the light breeze. Shit! Wouldn't it be nice to have that sort of money, mused Norton, stopping to admire a fat white cruiser that looked like a floating two-storey house. He went on, taking his time going through a wire gate to where it was now all blue water maxis and the like with all the latest ocean going equipment, radar, spoilers on the back, kevlar masts and stainless steel cables reaching it seemed to the sky. He was admiring a yacht to his left when he heard what sounded like two girls singing, their voices coming from a yacht opposite. It was a wide-beamed, twenty-five metre classic, all white fibreglass and cedar with a fat radar pod sitting on a spoiler above the stern big enough to drive a truck through. Splashed across the back in red and blue was Goodfellahs. R. 770. The two girls were parodying an old Elton John song.

'We're still sanding . . . yeah, yeah, yeah.'

'We're still sanding . . . yeah, yeah, yeah.'

Les moved over a little for a closer look. The two girls were in their mid-twenties, a beefy blonde and a better looking brunette, both wearing jeans and old T-shirts. They were standing in the stern next to some mops and buckets and tins of varnish, sanding back the cedar decking as if they were getting ready to paint it. Les recognised the brunette. Her name was Houston, though she was often referred to as Spare One. She worked up the game a couple of summers before leaving to work in the snowfields. She'd done a bit of modelling, liked to travel around and was a full-on Bondi girl. And after living there for a while Norton knew one thing: you can always tell a Bondi girl, but you can't tell her much. Houston fell into that category, though she had this kooky way of talking to people and a sardonic sort of sense of humour.

'Hello, Spare One,' said Les. 'What are you up to?'

The brunette turned around then smiled. 'Patooties. Well, what's your John Dory, Patoots?'

'Nothing much,' answered Les. 'Just looking around. I'm thinking of buying a yacht.'

'Yeah sure, Tooties. Where are you going to put it? In your bath?' She turned to the blonde. 'Jinny. This is Les. We used to work up the Kelly Club together.'

'Hi Les.'

'G'day Jinny,' smiled Les, before turning back to the brunette. 'So what are you up to Houston?'

'Ohh, would you believe working, Tooties. We've just scrubbed about five ton of mud off this rotten great thing. Now we're sanding it back to paint it.' Houston wiped some imaginary sweat from her brow. 'It's enough to send you spare. But the pay's good and Tooties needs the chops for when she hits the snow.'

'Shit! It's a bloody nice yacht,' said Les, stepping back a little to admire the fittings. 'Who owns it?'

Houston nodded to the name at the stern. 'Who do you think?'

'Goodfellahs?'

'Nizegy. Neville Nixon.'

'Neville Nixon,' said Les. 'I don't know him all that well. Isn't he a rock promoter or something?'

'That's him,' nodded Houston. 'Likes to keep a very low profile. This is his sneak go. Not many people know he owns it.'

'Not a bad sneak go,' said Les. 'I wouldn't mind owning it.'

'He just got back from two months cruising round the Whitsunday Passage and they got caught up in a storm near Laurieton and washed up on a mangrove swamp. That's why there was so much greasy, black, fucking mud to scrape off.'

'Was there fuckin' what,' added Jinny.

'But Nizegy's an old China. He knew we were both a bit short so he took us under his wing and he's paying us heaps. And believe me, Les baby, Patoot's can always do with the readies.'

'Can't we all,' agreed Norton.

'So what brings you down here anyway Tooties,' said Houston, going back to her sanding. 'You're not buying a yacht, surely. Though from what people tell me I reckon you'd have enough snookered away to buy the United States Sixth Fleet.'

'No,' laughed Norton. 'I'm having lunch with Price and George. In fact I'm running a bit late. I'd better bat and ball.'

'Okay. Hey, when you see Price, ask him if he

needs an ace waitress up there will you. And let me know.'

'I'll see that he gets the message,' answered Norton, starting to move away. 'I'll see you Spare One.'

'See you, Tooties.'

'Nice talking to you, Jinny.'

'You too, Les.'

Les had got through the wire gate and was half-way up the wooden ramp when he could just hear, 'We're still sanding. Yeah, yeah, yeah,' start up again. He went through the open-air restaurant back towards the CYC. That certainly was some yacht Neville. Some yacht. They say it's a long way to the top if you want to rock 'n' roll. But it must be okay once you get there. Anyway half your luck Nizegy; I suppose you deserve it, thought Les. A bit further on he turned into the CYC. A tall bloke in a white shirt and tie asked him to sign the visitors book, then Les went down a corridor past the phones and a row of coloured ensigns framed along the walls. Neville Nixon was standing against a small drink's table just inside the door, wearing a pair of jeans and a denim shirt with red and blue piping around the pockets and cuffs. His face lit up and his handshake was warm and sincere. Although it had been some time Norton couldn't help but feel good himself as soon as he saw Nizegy.

'Hello Les. Shit, it's good to see you again, mate.'

'Yeah. You too, Neville. It's been a while.'

'You look well, Les. Extra well. Anyway, what can I get you . . . beer?'

Les pointed to Nizegy's bottle. 'I might have the same as you, Nev. A mineral water.'

Nizegy was back from the bar in an instant and they clinked glasses. 'Well here's to . . . whatever Les.'

'To whatever, Neville.'

Nizegy took a swallow of mineral water and clapped his hands together. 'Anyway, why don't we order some food, sit down and have a yarn? I'm feeling a bit peckish.'

'Good idea. I've had bugger-all for breakfast.'

The bar faced a large dining area that looked over another marina full of yachts and around to their right was the kitchen with two blackboard menus and specials. Les went for some fish and chips, calamari rings and salad; Nizegy ordered a smoked chicken caesar and an extra salad. They took their food and sat down at a long wooden table with bench seats shaded by a large blue awning. A polite girl in a black dress and yellow T-shirt brought them two more mineral waters. The food was delicious, the atmosphere congenial and Les found it more than pleasant sitting amongst the other diners sipping and chewing away while he and Neville made a bit of small talk.

Nizegy, however, seemed more interested in what Les had been doing with himself; Neville Nixon was one of those naturally charismatic people who liked to listen to your story and somehow made you feel good in yourself at the same time. Les, however, never mentioned seeing the two girls working on his yacht at the next marina and Nizegy never mentioned he had it moored there. They finished their mains, then both opted for the mango and coconut cake along with two flat whites to wash it down. Between sips and bites Neville got quite a laugh out of Norton's story about the Irish scaffolder, and how he'd named his rock pool the Pool of Remembrance.

'I suppose if you were looking for a corny simile, Les,' said Neville, 'you could say instead of the Irishman being a few bricks short of a load, you're a few tiles short of a rock pool.'

'Yeah. Nice one Nizegy. That's about it all right.'

Les took a sip of coffee to wash down a piece of cake and looked directly at Neville Nixon. Neville did pretty much the same thing and looked directly at Les. There was a kind of pregnant pause between them which began to turn into almost an awkward silence. Above them the clouds drifted over the harbour, while behind them the yachts and cruisers barely rocked at their moorings in the sheltered breeze gently plucking at the clear, blue waters of Sydney Harbour.

'Well, Les. I suppose you're dying to ask me,' said Nizegy.

'Ask you what, Neville?'

'Where I got the idea for Extreme Polo from. And what's your end?'

Norton took another sip of coffee and put his cup down. 'All right Neville. Where did you get the idea for Extreme Polo and what's my end?'

Nizegy tilted his head slightly to one side and the flicker of a smile creased the corners of his eyes. 'Remember that night I lined you up with Miss Brazil.'

'How could I ever forget.'

'We drove over to North Sydney and when we parked outside the pool there was a game of water polo going on.'

Norton closed his eyes just for a moment. I knew it. I bloody well knew it, he thought. 'Yeah, go on.'

'And you said something about how you'd jump in with them and have a go if you could wear your webbs and fins.'

'Yeah.'

'Well at first I wondered what you were talking about. Then a couple of days later I bought a set and started swimming around with them. The next day I went down to Clovelly, got a couple of blokes I know from the surf club, gave them a set and got them to swim around tossing a gridiron ball to each other while I timed them and took a video. Then I went home and watched it on TV and had a think.' Nizegy leaned across the table a little. 'Now Les, you know how everything's going faster and faster all the time. Especially with sport on TV. I mean, rugby leagues's now Super League. You got one day cricket, golf is the skins, slam dunk basketball, extreme skiing. Boxing went to Karate, to Kung Fu, to kick boxing. Now they throw them in a cage and let them do what they like. Throw in some snazzy uniforms, rock 'n' roll, plenty of colour and the punters love it.'

'To be honest, Nizegy, I don't watch a real lot of TV. But I know where you're coming from.'

'Did you know, Les, that water polo is the oldest team sport in the Olympic Games? It started in Paris in 1900. It's played in over a hundred countries. There's five hundred teams in Sydney alone. It's a hard sport. But with webbs and flippers, anyone can play it – kids, old blokes, women, the handicapped – and have a ball.'

As briefly as he could, Neville Nixon went on to explain how he'd got in touch with some people he knew on a cable TV station, Oztel, and got them interested. Then he got some people together who he knew ran sports shows on TV and they organised a ten team competition. He knew plenty of musicians and people in the music industry and they got the rock 'n' roll music and the team songs together. He was good friends with a woman on the Central Coast who was a genius at making colourful, lycra outfits for aerobics teams and she knocked up those amazing-looking uniforms from this new Cobra Hologram Lycra. When Les asked Neville why he chose all those outback NSW towns, he said 71% of all the water polo teams in Australia were either in NSW or Victoria. Plus he had a lot of contacts in those towns from touring rock bands around the outback, and everybody was always battling in the bush so it was less expensive and more convenient than going national; for the time being at least. He put a heavy, Sydney team in because he needed some bad guys that everybody wanted to see get beat; and the rough and tumble Sydney Sea Snakes fitted the bill perfectly. The fans loved the Mud Crabs and as Australians always cheered for the underdog, they'd be sentimental favourites for the grand final on Sunday. When Les asked where all the money came from, Nizegy said he had sold some investments and also had a Singaporean banker backing him.

'I know I've made it sound simple, Les,' said Nizegy. 'But believe me, I went to some fucking around to get this thing together. Did I what. But it's been worth it. The game's developed an unbelievable cult following and it's good for the bush too. They do it tough out there.'

'You're talking to an old country boy, Neville.' Les

leaned back a little and folded his arms. 'So that's about all you've been doing for the last year or so Neville? Organising this thing?'

'That's it, Les. Just running around NSW like a blue-arsed fly getting it together. Been absolutely nowhere. I might shout myself a holiday after the grand final.'

Norton shook his head in admiration. 'Well I've got to hand it to you Nizegy. You're a dead set genius.'

'No, not really,' answered Nizegy, shaking his head. 'I just tap-dance pretty quick and I'm very perceptive. But the bottom line is that it was your throw away remark that gave me the idea. So I want to do you a favour.'

'My end Neville.'

'Exactly,' nodded Nizegy. 'Just give me a hand for the rest of the week and I'll see that you get two hundred grand cash.'

'Two hundred large? That's not a bad earn for a week's work. Who do I have to kill?'

'No one. All you have to do is drive out to Wagga Wagga, pick up the Mud Crabs, bring them back to Sydney and look after them till they go back straight after the grand final.'

Shit! This sounds all right, thought Les. Money for old rope. 'Okay Neville. You got me. But how do I get to Wagga Wagga? I'm driving a two hundred dollar banger at the moment that's flat out getting up Bondi road.'

'No worries. I'll give you a car. You can leave it with a bloke out there and bring the boys back in the team bus. They're staying at Coogee.'

'Okey doke. Which hotel in Coogee? Crowne Plaza?'

Nizegy shook his head. 'They're staying in a garage.'

'A garage?'

'Yeah. They're a funny bunch. They like to stick together and they hate the city. They just want to get in, do their thing, and get out. I got bunks and everything in the garage. It's all sweet.'

Norton shook his head. 'All right. A garage it is.'

'I'll bring the car round your place about ten. If you leave then you'll be there in the afternoon. Come back Thursday.'

'Fair enough.'

'All right. Now that we've got that sorted out, Les, there's one small catch.' Nizegy smiled and looked evenly at Les.

'A small catch?'

'Yeah. Have you got a thousand dollars?'

Norton returned Nizegy's even look but didn't smile. 'Not on me.'

'Okay. Just to keep you keen. I want you to weigh in a grand and I'll have it on the Mud Crabs for you. But win lose or draw you still get your two hundred thousand next Sunday.'

This is a bit odd, thought Les. But they don't call Neville 'Nizegy' for nothing. I'd trust this bloke with my car. 'Okay when do you want the thousand?'

'What are you doing tonight?'

Norton shrugged. 'Nothing in particular.'

'Remember how I said everything's moving faster and faster? How would you like to come to the Ultimate Event at Darling Harbour?'

'Where they fight in the cage? Shit! Me and Billy were only talking about that this morning. We were thinking of going. But we didn't have tickets and there'll be a million there.'

'No worries. I know the bloke running it. You can come up in the VIP room with me. The tickets'll be waiting out the front for you. Bring Billy.'

'Nizegy. You're a legend. Billy'll be rapt.'

Nizegy smiled then pulled a notebook and biro from the back pocket of his jeans. 'If there should be any stuff up with the tickets just ask for this bloke. And that's my mobile number. But it should all be sweet.'

'Ripper. Hey, while you're there Neville. Write down the address of that lovely garage in Coogee. Seeing as I've got to drive a bus in there, I'll make sure I know where it is.'

'The garage. Okay.' Nizegy scribbled some more then handed the piece of paper to Les and looked at his watch. 'Shit! Look at the time. I've got to get going.' He gave Les a tired smile. 'But I should see you in the VIP room tonight about eight.'

'Righto.'

They left their table and walked to the front door. Les pointed out the mighty Datty parked across the road and Nizegy made a joke about how Les would have to give it a new door and tyres just to get it put off the road. Les thanked Nizegy again for the tickets, said he'd see him down there, and drove off. As he did, he watched Nizegy in the rear vision mirror to see if he walked towards his yacht; instead, he went into the phone box at the front of the CYC. A few minutes later Les was heading up New South Head Road.

So just what exactly have I got myself into here, Norton asked himself, as the Datty gasped into second to take the rise past Edgecliff Station, then wheezed into top going down the hill towards Double Bay. I take a car out to Wagga Wagga, pick up some team of yobbos, bring them back to Sydney in a bus and shove them in a garage at Coogee. I'm promised two hundred grand yet I've got to weigh in a thousand. That's not a bad punt I suppose if the end result falls in. Funny though how Nizegy says he's been flat out all year, yet Patooties said he'd just been washed up in a mangrove swamp after sailing round the Whitsunday Passage. Then again Nizegy'd probably tell Spare One anything. In the meantime I've got to come up with a lazy thousand ... A bit of a smile creased Norton's eyes. That shouldn't be too hard, he thought. Before long he landed the Datty outside Earth Colony Seven and went inside.

There were no messages on the answering service. Les got a glass of mineral water from the fridge and no-one was around when he went out to the backyard. Les had another look to make sure, then got a pinch bar from the toolshed. Stacked against the back fence next to the end of the toolshed was a pile of timber with a tarpaulin over it sitting on two other pieces of wood. Les shoved the pinch bar under one end of the timber, levied it up and kicked a milk crate beneath the pinch bar. Settled into the ground was another flat piece of wood. Les moved that and beneath was a hole he'd dug into the ground big enough to hide a metal toolbox not quite a metre long, which he unlocked without taking it from the hole. Inside were all sorts of goodies including jewellery and a couple of guns with silencers. At one end of the box were bundles of fifty dollar bills tied with thick rubber bands. Les took one bundle of a thousand and poked it in his jeans; then, after carefully replacing everything as it was, he went back inside the house. Okay, he shrugged – as he put the money in a bedroom drawer and hid it under some T-shirts – so we got plastic money in Australia now and this is paper stuff and it's a bit molded and folded. It's definitely still currency of the realm. It's still kosher. Les closed the drawer and looked at his watch. Bloody Hell! Where did the day go? I'd better ring Billy and tell him what's going on.

'Shit! You got tickets for the VIP box. I already said I'd take Lyndy and the kids for a feed and then we're all going to see Star Wars. Wish I'd known earlier.'

'Oh well, don't matter Billy. I'll just have to tell you about it in the morning.'

'You're still keen for a paddle around six-thirty?'

'Yeah. Nizegy's not getting here till ten. We got heaps of time.'

'Hey if you've got a spare ticket. Why don't you ring up Kate the Tae Kwon Do queen? She might go.'

Les thought for a moment. 'Yeah, that's an idea. I might just do that. She's ten times better looking than you too.'

They talked a little more then Les told Billy he'd see him out the front in the morning and hung up. Tae Kwon Do Kate, smiled Les. Nothing wrong with her. And I'm still fairly sweet there I think. I was only talking to her last Sunday down the beach. I've got her number at work too, he recalled.

Ta Kwon Do Kate was Katherine Hannan, a

likeable almost-blonde from Bronte, where she part-
owned a home unit with one of her big brothers who
played first grade Rugby Union. She had frizzly, light
brown hair and soft hazel eyes in a pretty, if
sometimes slightly serious face. She was right into
health and like her brothers very fit with long,
smooth, sexy legs. She ran a travel agency in Rose
Bay. Kate also used to like running from her place to
North Bondi along the promenade. Les and Billy
bumped her one morning in the fitness station next to
North Bondi Surf Club doing some stretches and
tossing around all these fancy kicks. She wasn't too
bad either. Les didn't say anything, but Billy got a
mag on with her and told her he'd once boxed
professionally. Katherine said boxers didn't worry
her, men in general didn't worry her, nobody worried
her; she had a brown belt in Tae Kwon Do. Les and
Billy were suitably impressed and prayed their paths
never crossed.

One foul, cold morning early in the week it had
started to rain heavily and Les and Billy were in the
surf club, moving around downstairs with the gloves
on. Apart from the caretaker, a bloke they called
Uncle George, and one or two others, there was no-
one in the surfclub, when who should walk in to
get out of the rain but Katherine. She watched the
boys for a while, then for some reason challenged
Billy to a spar. Billy was reluctant, but then it was
yeah okay, if you want. Katherine shaped up and
started giving Billy all these shots. She knew what
she was doing and if Billy had just been some mug
he probably would have got shortened up. He kept
moving around – although a couple half slipped in

making Katherine think she was a world-beater. Billy didn't have the heart to move in, and slip a right rip under her ribcage followed by a left over the top and introduce Katherine to the real world. Which was her trouble. She'd never copped one on the snoot.

Billy let her go for a while playing Bruce Lee, though Les could sense he was starting to get a bit sick of it and she was interrupting his training with Les. Billy didn't hit her. Katherine shaped up to give Billy another spinning backfist, so the ex-boxer just put his arm straight out, stepped forward and Katherine spun round straight into it; she copped it right on the nose and fell on her arse, giving a shriek when she felt the slight pain and a trickle of blood. Billy apologised profusely and convinced her it was just an accident; the boys then cleaned her up and held her hand for a moment before continuing with their sparring. Katherine sat there with a few sheets of toilet paper dabbing at her nose while she watched the boys train and kept her mouth shut. But she seemed to cop the mild whack on the snoot fairly sweet and didn't cry or carry on like a sook and both Les and Billy liked her for that.

When they'd finished, Billy said he was married and had two kids and kidded to her a bit to make sure there were no hard feelings. Les said he wasn't married and seeing it was still pissing rain outside and her nose still smarted, maybe it might be best if he drove her home. Then, being such an urbane, sophisticated man about town, he suggested they might go out some time and got her phone number. Les took her out a couple of times and they enjoyed each other's company. Norton actually quite fancied Tae Kwon Do Kate as Billy nicknamed her. But Katherine liked a simple life: keeping fit, eating good food and getting plenty of early nights, especially during the week. With Norton's job it was the other way around. Katherine's big brother kept an eye on her, and evidently there was a bigger one again hovering around somewhere. So even if Les did get a chance to take the girl from the travel agency out it was pretty much home by midnight and no slipping the tongue in. Though Les was certain when he dropped her off after coffee and mud cake one evening that Katherine slipped the tongue in and Les had got hold of her left boob. Or was it her right one? But it was definitely one of them and Les felt that if circumstances were permitting and he was around a bit more often there might be a chance for a bit of tampering. He got his little blue book out then picked up the phone.

'Hello. Rose Bay Travel Service.'

'Could I speak to Katherine Hannan please.'

'This is Katherine.'

'Hello Kathy. It's Les Norton.'

'Les. Oh hello. How are you?'

'Not too bad thanks. How's things with you?'

'Good. It's a little quiet at work at the moment. So I'm kicking back with a nice cup of tea and a biscuit.'

'Half your luck. You still ripping into the training? You looked in terrifying condition when I saw you down the beach last week.'

'I sure am. I'm going for my black belt in a few weeks.'

'You'll romp it in, Kath. Especially living that Spartan lifestyle you do.'

'Yes. Well you know the old saying, Les. Early to bed, early to rise . . .'

'Makes a girl healthy, wealthy and wise.'

'That's the one, Les. Just like the show on TV.'

They made a little more small talk then Les dropped it on her.

'The Ultimate Fighting Championship. Sounds exciting. And you're in the VIP section as well as ringside tickets.'

'Yeah. I know it mightn't be your cup of tea. But you're sort of into that thing and I got some nights off . . . so I thought I'd give you a call.'

There was silence on Katherine's end of the line for a moment.

'All right, I'll come with you, Les. Why not. This could be good,'

'Unreal.'

Les said he'd call round her place at seven, leave his car outside and they could catch a taxi. He'd pick his car up when he brought her home. Katherine said that was okay, but that she was staying at her other brother Henry's home unit at Coogee while he was away for a few days. She gave Les the address and said she'd see him at seven. Well there you go, Les smiled at the phone. This could be a good night. There's something about Kathy I like. I hope she likes the fights.

After Norton had stuffed around the house and gone down and bought a few things they needed for the kitchen, it was time to start getting ready. Warren arrived home a little late and when Les came out of his bedroom all schmicked up in a pair of jeans, a maroon shirt and a black Wrangler jacket he'd bought in America, he found Warren in the kitchen staring over the top of half a bottle of Eumundi Lager.

'So how was the day at Cremorne, Woz? Did you get a root?'

'Almost,' replied Warren dryly. 'I had a wonderful chap called Reece up on the casting couch and the leg broke.' Warren sniffed the air then gave Norton a once up and down. 'Where the fuck are you going?'

'Warren, old mate. You ain't gonna believe this.'

About ten minutes later Les was looking at his watch and Warren was shaking his head over another bottle of beer.

'You're right, Les. I don't fuckin' believe it. Bloody Neville Nixon ringing you up just like that.' Warren shook his head again. 'I don't believe it.'

'So if you know what's good for you Croden. Keep that groupie girlfriend of yours away from the Mud Crabs when I bring them to town.'

'Shit. Wait till I tell her. She'll start frothing at the mouth.'

Norton looked at his watch again. 'Yeah, well if I don't get going, I know somebody else that'll start frothing at the mouth. I'll probably see you in the morning.'

'Yeah righto, Les,' replied Warren, still sounding a little dazed. 'I'll see you then.'

Les climbed into the mighty Datty, checked the address again and thundered off towards Coogee.

Brother Henry's home unit was in a side street to the right of and just behind Coogee Surf Club. There were six in the block, all beige-painted brick with coloured awnings over the sundecks, stained glass windows on the stairs and a huge frangipani tree dropping white and yellow flowers everywhere out the front. The unit was on the second floor. Les parked the Datty in front of some Otto bins, skipped happily up the stairs and knocked on the solid wooden door. Katherine opened the door wearing a pair of Levi 501s, K. Swiss gym boots and a green Wallabies Rugby Union sweat shirt, carrying a glass of wine in one hand and a CD cover in the other. She didn't say hello or anything to Les, instead seeming to turn away from him. Les closed the door behind him and followed her down a hallway into the lounge room. The unit was done out in solid wooden furniture, solid wooden landscapes on the walls, and solid stone bric-a-brac. Everything was tidy and in good taste but left little doubt that a man of some description lived there. Katherine still didn't say anything, keeping her back slightly to Les; he wasn't sure, but it looked to him like she'd been having a tiny weep. A song was playing from an expensive stereo against one wall; Les recognised the tune and smiled knowingly.

'Yeah. He sure knows how to string them together. Doesn't he, Miss Hannah?'

'No he does not.' Katherine sort of snapped at Les for catching her out and placed the CD on the kitchen benchtop. 'I've been playing it all afternoon. I'm going to buy another first thing in the morning.'

Les picked up the CD. Graeme Connors – 'The Road Less Travelled'. Norton had it at home with all Graeme Connors' other CDs. The track finishing was, 'I Won't Forget Loving You'. 'He named this CD after me you know.'

Katherine spun around. 'What?'

Norton pointed to the cover. 'The road Les travelled. That's all about me.'

'Oh don't give me the . . .' Katherine took the CD from Les then smiled through the mist in her eyes. 'Actually he looks a bit like you leaning against the wall. That red hair and those cheeky sort of eyes.'

'Get out. I'm better looking than that.'

'Oh you think so do you?'

Norton looked at Katherine for a moment then shook his head. 'No. About the only bloke I'm better looking than, Kathy, is your brother Steve. What about the one who owns this? Is he any bigger or uglier than Steve?'

'Henry? Or as they called him at school, Hogs Head Hannan. The prefect from hell. You'd better believe it, Les. Anyway, I'm going to have another glass of wine. Would you like a beer? We've got time.'

'Yeah okay. One'd be nice. Thanks.'

Kathy poured herself another glass of mozell then handed Les a bottle of Coopers Stout from the fridge and they made a bit of small talk till she rang for a taxi. Henry, who ran some marine engineering company, had to go to Port Kembla on Sunday and would be back Thursday morning. Les told Kathy he was going to Wagga Wagga the next day to pick up the Mud Crabs; she missed the game on TV, but she'd heard about it somewhere.

The taxi arrived, Kathy locked up the home unit, and they walked down and bundled into the back. Kathy appeared to be in quite a good mood now, laughing and looking forward to the fights, and Les was glad he'd rung her up. He also had a feeling, the way she was shadow boxing and bouncing around on the back seat, there was a good chance Kathy'd had more than just two glasses of mozell. Whatever the case, it was shaping up to be a good night. Before long they arrived at the rear of Darling Harbour and Les paid the driver.

'I like it down here,' said Kathy, as they started walking towards the exhibition halls.

'Yeah. It's a good spot all right,' agreed Les. 'I want to come down and check out that IMAX screen.'

'I'll come with you.'

'Okay.' Whether it was the way Kathy said it or how she slipped her arm inside Norton's, the big Queenslander couldn't help but get a bit of a glow inside as they strode happily along the corridor.

When they reached the venue, there were hordes of people milling around or queued up waiting to buy their tickets – mainly hard-looking men who probably wouldn't take too kindly to some mug and his trendy-looking tart in her rah-rah sweatshirt pushing in front of them. Across the queues Les saw a man in a green coat who was standing next to a table in front of the long glass doors that separated the punters from inside. Les pointed him out to Kathy and like a true gentleman let her go first. The horde parted amicably enough and Les followed politely behind.

'You got the tickets for the VIP box mate?' The bloke nodded. 'Is there two there for Norton?' The man in the green coat flicked through a box of envelopes on the table and pulled out two tickets plus a green, plastic ID to go round their wrists. Les gave Kathy a wink as they slipped them on, the bloke opened the door behind him and they were inside with the thousands of other eager fight fans.

Right in the middle was the cage; an eight-sided, open wire grill with black padding around the top and two doors at either end. The ringside seats were level with the cage, the others spread up and out like a coliseum with the scaffolding holding the lighting overhead. An eight piece rock 'n' roll band in tuxedos was belting out some old Motown favourites from a stage in one corner while the punters streamed noisily to their seats creating a noticeable hub-hub of excitement that hung in the air above the music. Behind and above them was the VIP box.

'Why don't we check out our seats first?' suggested Kathy.

'Yeah, good idea,' agreed Les.

A woman attendant led them over and the seats were on the aisle about ten from the front so the view was quite good. They sat down, looked at each other and began checking out the punters; Kathy obviously couldn't quite believe what she was seeing and Les had to admit it was a bit of an eye-opener too. There were blokes with wasp waists and shoulders like the back of armoured personnel carriers, with necks that started somewhere on the tops of their heads and rolled down their backs in thick waves of muscle. Ringside wasn't quite packed and just down from them a big man in a jacket with a broken nose and tattoos all over his hands was eating two sausage rolls on a paper plate; except instead of eating them he was attacking the two sausage rolls with his head like a shark. On the other side a bunch of about fifteen kids in zip jackets, sunglasses and caps on back to front were sprawled around as if some giant hand had scattered them into their seats and said sit there gang and show some attitude. If you were a people perv it was paradise; providing you kept your mouth shut and didn't make too much eye contact. The band stopped, the lights faded momentarily and just as some heavy dance music started up five ninjas in black entered the ring and started kicking and punching, rolling and tumbling around. The lights dimmed momentarily again and the ninja gear came off to reveal five well-stacked, sexy blondes in G-strings who started wiggling their bums and shaking their boobs to the howls and roars of appreciation from the audience.

'Hey this is more like it, Kathy,' cracked Les. 'Bugger martial bloody arts.'

'Filthy animal.'

The dancing girls finished doing their thing and left in a storm of whistles and cheers from the audience, then an MC in a tuxedo entered the ring to announce the first fight and explain the rules. There was no immediate hurry to meet up with Nizegy so Les thought they may as well stay where they were for the time being and watch the opening bout. Les didn't have a programme but it appeared there were eight fighters from around the world who eliminated each other till there were two left, then it was winner take all twenty five thousand dollars. The rules were: no biting, no gouging, no knees and no elbows to the back of the neck. That was about it.

'What? No knives?' said Kathy. 'I'm disappointed.'

'Yeah. That is a bit of a let down,' answered Les. 'I was hoping they could use axes.'

The first fight was between a black American kick boxer and a Brazilian Jiu Jitsu champion from the famous Gracie stable. Both men looked as hard as rocks and both wore knee length, black lycra tights. The American stepped into the cage when he was announced, to the claps and cheers from the audience. When the big Brazilian was announced, it was like carnival in Rio. He came down the aisle flanked by his handlers and followed by a Brazilian drum band going off and a squad of gorgeous Brazilian dancing girls in blue and green boas and bikinis carrying a huge, blue and green Brazilian flag. It looked and sounded sensational. The hyped-up Brazilians blew their whistles, banged their drums and boogied around the ring. There was a bit more hoopla then a bell rang and the two willing contestants got into it.

The two big men carefully circled each other for a moment then the American kicked the Brazilian in the stomach, punched him in the head a couple of times, then kicked him in the leg and gave him another one on the jaw. Les felt Kathy's hand dig into his arm and he noticed her jaw had dropped a little and her eyes were wide open. The American kicked the Brazilian in the leg again, the Brazilian threw a couple of punches back, then quick as a snake ran in, grabbed the American, spun him up in the air and slammed him down on his back. Somehow the American managed to wriggle out from under the Brazilian, sit up on his chest and pin his arms with his knees then start punching him in the head at about eighty punches to the minute. He got a good twenty in before the Brazilian flicked him off. Straight away they charged at each like two buffaloes, then spun across the ring slamming into the wire nearly ripping the cage off its stands and sending a few bits of wire spinning into the crowd. Then they started grappling around the mat with the Brazilian trying to use his Jiu Jitsu to either choke the American out, break an arm or a leg or dislocate something, while the American was trying anything he could think of within the rules.

The crowd at ringside was on its feet now with excitement. The trouble was, as the seats at ringside were level with the cage, once the fighters started grappling on the mat and the people in front stood up it was a bit hard to see what was going on. So there was plenty of 'fuckin' sit down in front you cunts' coming from behind and a torrent of even viler abuse accompanying that. Even though the Brazilian couldn't choke the wily American out, he still gave him an awful hiding and won the first fight fairly convincingly. The Australian audience, however, was more in the mood for stand up kicking and punching rather than grappling and Les figured that as well as the horrible language being a bit too much for Kathy's two sweet shell-likes, if the crowd's view kept being obstructed and there were one or two bad decisions, they might go a bit berko and start throwing chairs along with the abuse. So he suggested to Kathy that they go up to the VIP box. Kathy nodded in agreement and they headed for the far wall and a set of concrete steps with a metal railing where a man in a green jacket checked their ID tags.

The VIP box was spacious and carpeted with a bar in the corner and a long balcony dotted with chairs that faced out over the cage. The other punters were just as hard-looking as the ones downstairs, the only difference was they were possibly a little better dressed. What remained of a tray of nibbles sat in the middle, which made Les glad he wasn't hungry – because the way the punters attacked a tray of chicken wings when it landed, if you were a bit slow in the scrum you could lose an arm up to the elbow. One beer after the first fight wouldn't go astray, however, and Kathy fancied another wine. So Les went and got a can of VB and a glass of white and they moved out onto the balcony. As there was no sign of Nizegy, they found a seat amongst a scattering of more bull-necked, barrel-chested monsters and sat down.

'My word', said Kathy. 'I think a girl would need more than a black belt in Tae Kwon Do to handle some of these men.'

'Yes, they're an unsavoury-looking lot all right,' agreed Les, returning a few discreet nods and winks behind her back. He didn't quite have the heart to tell Kathy he knew most of them and the girls they were with from working at the Kelly Club.

'I'm still enjoying it though,' she smiled, giving Norton's arm another squeeze. 'And thanks again for bringing me, Les.'

'My pleasure, Kathy.' Les pointed to her glass of wine. 'Just don't get too full of plonk and go picking any fights that's all. 'Cause you're on your own Tiger. I don't fancing getting my jacket ripped.'

Kathy looked around. 'That's okay. I'd just ring Henry.' She had another look around. 'Yes. Hogs Head would give any of these boys a run for their money.'

The band finished the song they were doing, the attendants wiped the blood out of the ring from the previous fight, and it was time for the next one. A big Maori in a pair of Thai boxing shorts and a white boy from Newcastle wearing what looked like King Gees. They charged into the middle of the cage and immediately started punching and kicking the soul case out of each other, which straight away brought the crowd to its feet again; this was more what they'd come to see. The big Maori seemed to be doing most of the kicking and punching, giving the Newcastle boy all sorts of trouble; especially when he'd knock him down and boot him straight in the face every time he tried to get up, then jump on him and try to choke him. But they breed them tough up around the Hunter Valley. Somehow or other the Newcastle boy got a second wind and finished up smashing the big Maori, knocking him out for good measure. Unfortunately the Newcastle boy couldn't continue into the finals as he broke his jaw in the process.

The band kicked into another song, the attendants wiped the blood from the ring, then the lights dimmed and a bunch of men in black Tae Kwon Do outfits piped with coloured edges got up and gave a lightning fast display of martial arts, complete with swords and spears, under a strobe light. It looked sensational.

Next fight was a hulking Canadian and some Aussie bloke called Elvis something or other. Elvis absolutely blitzed the Canadian; smashing, choking and knocking him out in the first round. The ring attendants wiped away the blood, the dancing girls in the G-strings did some more bump and grind, then a big Aussie boy from Queensland jumped up and flattened Elvis even quicker than Elvis had flattened the Canadian. Naturally, the ring announcer had to say it as they carted Elvis off on a stretcher:

'Ladies and gentlemen. Elvis is now leaving the building . . .'

The blonde-haired bloke from Queensland looked the goods, obliterating everyone in his path. All the time though, the Brazilian was wrapping himself around his opponents like a lantern-jawed boa constrictor crushing them with his strength and choking them out with his Jiu Jitsu techniques. The eliminating fights seemed to end fairly quickly now, which was only natural. Most people would be lucky to have two or three horrible, knockdown, drag 'em out fights in their life, let alone a night. Finally, the last ones standing were the blonde bloke from Queensland and the Brazilian. Norton's heart was in the right place. But he hardly had time to cheer. The Queenslander came out of his corner and tried for a flying head scissors – and missed. The Brazilian grabbed an arm and a leg, wrapped the Queenslander up and choked him out in what seemed like seconds. Norton couldn't believe it. The Brazilians could. No sooner did they hold the winners hand up than the Brazilian band, the dancing girls, the entourage and the supporters came partying and howling down the aisles banging drums, singing and blowing whistles. It was complete pandemonium again.

Les stood up. 'What do you reckon, Kathy? We make a bolt for the cab rank before the hordes get there?'

'Yes. Good idea.'

They walked briskly to the stairs then out the front and began a fast walk, which finished up in a jog, to where they came in. Les was glad he'd only had the one can of beer because Kathy wasn't setting too bad a pace. Her big, rugby union-playing brothers must have trained her well, because as they zig-zagged through the other punters she showed a neat sidestep that would have got a nod from the Ella brothers. They burst through the glass doors elbowing four young blokes and some Japanese tourists aside to get the last taxi waiting on the rank.

'Coogee mate,' said Les, as they piled in the back.

'Righto,' said the driver. They took off leaving a string of curses hanging in the air along with something unintelligible from the Japanese.

The conversation was fairly incessant on the trip home. Although Kathy still kept her arm inside Norton's, she was bubbling away about some of the fights they'd just seen and it was obvious she'd enjoyed both a night with a difference and Norton's company. Sitting so close to him she looked quite sweet and sparkling, and every now and again the passing lights of the city would wash over her squizzly brown hair or play little tricks in her soft, hazel eyes. Les could feel that warm glow inside him again and as he placed his hand over hers, was wondering what his next move should be. Kathy made it for him after Les paid the driver outside her brother's home unit.

'Would you like to come up for a beer or a coffee before you go home?'

'Yeah, all right. Thanks.'

Kathy said she'd had enough wine for the night and Les didn't particularly feel like another bottle of Coopers, so Kathy brewed up some nice, relaxing herb tea. While the kettle boiled Kathy slipped on the same Graeme Connors CD and before long they were seated on Henry's solid, black leather lounge with just the music and the light from a table lamp in one corner for company.

'One of the reasons I went out tonight was because I don't have to start work until twelve tomorrow,' said Kathy. 'Normally I never go out during the week.'

'Yeah. It makes a difference if you don't have to get up in the morning.' Les took another sip of herb tea and tried to swallow a yawn as he put the cup back on the coffee table. Whatever the tea was, as well as having a nice taste it was very relaxing.

Kathy seemed to notice. 'What about you? You're not working tomorrow are you?'

'No. But I have to get up early. I'm going training with Billy.'

'How early?'

'About six-thirty.'

'Six-thirty? Mmmhh. That is early.' An odd smile seemed to flicker across Kathy's eyes. 'And Billy likes to train hard too. Doesn't he?'

'Does he what. He can be a monster at times.'

'I like your friend Billy. He's a good bloke.'

'Yep. One of the best.'

'And you'd never let Billy down. Would you?'

Les shook his head adamantly. 'No. Never.'

'You'll be there tomorrow morning at six-thirty. No matter what.'

Les nodded. 'My word is my bond, Kathy.'

With a kind of twinkle in her eye, Kathy put her cup of herb tea down on the coffee table too. 'Have you ever done any Jiu Jitsu, Les?'

'Jew Jitsu? Isn't that some kind of Israeli folk dance?'

'What would you do if I started to do this?' Kathy got up and sat on Norton's knees, facing him with her legs either side of his waist, then put her hands round his neck and started softly squeezing.

Les looked at her for a moment. 'I'd just put my arms up through yours. Push your right arm down with one elbow. Take you by your lovely, thick brown hair with my left hand and pull your head to one side. Then do this.' Les started kissing Kathy on the neck. Up and down, under her chin, round her ear lobes, giving the smooth sweetness of her skin a little flick with his tongue now and then.

'Mmmhhhh.'

Les let go of her hair and started running his fingers through it, lightly massaging her scalp. 'I might even throw that in too,' he said quietly, still softly kissing her neck.

Kathy had her eyes closed and was starting to purr. 'That's fighting very dirty you know.'

'It's the only way I could win Kathy. You'd kill me in a fair fight.'

Les straightened Kathy's head up a little, she opened her eyes for a brief moment, then Les brought his lips down lightly onto hers; and Kathy didn't seem to mind one bit. Her mouth opened a little as she returned Norton's kisses and Les deftly slipped the tongue in about the same time Kathy deftly slipped the tongue out. After that it got very steamy, very quickly. Kathy laced her hands behind Norton's neck and got him in some grip not even the big Brazilian could break. Les slipped a hand up under the back of Kathy's sweatshirt and began rubbing his hand around the small of her back then in between her shoulder blades; he got a bit of surprise to find she wasn't wearing a bra as he hadn't noticed all night. When he moved his hands under the front of her sweatshirt he remembered why; Kathy's set wasn't all that big, but you could flick a two dollar coin off it. As he continued kissing her he placed his hand on her thigh and gave the inside of her leg a rub. Kathy returned Norton's kisses and began undoing the front of his shirt. Then she stopped everything and drew back.

'Who was the last girl you were with?' she demanded.

'Huh?' Les gave Kathy a double blink. 'There was no girl. It was a bloke.'

'What?'

'No, seriously Kathy, I don't think I remember. It's been a bit of a while between drinks.' Les placed his hand over hers. 'But whoever she was, she had nothing on you, Kathy. And I mean that from the heart mate.'

Kathy took hold of one of Norton's fingers. 'Well it's been a long time between drinks for me too, Les. But. I've been taking the pill lately to regulate my periods. So . . .'

'Well, I'm not on the pill Kathy. But my doctor said I was A okay in all departments last time I saw him. And just a regular kind of guy.'

'And a bit of a bastard.'

'A bit,' admitted Les. 'But I have been taking my evening primrose oil. Which is your bedroom?'

'The one closest to the door.'

'Shall we go?'

Kathy left the door half-open and by the light

coming in from the lounge room Les could see brother Henry also used the spare room as a gym. There was a set of weights and a bench press next to a wardrobe against one wall then a dressing table and a double bed with a check doona on it. Les also noticed, that if Kathy looked good down the beach in her one piece, when she got down to a pair of shiny, mauve knickers, she looked that good he fell into Henry's weights with a great, clunking rattle. Les kept perving on her as she slipped her sweatshirt over her head, while he was standing on one leg trying to get his jeans off. Kathy switched a lamp on next to the bed, rolled the doona back and Les got into bed with her. Kathy wrapped herself around him and immediately they started kissing up a storm.

Les massaged Kathy's hair and the back of her neck, ran his hand around the flat of her stomach then began stroking the mound under her knickers. It began to swell delightfully so Les slipped a hand somewhere between her knickers and her bikini line, found an erogenous zone and let his fingers do the walking. Before long Kathy had her tongue in his ear, a hand on his knob and was starting to softly moan a little and grind against him. Les didn't need Mr Wobbly to tell him Kathy was starting to sizzle and it was time to stick a fork in her to see if she was done. She brought her knees and ankles together as Les delicately slipped her knickers off then spread her legs and brought her knees up. Les got in between and kissed her again. It took a couple of gentle pushes at first, then a few more followed by a couple of shoves, then Kathy gave a couple of squeals followed by a tiny scream, then Les was in and they began moving together.

Norton didn't know what to think. He'd always fancied Kathy in a strange sort of way and often fantasized about making love to her when he'd given her a bit of cheek on the odd occasions they either went out or they'd bump into each other somewhere. But in his wildest dreams he didn't ever think it would come to this and, when it did, be this good. After a while Les didn't bother thinking about anything. He just concentrated on what he was doing. About the only thought that did cross his mind was that somehow he had momentarily slipped into heaven. Like all good things, however, it had to end sooner or later. Kathy started to scream a little louder as she pushed up and scrabbled at Norton's red hair. Les ran his hands up along her ribs to her shoulders, pushed her arms straight back behind her and got a brief glimpse in the darkness of Kathy's thick locks of brown hair thrashing from side to side as she screamed some more and threw her head against her arms. Then Les emptied out for what seemed like an eternity, till it felt as if every piece of marrow and every drop of blood had been drained from his bones and veins. His heart was thumping and his eyes were still spinning when Kathy went to the ensuite and came back with a towel about five minutes later. They straightened the bed a little and out of the sides of his eyes Les could see the white of Kathy's smile next to his face shining at him in the soft light from the bedlamp.

'So how are you feeling, Les?' she purred. 'Would you like another cup of herb tea?'

'I need more than a cup of bloody herb tea,' replied Norton. 'How about a couple of litres of blood and an oxy-viva? You've destroyed me, woman.'

Kathy chuckled and picked at a hair on Norton's chest. 'You were easy meat. I've had harder games of noughts and crosses.'

'Yeah. I'll bet you say that to all the boys.'

'What?!!'

Kathy gave Les a light clout over the ear and Les was thinking of some other smart remark to stir her up when the building started to shake like it had been hit by a small earth tremor. The shaking seemed to intensify as if the epicentre was now on the landing right outside the door. The noise stopped suddenly, there was the sound of a key rattling in a lock, then the door opened and slammed shut. The unit shook and rumbled again, then the noise stopped and was followed by a strange bellow, as if something had just broken loose from Jurassic Park.

'RROOARGGRSSHLLNMPHPH!??'

'Jesus Christ! What was that?'

'Oh God. It's Henry.'

'Henry? What the . . .'

Kathy put her finger over her lips and her hand over Norton's at the same time. She got up, slipped quickly into a pair of tracksuit pants and the same top she'd worn that night and moved across to the half-open door. Then a shadow fell over the door, blocking all light coming into the room except for a tiny shaft near her face.

'Henry. You gave me a bit of a start. I wasn't expecting you back so soon.'

Henry's voice sounded like Darth Vader gargling blue metal. 'We closed early at Port Kembla. So I drove straight home to catch the test. What are you doing anyway? Are you all right Katherine? What's the light doing on in the lounge room?'

A trickle of sweat ran down Norton's neck as Kathy started tap dancing. 'One of the girls from work called round earlier. I was reading a book on the bed and dozed off.' She threw in a yarn. 'Actually I'm glad you woke me up. I'll get into bed now.'

'All right Katherine. I might watch TV for a while. But I'll keep the sound down so I don't wake you up.'

'Okay.' Kathy yawned again. 'Well, goodnight Henry. I'll see you in the morning.'

'Goodnight Katherine.' The shadow moved momentarily and a little more light fell on Kathy. 'Oh, mum rang earlier. She wants to talk to you about that cruise her and Aunt Lilian are taking to New Zealand.'

'I'll ring her first thing in the morning. Goodnight Henry.'

'Night Katherine. Sleep tight.'

Kathy closed the door gently, turned off the bedlamp, then took her clothes off and got back into bed with Les. All the time Les had been laying there stiff as a running board trying to disappear into the doona and praying his almost imperceptible breathing, the banging of his heart and the whites of his eyes bulging out in the dark didn't give him away. If that was brother Henry, who did her mother marry? Jabba the Hutt? The home unit shook and rattled some more, there were noises in the kitchen, then the lounge groaned in protest and Australia vs South Africa at Rugby Union came on with the sound barely audible. Though you could bet there'd be nothing wrong with Henry's hearing, thought Les.

He'd probably have ears big enough to swat flies with.

Norton lay there wondering what to do. His guilt feeling as well as the monster in the next room had him too terrified to move let alone speak. Apart from a few slivers of light coming in under the blind the room was in complete darkness. But he could sense Kathy smiling at him in the dark. Then he felt her tongue in his ear and her hand move down onto Mr Wobbly.

'Kathy don't!' Les breathed urgently.

Kathy ignored Les and started kissing his neck, like he did to her earlier, while she continued to stroke Mr Wobbly. And Mr Wobbly didn't seem to mind one little bit. In barely moments he was up and about looking for some more action.

'Kathy. For Christ's sake don't.' Les took her wrist and held her hand away from Mr Wobbly. 'Don't!'

Les felt her warm breath in his ear. 'I'll scream.'

'You'll scream anyway, you stupid . . .'

It was useless. Kathy moved her mouth down onto Mr Wobbly and got him harder and meaner than he already was, then eased herself down on top – as if she was slipping gently into a nice warm bath – and slowly but steadily started having the time of her life. But Kathy definitely didn't scream. She closed her eyes and shuddered and sighed a bit, but she definitely didn't scream. In fact, the only one having trouble not screaming was Norton. He wanted the world to know. It was nothing short of sensational; sweat ran into his eyes and tears ran out of them. Somehow he managed to wrap the towel around his face and gag himself, while also shoving the pillow over his head;

he almost bit straight through the towel into the pillowcase as he joined Kathy in the home stretch for the run to the judges.

Roughly an hour or so later Kathy was cuddled up against Norton's chest snoring softly and Henry was still in the lounge room watching the rugby union. Every now and again the unit would shudder and shake if Henry got up for a beer; and when he took a leak the gurgling and splashing coming from the bathroom sounded like there was a draught horse in there letting go. Australia scored a try and during the conversion Henry let loose this unbelievable fart that went for about a minute. Christ! I hope he doesn't smoke, thought Les. He'll blow the whole building up if he lights a match. Norton lay there staring at the ceiling and looking at his watch now and again. Then the TV went off. There was more shaking and shuddering, more gurgling and splashing followed by another horrendous fart, a door closed then silence. You fuckin' beaut, thought Les. I'll give him fifteen minutes then bolt. Les only had to wait five minutes before it sounded as if there was a herd of hippos in Henry's room all stuck in a mud hole trying to get out at once. That'll do me.

Les got out of bed and started trying to put his clothes on in the dark. Some money fell out of his pockets, but Les thought he might leave it for the cleaners. In the fraction of light creeping under the blind Kathy still looked gorgeous laying on the bed, the outline of the doona against her tight rump and one shoulder exposed. Les smiled at her and couldn't quite help himself. He crept over, tucked the doona around her then kissed her lightly on the lips. Her eyelids flickered for a second so he kissed them too, then snuck out the door closing it behind him. Les didn't have to do too much sneaking. Out in the hallway Henry's snoring would have blanketed him kick-starting a Harley-Davidson. He eased the dead-lock then slipped down the stairs into the night.

Sitting in the car Les looked at his watch again. It was late and he was tired, but after the drama up in Henry's home unit his adrenalin was still pumping and his mind was racing. Christ! What did Kathy say up in the VIP box? Yes. Henry'd give any of these boys a run for their money. Imagine if that monster had walked in the room and found me there with no gear on. He'd have tried to kill me. Les looked up at the night sky and offered a silent thanks. He fired up the mighty Datty, drove back down to the corner then stopped for a moment and looked up at the street sign. This is the street where the garage is. I'm sure of it. Nizegy wrote it down on that piece of paper. Number 171. S'pose I may as well check the bloody thing out while I'm here. Save me going out of my way in the morning. The lights were green at the next inter-section, so Les drove straight through. I wonder what happened to Nizegy tonight anyway? Probably too busy. Oh well. He kept going and found it roughly a kilometre past the hotel.

It was just one skinny garage on the bottom left of what was either a large house or a small block of flats built from old, purple bricks. The flats or house were on a corner in front of a roundabout just up from a tatty bus stop and a small, barren-looking park with a few tired-looking palm trees separating it from a dead-end street behind and the surrounding,

69

Federation-type houses. A set of steps on the right ran up to a glass door and a verandah with another storey above that; there was an odd, angled brick fence out the front and a rusty, wrought iron gate in front of the garage roller door. It looked old and cramped and hardly the place you'd park a decent-sized car let alone a team of swimmers. How's he going to fit seven blokes in there, thought Les? Maybe it's bigger inside and goes back. Les gave a shrug. May as well have a closer look I suppose. He got out of the car, walked across and stepped over the wrought iron gate.

The lock on the bottom looked like one of those cheap things you could open with a Paddle Pop stick and Les was surprised to find it wasn't even locked. He's fuckin' kidding. Les reached down, removed the lock from the clasp and slid the door up. There wasn't a great deal of light entering, but enough to show there were no bunks, no portaloo, or shower or whatever. The only things in the garage were what looked like a stack of shiny, metal tea chests against the back wall, half-a-dozen or so, small suitcases on the left and about the same number of small wooden boxes sitting on a table alongside the wall opposite. On top of the boxes was an oblong-shaped parcel wrapped in a piece of old oilskin. Les couldn't make out anything written on the boxes. But across the folds of the oilskin was what looked like a K then RAND. The bulb above Norton's head lit up for a second and he gave the parcel a light nudge.

He couldn't believe it. It was the parcel of tiles he'd been after. It was a bit hard making out the shape in the dark. But under the oilskin Les could feel they were the same shape, same size, same weight and there would have been about sixty as well. That was Kandos Grand written across the top of the oilskin and folded over. Les laughed to himself. Forget the luck of the Irish, his own stupid luck was enough. He'd stuffed up on the address and stumbled instead across the garage where the Irish scaffolder had left the parcel of tiles that was over. Well I'll be buggered, thought Les. Somebody up there does love me. Anyway, they're uncle Les's now.

He carefully wrapped the delicate little tiles up a little tighter in the oilskin so they wouldn't chip, closed the garage door and walked back to the car. Top of the morning to him anyway, smiled Les as he put them on the front passenger seat, walked round and got behind the wheel. That certainly saves me a lot of rooting around, he thought. All I have to do now is get the tiler back when this rattle with Nizegy's all over and my rock pool's as good as finished. Unreal. He fired up the mighty Datty and headed for home.

By the time Les got to Bondi he couldn't believe how tired he suddenly was. Then, when he pulled up out the front of Chez Norton, he remembered he had to get up at six-thirty and go training with Billy. Shit! Les cursed to himself. That's going to be fuckin' nice. I'm absolutely rooted in more ways than one. Norton's earlier joy now turned into irritable moodiness. He kicked the car door shut and went inside taking the tiles straight out to the toolshed and placing them on the workbench where they'd be safe. Walking back inside Les was now dog-tired and stumbling into things. Fuck it, he thought. I might ring Billy and leave a message saying forget the whole idea. I'll be too stuffed. I think I can live without spending a morning paddling around Sydney bloody harbour. Will I, or won't I? There was one message blinking on the answering service. Les pushed the button and it was the man in question himself.

'Les. It's Billy. Mate, you're not gonna believe this. I dropped the fuckin' steering lock on Lyndy's foot after the pictures and I think I broke her toe. Anyway I'm taking her down for an X-ray first thing in the morning, so the paddle's brushed. Sorry old fellah. I'll probably ring you in the morning or whatever. See you mate.'

Norton raised his hands above his head. Praise the lord. I'll get up around nine. Les didn't even bother to clean his teeth. He just crawled straight into bed. Before he crashed out into a deep, deep sleep he had to smile one smile though. It hadn't been a bad start to the week.

It was getting on for half-past-nine when Les blinked his way out of the bathroom into the kitchen and started getting himself together. Warren had gone to work, there were no phone messages, and outside it looked cloudy with a southerly blowing, much the same as the day before. He had a quick breakfast, climbed into a clean pair of jeans, a mambo T-shirt and his vest, threw some things into a gym bag plus a small overnight one. He was wondering what the weather would be like in beautiful downtown Wagga Wagga, when Nizegy arrived at the front door in a pair of brown jeans and matching jacket; he had double-parked a white Holden Statesman out the front.

'You ready?'

'Sure am.'

'Okay. I'll see you out the car.'

Les turned the radio off in the kitchen, picked up his bags and, after making sure the house was locked, joined Nizegy out in the street. He was standing at the back of the Statesman with the boot open; inside were two overnight bags and Les threw his biggest bag in next to them.

'There's four hundred grand in those bags, Les. That's to pay the other teams. A bloke in Wagga Wagga will get them off you when he picks up the car.' Nizegy smiled at Les. 'It's all kosher so you needn't worry.'

Les shrugged indifferently. 'Talking about money, here's one thousand drops of my precious blood.' Norton slipped the money from inside his vest and handed it to Nizegy. 'Four hundred grand in the boot and I'm giving you one of mine. I must have a pumpkin for a fuckin' head.'

Nizegy kept smiling. 'Don't worry about it, Les,' he said. 'You'll be sweet on Sunday. This just keeps you keen.' Nizegy tucked Norton's thousand into his jeans, closed the boot and handed Les the keys. 'Righto mate,' he said. 'Drop me off at the Diggers. I got to meet someone for a cup of coffee.'

After having to jemmy himself into the mighty Datty the plush roomy console of the Statesman felt like the flight deck on the star ship Enterprise. And warp drive too, mused Les, noticing the Statesman had a V8 motor. Hitting hyperspace down the Hume Highway should be very interesting.

'Hey, that's a nice vest, Les,' commented Nizegy. 'Where did you get that?'

'Actually it was given to me. Some bloke up the Central Coast makes them.'

'Not the Shamash?'

'That's right. How . . . ?'

'I know his style anywhere. His wife makes the teams' outfits.'

'Fair dinkum.'

'Yeah. She's a real good sort too. A blonde. Does heaps of Tai Chi.'

'Go on. Anyway,' Les started the engine and began turning the car around, 'exactly where do I have to go? And exactly what do I have to do?'

'It's easy.'

Nizegy pulled out a notebook and wrote down the name of the hotel Les was staying in and the bloke he had to meet. It was all charged to Nizegy's company, Borderland Touring. Any dramas and there'd be a message at the desk. The bloke would drop the bus off at the hotel at 8 a.m. with the team in it, then pick up the Statesman and the money. Leave the money in the safe at the front desk. While he had his biro out Les got Nizegy to write down his mobile phone number and the address of that garage again, saying he'd left it somewhere in his room and couldn't find it. Les didn't mention anything about the previous night, figuring Nizegy might think him a bit of a wally driving around in the early morning getting the address mixed up. He'd tell him about it Sunday night when it was all over and they were having a drink or whatever. When he asked Nizegy what happened to him last night, Nizegy said he got tangled up with a couple of TV producers and couldn't make it. Les said he missed a good night. By the time Nizegy commented about how Bondi didn't look the same without the baths, and Les sagely agreed with him, they were outside the Bondi Diggers.

'Okay Les,' said Nizegy getting out of the car. 'Take care and I'll see you back in Sydney tomorrow afternoon.'

'Righto Neville. See you tomorrow.'

Les watched Nizegy disappear into the coffee shop beneath the Diggers, drove on a bit further, then did a U-turn at North Bondi Surf Club and came back up Campbell Parade. The lights were red opposite Curlewis Street so Les checked out the piece of paper Nizegy had given him. The hotel was called Romero's and the bloke he had to meet there was named Coyne Stafford. Well that's not too hard to remember, thought Les. As the lights turned green he had a look at his watch. I'm in no mad hurry. I may as well go and check this garage out, then I know where it is for certain. Les tucked the piece of paper back in his jeans, then took the scenic route past Tamarama and Bronte and headed up Hewlett Street towards Coogee.

The garage was in a three-storey block of home units, first on the right at the bottom of Mount Street about two hundred metres from the corner and directly opposite Coogee Oval. The units sat on the corner of another street then ran back up the hill and each was surrounded by glass balconies with a row of five garages facing the street below and the oval. The garage was on the end right and seemed a little bigger than the others; it had a flat, concrete deck on top and a small door built into the roller so you didn't have to open the roller all the time to get inside. A grimy, narrow passageway separated the last garage from an equally grimy, old block of flats next to it. Les glanced from the garage across Coogee Oval, where he could see McDonalds and several other shops and the Coogee Bay Hotel a little further on. Nizegy had given him the key but Les thought he'd check it out when he came back with the Mud Crabs. He glanced at his watch. Righto beautiful downtown Wagga Wagga. Town of good sports. Here I come. Les headed back towards the city and Parramatta Road.

After a bit of ducking and diving through the traffic, Les found Liverpool Road past Ashfield and Enfield and was heading towards Campbelltown and the M5. The traffic was fairly heavy so he didn't bother with his tapes but just hit the tuner in the Statesman and listened to whatever glurge was playing on Sydney FM. He yawned a couple of times and rubbed his eyes. Still feeling a little grainy from having to rush this morning and not quite getting a full nights sleep. Les smiled to himself. But it had certainly been worth it and he'd give Kathy a ring as soon as he reached Wagga. Would he ever. Despite only having a cup of coffee and a muesli biscuit for breakfast Les wasn't all that hungry. He'd have a big feed when he reached Wagga but he'd stop at Goulburn and grab some nibblies and a drink when he got some petrol. Before long the traffic started to ease and he was on the M5. The Statesman was perfectly air conditioned but outside it was quite cloudy and the wind whipping across the rolling dry brown hills and through the trees looked cold and uninviting. Les took an apple from his overnight bag and slipped a tape into the cassette player. The Warumpi Band's 'Jailanguru

Pakarnu' slipped into Graeme Connors' 'An Old Piece of Wood' and whistling happily while he tapped his fingers on the steering wheel Les zoomed on towards Goulburn.

Norton wasn't wrong about the cold. When he stopped for petrol at Goulburn he got out of his vest, climbed into a Levi jacket and buttoned it up to the collar. The wind coming down from the mountains across the petrol station was colder than the proverbial well digger's. He paid the garage attendant, stocked up on nibblies and fruit juice and proceeded on towards Yass and Gundagai.

A packet of burger rings and a bottle of orange mango juice later, Les couldn't believe what absolutely splendid time he was making. He'd be in Gundagai before he knew it. Then Les looked at the speedo. He was sitting on 170 klms an hour and it didn't feel like he was moving. Shit! I don't believe it. If some fat-arsed speed cop pulls me over and finds that money in the boot, kosher or not, I'll be pretty cold sitting in some gaol in Goulburn by the time I sort it out. Les brought the statesman back to 110 klms just as a police car seemed to come out of nowhere and pass him as the Fabulous Thunderbirds' 'Work Together' went into John Mayall's 'I'm A Sucker For Love'. Before long he'd cruised through Bookham with all the rusty, old steam engines and tractors parked by the side of the road, the rolling drab hills around Coolac, a few puddles of water that passed for Muttama Creek and he was getting ready to bypass Gundagai. One tape finished, more tunes blended into other ones, and around five or so Les was on the outskirts of Wagga Wagga. Now it was wheat silos, rolling hills in the background, car yards, tractor depots and water pump dealers on either side of a long tree lined road. A Canberra bomber loomed up on the left outside the Air Force Museum at Forrest Hill. Further on a big yellow, Murray cod announced the hatchery at Gumby Gumby, then Les stopped at a set of lights; across the road a sign on a railway bridge said Welcome To Wagga Wagga. A bit further on Les turned right into Baylis Street.

It was just starting to get dark as Norton cruised slowly down the long, wide boulevarde that forms the main street of Wagga Wagga to try and find his hotel. Except for the smaller cars, the low rise buildings and the wide sweep of road reminded him of Sarasota, Florida in an odd sort of way. Whatever Wagga Wagga reminded him of, it all looked very neat and tidy; no graffiti or rubbish and a wide variety of shops with neat, tidy-looking shoppers or whoever they were strolling around. As he stopped for a set of lights, Les felt momentarily sorry he wouldn't be in town a little longer; you'd probably be able to pick up some good country and western music and jeans. He drove past a carefully restored post office and near a little bridge saw a sign saying Wagga Wagga Beach, 600 Metres. What a shame, he thought. I forgot to toss in my Speedos and the banana chair. He zapped his window down a few inches then zapped it straight up again as a blast of cold air hit him in the face. Yes, well we might just put the beach on hold for the time being.

At the bottom of a small hill Les found what he was looking for on the opposite side of the road next to an intersection and a set of traffic lights. A lovely old, beige brick hotel with tan awnings and a white sign saying ROMERO'S wrapped right around one corner of a side street and the local courthouse wrapped around the corner facing it. For some reason there seemed to be a lot of activity around the courthouse. There was another wide, side street on the left and a sign saying No Right Turn. Les moved the Statesman on about another hundred metres past the lights, did a U-turn and, although there was parking at the rear, turned left and got a parking spot almost outside the leadlighted, front door of the hotel next to a hairdressing salon. Les buttoned up his jacket and was about to get out of the car when he noticed the people he'd glimpsed driving past earlier were all journalists swarming between the courthouse and the police station alongside it in a maze of TV cameras, sound crews and other media lizards. Shit! What's this? They're not waiting for me are they? I haven't been busted with a dodgey four hundred grand have I? Norton waited a few moments then cautiously got out of the Statesman and stretched his legs. No one gave him a second look; they were all too busy concentrating their lizard minds on whatever action it was they were concentrating on around the courthouse. Oh well, shrugged Les, at least it ain't me. He gathered all the bags up out of the boot and stepped inside the hotel.

The hotel foyer was very warm and plush, with thick red carpet, green trim on the walls, potted palms and a small lobby area with white lace railing. A cedar staircase angled up in one corner with a pay phone below, a sign to the left said Rugby Bar, and to the right another sign said Romero's Cafe. The old hotel had been carefully restored and the cedar panelling, hanging lights and a small lift around from the front desk gave the place an air of gracious charm and old-style luxury from another era in Australia's history. Despite the swarms of reporters across the street the hotel appeared relatively deserted. Les walked over to the desk, knocked on the counter and a blond-haired man wearing cord trousers and a Riverina Waratahs polo shirt appeared from a side door.

'G'day mate,' he smiled. 'What can I do for you?'

'Yeah. Have you got a room booked here for Norton.'

'Just a sec.' The bloke checked a register on a table and came back. 'Are you Mr. Norton?'

'That's right,' answered Les.

'I got a nice ensuite for you on the second floor.' He handed Les the key and pointed to the corner. 'It's just up the stairs, or you can take the lift.'

'I'll take the stairs.' Les placed the two overnight bags on the counter. 'Can you put these in the safe for me?'

'Sure mate.'

'And keep an eye on them too will you. They're full of money.'

'Yeah sure,' smiled the bloke, adding a nod and wink.

Oh well. It's not as if I didn't tell him, thought Les. 'Hey what's all the commotion across the road?'

'The local cops arrested that paedophile Ken Fisher in Khancoban and they've brought him up to Wagga Wagga lockup to front court.'

'That rock spider that was in the papers?'

'That's him,' said the bloke. 'Let's hope his cell's a nice, cold hard one.'

'And full of rats and cockroaches,' agreed Les. 'So he'll be in good company.'

Les took his bags and began walking up the stairs, which still had their original creak from the turn of the century. The rest of the hotel was more thick carpet, paintings and mirrors on the walls and beautiful old, red-quilted leather chesterfield lounges. Amongst the mirrors and paintings were old sepia photos of Wagga Wagga and the hotel during the floods and in its heyday, giving the establishment even more ambience. Les rounded a corner on the second floor, went through a small TV room, found his room in the corner and stepped inside.

Hey this is all right, thought Norton, tossing his bags on the floor. There were two rooms. One full of bamboo furniture plus a fridge, TV, heater and toilet. The other had two old brass beds, a double and a single covered with thick doonas, electric blankets and heaps of scrunchable, fat white pillows. There was a dressing table, a shower, bedlamps, a radio, and a window overlooking the main street. Les walked across to the window, drew the curtains and raised the holland blind. The street lights were coming on but Les could still make out an empty shop on one corner, a travel agency on the other near a paper shop, and further down the side street opposite the red and gold of a fairly large Chinese restaurant. So that's beautiful downtown Wagga Wagga eh, thought Les. Looks all right to me. He let go of the blind and lay down on the double bed. Ohh yeah. How good's this? It had to be about the most comfortable bed Norton had ever felt. Even better than the one at home. This is what I need, you know, a holiday out in the countryside. Stuff the glitzy resorts, see a bit of the real Australia. He switched the radio on and got a local FM station playing a Sound Garden tune. Mmmhh mmhh. What about these pillows? This is heaven. I might just lay here for five minutes and have a think. About what? I dunno. Nothing.

Five minutes later Les jerked his head up from the pillows to find the room in total darkness and quite cold. 'Shit! What time is it?'

The radio was still playing. Les switched one of the bedlamps on and blinked his watch. It was getting on for seven. Bloody hell! I must have been tireder than I thought. He swung his legs over the bed, rubbed his shoulders and yawned at the floor. I suppose I'd better have a shower and see if I can wake up – a great grumble rolled through his stomach – then get something to eat. He went to the other room, turned on the heater and the TV then stripped off and got into the shower. After a long shower and a shave Les was drying off in front of the heater and watching the ABC news.

First up was a murder-suicide in Queensland, then the cameras switched to Wagga Wagga and the local courthouse for the story on the arrest of Fisher; and sure enough, if you looked behind the scenes, there was Norton getting out of the Statesman, looking around then going into the hotel. Well I'll be buggered, chortled Les. I've made the news. I'm famous. He dried off then got back into the same pair of jeans and Levi jacket and a clean, blue polo shirt. He got his keys, shoved some money into his front pocket, then walked downstairs thinking he might check out the Rugby Bar and maybe have just the one before dinner.

Being an ex-footballer Norton immediately liked the Rugby Bar. There were photos of local rugby teams and other memorabilia all over the walls and international guernseys and team photos signed by the Wallabies above a sign saying, Romero's Hotel Proud Sponsors of Riverina Rugby. A whole panel above the bar was pinned with colourful guernseys of all the local rugby teams, and on one wall was a vicious-looking, Polynesian war club donated by a visiting rugby team sitting beneath an equally vicious-looking, stuffed boar's head. Double windows looked out over the main street and the courthouse opposite, and there was no shortage of chairs or stools and tables crammed with people enjoying a few drinks and cigarettes while they listened to Steve Earle's 'Copperhead Road' – coming from a small CD juke box on one wall. Les went to the bar and ordered a middy of VB from a whippy little blonde barmaid who seemed to walk on her toes all the time. Les returned her pleasant smile when he got his beer, then went over to a vacant stool near a corner window and checked out the surroundings and the punters.

They all seemed to be a hale and hearty looking lot. Everyone was well-dressed and there were quite a number of attractive-looking women amongst them. Whether they had just knocked off from work or not Les couldn't tell, but they all seemed to be enjoying themselves, laughing and talking over a few cool ones early on Wednesday evening. Les was enjoying his middy too, and was almost to the bottom and seriously thinking of ordering another one when he felt a tap on the shoulder and a soft woman's voice in his ear.

'Hello Les darling.'

Norton looked up. The woman was a beefy brunette of about twenty-eight with short hair and a pretty, if tired, sort of face almost devoid of make-up except for some light lipstick. She was wearing a bulky-knit, red top, black jeans and black Doc Marten shoes. It had been a while, but he was certain it was a nurse he knew from the casualty ward at St Vincents who'd helped stitch him up when he got hit over the head with a bottle at work one night. Les got to take her out a few times and won her heart when he gave her a small, gold and pearl, ankle bracelet some hooker left up the Kelly Club to go with a dainty ring of flowers she had tattooed round one of her ankles. She originally came from Junee and lived at Stanmore, if Les remembered right, before she disappeared out of his life after a brief fling; she also looked as if she'd packed on a few kilograms since the last time he'd seen her too.

Norton pursed his lips for a moment. 'Evelyn?'

The girl smiled. 'You still remember me.'

'How could I forget you, Evie baby? Every time I comb my hair I think about you.'

'And I couldn't forget you. Apart from our fling, you're the only man I know that wore a tuxedo and read a magazine while he got his head stitched up.'

'I was filthy on you giving me local anaesthetic. So what are you doing in Wagga Evie? And may I say you're looking just as vivacious as ever too.'

Evelyn smiled coyly. 'I've put on a little weight.'

'Fair dinkum?' said Les. 'I wouldn't have noticed.'

'Actually. I'm down here with an ABC news team.'

Les nodded out the window towards the courthouse. 'Covering that rock spider.'

'That's right.'

'So you've give nursing away?'

'Sort of. I've been with Aunty about five years now.'

'No wonder you're beginning to blossom. You wouldn't raise a sweat if you had malaria, working at the ABC.'

Evelyn shrugged. 'True. But it shits on pumping vomit out of drunks and pulling vibrators out of poof's dates in a casualty ward at three o'clock in the morning.'

'Jesus! You're still a hard woman. Aren't you Evie?' laughed Norton.

'Anyway what are you doing in Wagga Wagga, Les? It seems a long way to come to punch some poor bastard's teeth in.'

Norton told her the truth, and that he was staying at the hotel and going back in the morning. He even nodded towards the Statesman out the front and thanked her for blabbing him all over the seven o'clock news. 'Who are you in here with anyway, Evie? Why don't you pull up a seat and let me buy you a drink. It's good to see you again.' Les gave Evelyn's hand a squeeze. He *was* pleased to see an old friend; and a bit of good company, especially the female kind, was always better than drinking on your own.

Evelyn nodded towards a table of about five very tweedy, very politically correct, ABC-looking types. One bloke with a pepper and salt beard and corduroys was sucking furiously on a pipe. 'I wouldn't mind. But they're all leaving soon to find a cheap nosh. And I have to jump in on my ABC allowance.'

'I'm having dinner in the hotel restaurant shortly. Why don't you join me and I'll shout you a decent feed?'

Evelyn gave Les a double blink followed by a heavy once up and down. 'Don't go away big fellah. I'll be right back.'

Evelyn went over to the table and Les smiled inwardly as the ABC types frowned over at him. Well this is all right, thought Norton. Looks like I've got a friend to have a drink and a feed with. And if I remember correctly, Evelyn didn't mind a laugh when she got a few drinks under her belt. Evelyn returned and sat down just as Les finished his middy and stood up.

'Okay sexy,' she said. 'I'm hard to get. But you got me.'

'They don't call me lucky Les for nothing,' smiled Norton. 'So what would you like to drink, Evie? I'm just about to stagger back to the bar.'

'Scotch and lemonade, thanks Les.'

'Ice and slice?'

'Yes please.'

Les returned with the drinks and sat down. 'Well, what's doing, Evie me old?' he said, clinking her glass. 'How's life treating you?'

'Pretty good,' replied Evelyn, taking a sip of scotch. 'I can't say the ABC tickles my fancy or flips my flaps. But I don't miss St Vincent's all that much either.'

'I don't know,' shrugged Norton. 'Me and Billy used to send down a few customers to keep you going.'

'Yes. I could always tell your handywork, Les,' said Evelyn. 'If their front teeth were all smashed in, that was you. If their ribs were all broken, that was Billy. Is it still as bad up there?'

Norton shook his head. 'Naahhhh. It's getting like a retirement centre. We'd be flat out having six fights a night and two murders a week in the joint now.'

Evelyn's workmates left, more cool ones went down, and before long they were both talking and joking away like old pals. Evelyn was sharing a room in a cheaper hotel up the road, the crew were heading back to Sydney in the morning, but she was getting a lift to Junee at ten to see her family. She was sharing a house at Willoughby now because it was closer to work, though the way things were going at the ABC, she'd probably end up going back to nursing.

'Jesus Evie. You'll do it tough working in a hospital again,' said Les, 'after shuffling around Aunty's glorified, sheltered workshop for the last five years.'

'Probably,' conceded Evelyn. 'But not as tough as some. You ought to see them Les. They're almost suicidal at the thought of having to go out into the real world.'

'I know just how they feel. I'd be the same if I ever had to leave the Kelly Club.'

Les told her a bit more about how he met Nizegy, how he was still living with Warren, how he managed to pay off the house and about the couple of crazy trips overseas he'd had. Evelyn said he should call over her place one night and bring his photos. Norton said he would. After a few beers on an empty stomach Les was starting to feel more than pleasant. His stomach was rumbling, however, and he was also feeling ravenously hungry.

'Well, what do you reckon Evie old mate? You getting hungry? I'm bloody starving.'

Evelyn took another mouthful of scotch and waved the glass. 'As a matter of fact, Les, I am getting rather peckish.'

'Then let's leg it for the restaurant. Before I start chewing on your arm.'

'Ooooh Les. You absolute animal.'

'Gggrrhhh!'

They finished their drinks and left the Rugby Bar. As they stepped through the doorway into the foyer, Evelyn gave Les a cuddle and a peck on the lips. 'Hey, thanks for this Les. It's really nice of you.'

Norton returned her cuddle with a bigger peck on the lips. 'It's an absolute pleasure, Evie my dove.' Les meant it too. Being an old blue collar worker who'd been patched up and stitched up in hospitals, he always had a deep respect for nurses, whether they were old friends or not.

The hotel restaurant was bright and clean with solid wooden tables and polished wooden floors. Two extensive blackboard wine lists sat on one cream wall beneath a white ceiling, and at one end a well-stocked bar meandered around from the kitchen, past a coffee machine and the desk. A pleasant, dark-haired girl wearing a dress, with a white shirt and a tartan tie came over. Les jangled his room key and the girl got them a nice table beneath the wine blackboard leaving them with the menus.

'You fancy a bottle of wine Evie?' asked Les, pointing to the two blackboards.

'Mmmh. That'd be nice.'

'Okay. You pick it.'

'Me?' Evelyn turned to the blackboards.

'Yeah. Ladies choice. I'll help you drink it, no matter what.'

Evelyn's face lit up a little. 'Okay.'

After staring at the wine list for a few moments Evelyn whittled it down to either the Wynns Coonawarra Cabernet Sauvignon. Or the Penfolds Kalimna Bin 28. She finally chose the Bin 28. In the tucker department, Les went for scallops fennell flambe for starters and pork fillets in mandarin brandy sauce for mains. Evelyn chose king prawns and avocado with Thai dressing and chicken kebab skewered with pineapple and mango sauce and roast coconut. The wine arrived, and Evelyn gave it the Leo Schofield treatment; then they filled their glasses, clinked them together, took a slurp each and settled back.

'Actually I've been on a diet,' said Evelyn. 'It's bloody hard.'

'Yeah I know,' answered Les. 'It's not as easy for women. But I wouldn't worry too much if I were you. You're just a big, healthy girl Evie. You've got a big frame.'

'I've been doing a lot of swimming.'

'That's as good as any exercise going. Do that, jump on an exercise bike now and again while you watch a video, and the weight'll fall off you.'

'And watch the food.'

'Yes. But only at home, Evie. Not when you're out with Joe Cool Norton in a grouse restaurant in Wagga Wagga.'

'Exactly.' Evelyn raised her glass. 'One look in your eyes Denzil Dreamboat and I'll start eating like I'm going in a Sumo contest.'

Evelyn put her glass down, undid the front of her bulky knit top and Norton's eyes nearly fell out of his head. Underneath she was wearing a low-cut, tight white singlet that held in a set of the biggest, solidest hooters Les had ever seen. They were massive. She undid two more buttons while she gave her shoulders a wiggle; Les was expecting them to wobble around a bit, but they simply sat there looking like they wouldn't move if you hit them with a shovel.

The food arrived and they started eating, with Norton trying not to spill too much while he forked food into his mouth and ogled Evelyn's front porch at the same time. Everything they ordered was absolutely delicious and went down exceptionally well, along with the choice wine and bubbly conversation. When they had finished Les was in a pretty good mood and felt like kicking on a bit. Evelyn appeared to be the same.

'Well I don't know, Evie,' said Les. 'Maybe it's the wine. But I feel like going out somewhere and giving my tail feathers a bit of a shake. Is there anywhere to go in beautiful downtown Wagga Wagga on a balmy Wednesday night?'

'Actually,' replied Evelyn, taking another sip of wine, 'Wednesday night is students night. There's a big university just out of town and the hotels give the students a bit of a break on the prices tonight.'

'Go on.'

'Well, there's a pub just round the corner called

The Visitors. All the art students hit it tonight and across the road is a nightclub called Stintsons that goes till two.'

'Have they got a dance floor at this Stintsons?'

'Of course.'

'Will you have a dance with me, Evie?'

'Will I have a dance with you, Les? Does Batman drive a Batmobile?'

'Good. Then let's finish this plonk and see what the arts students are up to.'

They downed their glasses and Evelyn did up her top. She gave Les a half-drunk once up and down over her empty glass as he signed the bill, then they headed for the front door.

Outside, the night was quite cold. Evelyn snuggled up to Les, he put his arm around her shoulders, and they ambled down to the Visitors Hotel. It was just an unimposing row of windows and some glass doors against the footpath about a hundred metres round the corner from Romero's. Les pushed open the door and they entered.

Inside was just one fairly crowded room split into two sections by a bar built against a wall on the right with a shelf of bottles running around the top. There were posters on the walls, a row of video machines on the left, a covered-over pool table as you walked in, and a three piece band on the right consisting of a girl on conga drums and two blokes on guitars all aged about nineteen if they were lucky. Most of the clientele were feral-looking art students drinking beer, smoking their heads off and trying to look sort of acid funk, semi-psychedelic, post-hippy. The girls had either scraggly hair and no make-up or scraggly hair tucked up under woollen beanies and make-up laid on with a trowel. Most wore daggy cardigans or V-neck jumpers with the elbows out and the sleeves too long à la Johnny Rotten; there was also a smattering of daggy jeans, Blundstone boots or cheap gym boots and striped socks. The blokes dressed much the same – op-shop clothes, army disposal gear, Van Dyke beards and John Lennon glasses. Scattered amongst the ferals were what looked like the regular punters, wearing flannelette shirts, jeans and trainers and sucking schooners.

'Why don't we go down the other end?' suggested Les. 'There seems to be a bit more room.'

'Good idea,' answered Evelyn.

They eased their way through the crowd, past the video machines and a What's On board pinned mainly with Larsen *Far Side* cartoons, to another section with a few chairs and tables, a fireplace, some RAAF and Vietnam War memorabilia on the walls, more video machines and tucked away in the corners a phone and the toilets. The chairs and tables were all taken by more ferals, but there were two vacant stools against the bar facing the front. Les steered Evelyn towards them and they sat down.

'I might have a Jack Daniels and unleaded,' said Les. 'What about you Evie?'

'Yes, I might have the same,' replied Evelyn. 'I'm getting sick of Scotch.'

Les ordered two Jack Daniels with diet coke and plenty of ice, Evelyn undid the front of her top again, and they settled back to watch the punters and listen to the band.

The band didn't appear to have a name behind

them, but you could describe them simply in two words. Un-bearable. In fact, Les couldn't believe anything could sound that bad or that anybody would have the audacity to get up and do whatever it was they were doing and call themselves musicians. No-one in the trio could sing and no-one could play a note. A bunch of Neanderthals in a cave banging rocks together round a fire would have sounded better. They seemed to be singing or butchering a song of protest that could have been an original.

'Sittin' down by that river. Ooh-ooh.

That dirty, dirty river. Ooh-whoo.

I hate that river. Whoo-ooh.

Dirty, dirty river. Yeah-ooh.'

Norton, thinking maybe it was just him, winced and turned to Evelyn. 'Have you ever heard anything like that?'

Evelyn winced back and shook her head. 'Never. Ever.'

But the ferals seemed to be enjoying it. Some were even shuffling from one foot to the other and mumbling along with the lyrics.

Naturally, in every hotel and in every crowd there has to be a mug and The Visitors Hotel was no exception. This one was a tall, ugly bloke in his mid-twenties with a goatee beard and his hair pinned back in a ponytail, wearing jeans, trainers and a chunky, red, flannelette shirt. Les had been watching him push his weight around, with a cigarette in one hand and a schooner in the other, annoying all the art students; trying to hit on the girls and putting all sorts of shit on the inoffensive blokes.

The people he annoyed most, however, were the

three kids in the band. He kept pulling a mouth organ from the top pocket of his shirt, jumping in with them and playing a few licks. Somehow or other they'd manage to get rid of him, only to have him put down his schooner, pull out his harp and jump back up again and start blasting away louder than ever. The most offensive thing about him, though, was that he could actually half-play his mouth organ. When the trio would hack off another barrage of clunkers, Ponytail would let go some fairly good notes, making them sound even worse than what they actually were, and managing to murder the whole scene, if that was possible. Evelyn picked up on him about the same time as Les and both commented that in a paradoxical sort of way he reminded them of that cartoon on the Bugs Bunny show where the big bad wolf's got a trumpet and keeps trying to join the three little pigs' band before he blows himself up with gunpowder.

The band finally got rid of Ponytail again and he went back to his schooner. Then, from across the bar, he noticed Evelyn's boobs and his eyes started rolling around like they were on springs. Les ordered two more drinks, while Ponytail got a fresh schooner and decided to come round to their side of the bar and have a real good perv. He propped about six feet away blatantly ogling her while he slurped and drooled into his beer. After about five minutes Les turned to Evelyn.

'Friend of yours?' he asked.

Evelyn shook her head. 'I think he's trying to get to you through me.'

Ponytail puffed out his chest a little belligerently. 'You say something?'

Norton shook his head. 'No. Didn't say a word.'

'Me either handsome,' said Evelyn. 'But gee, I wish I had.'

Ponytail ignored Les and gave her a drooling once up and down. 'You from round here?'

Evelyn shook her head. 'No. I live locally.'

'I live in North Wagga. Just over the bridge. Got a house with me two brothers.'

'Yeah? How exciting,' said Evelyn. 'Are all the family as good looking as you?'

Ponytail gave Evelyn a slow, double blink over his schooner. 'Who are you here with?' he asked.

'No-one. I'm on my own.'

Ponytail nodded at Norton. 'You're not with him?'

'No way. I've been trying to get rid of the creep all night. But he won't go away.'

'He won't? Just tell him to piss off.'

'How can I? I'm just a poor defenseless woman.' Evelyn gave Norton a frosty look then batted her eyes at Ponytail. 'Unless you could get rid of him for me. Then maybe you and I could have a drink together.'

'All right. I will.' Ponytail puffed out his chest and gave Norton a very heavy, once up and down. 'You heard her. Piss off.'

Les shook his head adamantly. 'No. I'm not going till I get my cardigan back.' He nodded to Evelyn's red top. 'That's my cardigan. I knitted it. And I'm not leaving here without it.'

'What!?' howled Ponytail. 'You knitted yourself a cardigan? What are you. A bloody POOFTER!?'

'Doesn't matter what I am,' said Les. 'That's my cardigan, and I want it.' He turned to Evelyn. 'So give it back to me. You fat bitch.'

Ponytail puffed himself up some more. 'Listen. I ain't gonna tell you again. Piss off.'

Norton shook his head. 'No. Ain't going nowhere. Not without my cardigan.'

'Oh belt him one will you?' said Evelyn, looking up at Ponytail. 'He's nothing but a big cat anyway. He drinks his milk out of a saucer.'

Ponytail seemed to think for a moment. He looked at Norton then took another look at Evelyn's boobs. 'Okay. I bloody well will.'

Ponytail put his beer on the bar, shaped up to Norton and speared out a very wooden, right hand, Karate type of punch at Norton's chin. About halfway before it landed Les clamped his left hand around Ponytail's wrist, prised his right fingers inside Ponytail's fist and started crushing his knuckles together, while twisting his wrist backwards and down at the same time. Ponytail's face turned white and his jaw gaped open in silent disbelief at the amount of pain he began suffering in such a short space of time. Les kept squeezing and twisting, forcing Ponytail down onto the floor till he was sitting on his behind with his back against the bar. Just as Ponytail's bladder started to go, Les let go of his wrist and gave him two quick backhanders under the ear then stood him back on his feet. Ponytail could still scarcely believe what had happened, it had been that quick; at the same time hardly anybody in the hotel had noticed it.

'Now listen you fuckin' goose,' said Norton, his eyes about an inch away from Ponytail's. 'Piss off. And don't fuckin' come back.'

Norton let go of Ponytail, turned him round and

gave him a slight push in the back propelling him through the crowd. Ponytail bumped into a few people, then half-limped, half-walked out the front door clutching at his hand while a little more dampness spread across the crutch of his jeans.

'Thanks Evie darling,' said Les, sitting back down and picking up his drink. 'Be nice if the prick could fight and knocked me out. Where would you have been then?'

'Sitting here having a drink with him I imagine,' replied Evelyn. 'Where do you think I'd be?'

'Wouldn't surprise me,' sniffed Les. 'If you ask me, I think you secretly fancied him.'

Evelyn jabbed her finger into Norton's shoulder. 'And what's this – "you fat bitch"? How dare you. You crude, rude bastard.'

'What!? Up yours hairy legs,' replied Norton. 'I come in here just to have a quiet drink and enjoy the band. You start running off at the mouth, now everybody in the place knows I'm a POOFTER. Thanks a bloody lot. And I still want my cardigan back.'

'Oh Les, I'm sorry.' Evelyn threw her arms around Norton and kissed him on the lips. 'But what could I do? He was such a fuckin' idiot. And you sorted him out so beautifully.'

'Yes,' replied Norton casually. 'I admit I did handle him with a bit more panache than he deserved. But a mug like that, sooner or later he'll pull that caper with a real nutter one night and wake up the next day in hospital with all drips hanging out of him wondering how he got there?'

'Serve him right. And hopefully this little nurse

won't be there to change his dressings and take his temperature.'

'Talking about temperature,' said Les, finishing his drink. 'Do you think it's time for another cool one?'

'I don't see why not?' replied Evelyn, draining hers also. 'And let's make them doubles. My shout too.'

'No. I'll get them. You can shout me one when we get to that nightclub you're taking me to.'

'Okay.'

They stayed at the bar a while longer and a couple more drinks went down. Somehow the band seemed to get worse, if that was at all possible, and the air began to feel like all the smokers were lighting two cigarettes at a time. Les started getting to the bottom of another Jack Daniels and diet coke.

'Well, what do you reckon Evie,' he said, turning to Evelyn. 'This band's starting to give me corns on my ears. We hit the toe?'

'Yes,' agreed Evelyn. 'I'd just as soon have boiling lead poured in mine than listen to any more, and the cigarette smoke's starting to get a bit bewildering too. We'll go to Stintsons.'

'Splendid idea.' They finished their drinks and left the hotel.

Outside the warm pub, the main drag in Wagga Wagga felt like Camp Mawson. Les and Evelyn grabbed each other and headed off into the night with Evelyn leading the merry way. It wasn't far to Stintsons, barely two hundred metres down the street on the opposite side of the road.

The entrance was a maroon marquee with STINTSONS in gold across the front, then double glass doors beneath with a sign saying Open; above, a blue neon sign on a window said Restaurant and Nightspot. There was no-one much around, as a young solid bloke in a white shirt and black bow tie smiled then stepped back to let them inside. They went up an angled staircase with posters and mirrors on the walls, to a small foyer with a coloured poster of Humphrey Bogart on the wall. Inside was one big room split by a dance floor with a DJ stand behind next to a mirrored wall that gave the place an illusion of being bigger than it already was. There were plenty of chairs and tables, and a bar on the right cornered around to the wall where some stools, chairs and tables sat alongside a row of double windows overlooking the main street. There wouldn't have been more than thirty people in there, including half-a-dozen girls on the dance floor, shuffling around to 'Where Are All the Cowboys From' by Paula Cole. Evelyn nodded to the ladies, Les nodded to the gents – which was right of the DJ stand.

'Whoever gets back to the bar first buys the drinks,' he said.

'Okay.'

Les headed for the gents. While he was getting rid of several beers, half a bottle of wine and an unknown number of delicious, he got an idea. On the way out he dug a ten dollar bill from his jeans and folded it in his hand.

The DJ's stand was the usual thing with the usual type of DJ – trying to look happy while wishing he was somewhere else. Pinned to a sheet of perspex was a sign saying All Requests Will Be Played Within Reason, eg, We Draw The Line At AC/DC, Cold

Chisel, Dragon, Barnsy and Farnsy. Les caught the DJ's eye.

'Hey mate,' he said. 'If I give you ten bucks will you play two songs for me?'

'Mate,' replied the DJ. 'For ten bucks I'll play you Tiny Tim singing A Pub With No Beer in Vietnamese.' Les leant over. 'Yeah, no worries. I got the other one in there somewhere.'

Les gave the DJ the ten dollars and walked across to the bar where Evelyn was waiting just around the corner with two delicious and two stools underneath a sign for a couple of local bands, Wobbly Boot and Cordidegoon.

'Well done Evie,' said Les. He sat down, picked up his drink and clinked their glasses. 'Cheers mate.'

'Yep. Cheers mate.' Evelyn took a mouthful of Jack Daniels and smiled at Les. 'Hey, do you know I've still got that ankle bracelet you gave me?'

'Fair dinkum. You haven't got it on tonight?'

Evelyn nodded. 'Well I'll be buggered,' said Les with a grin.

They toasted Evelyn's bracelet, and Les watched her eyes spin as more Jack Daniels hit home. Then they settled back and started joking and laughing while they checked out the punters. Before long Les heard the familiar riff of a popular song start up.

'Righto Evie,' he said putting his drink down. 'Let's show these disco ducklings what hotfootin's all about.'

'Oh yes. I like this one.' Evelyn left her top on her stool and they headed for the dance floor and started sashaying into 'Your Woman' by White Town.

Les knew he'd had his share of booze, but Evelyn

was more than just a bit drunk. She whirled herself around in Nortons arms and if Les hadn't have grabbed her on several occasions she would have gone crashing through the other dancers and off the floor into the chairs and tables in an avalanche of giant boobs and healthy, well-fed woman. They got through that song, gave themselves a clap then the DJ winked at Les and slipped into Stevie Wright's 'Evie'.

Les took Evelyn's hand and spun her back. 'Righto Evelyn. This is your song baby.'

'Oh yeah. Evie. Evie. Evie let your hair hang down.'

'Go for it hip shakin' momma.'

Evelyn went for it all right. She grabbed herself behind the head, got down on her haunches, shimmied and shaked and shook her gigantic boobs from one end of the dance floor to the other. Les went with her, grabbing her when she wanted to be grabbed, shuffling when she wanted to be shuffled and spinning her when she needed spinning. It was sensational. They put on that good a drunken show the DJ was almost tempted to give Norton his ten dollars back. When they finished the DJ settled everyone down with 'I Will Survive' by Cake. They finished off to that then went back to their stools at the bar. Les was puffing a little but Evelyn was starting to look rather knackered. She was rocking around on her stool, and her eyes were spinning as if she was having trouble trying to focus. She looked out the window, around the bar then blinked back at Norton.

'Are you okay?' asked Les.

'What's your room like back at the hotel?' asked Evelyn.

'Room,' said Les. 'I got an ensuite. Two beds, a lounge room, TV. The grouse.'

'Then why don't we go back there?' said Evelyn.

'Alright' said Les. 'If you want.'

The DJ slid into Blur, 'Song 2'. Evelyn slipped into her woollen jumper with a little help from Les then they slipped out of Stintsons into the cool Wagga Wagga night.

There was no-one out the front of the nightclub and there didn't appear to be anyone else around as they strolled along the footpath on the nightclub side of the road towards the hotel. Evelyn was half-asleep, snuggled up against Les who had his arm around her. He was still feeling merry from the drink and quite happy at the way things were turning out. They went past a shop full of country things – pumps, big hats, tools etc – with not a worry in the world between them, when Les sensed a movement in an old blue Ford a few metres in front of them. Then the hair on Norton's neck bristled as the car's doors opened and four men got out. It was Ponytail and two blokes dressed like him who were probably his brothers, plus a fatter bloke in a pair of overalls and a leather jacket carrying a baseball bat. They all had beady little eyes sunk into mean, bony heads and looked like something out of Deliverance. Evelyn's eyes snapped open as Les suddenly propped.

'What . . .?'

'Okay Evie,' said Les, pushing her into the shop doorway. 'Stay here. It's that idiot from the hotel with his banjo-playing mates.'

'Shit! What are you going to do?'

'I dunno. But I know one thing for sure – I ain't got time for any panache.'

'Oh God.'

Norton let Evelyn go then turned around and, with his adrenalin hitting hyperdrive, roared at the top of his voice and charged straight at the mug with the baseball bat.

When Ponytail had gone back to the house and told his brothers and his cousin about the bloke in the hotel king hitting him for no reason, they jumped in the cousin's car and come back for a square up knowing four of them could give it to him easy. Then, when one of the brothers snuck up to Stintsons and saw Les flopping around on the dance floor, they knew he was drunk and it would be easier again. And when he came weaving up the street with his girlfriend they knew once he saw them he'd start shiting himself and try to get out of it. Instead he'd get the worst bashing he ever got in his life. As for the girl? She was all right. They'd throw the moll in the back of the car and have a bit of fun with her down in that special spot up along the river; then leave the bitch there with no clothes. The last thing they were expecting was for the bloke to come screaming at them like some enraged, red-headed rhinoceros.

Before the fat mug with the baseball bat even got a chance to raise it, Norton ran up, slammed his fists down on either side of the mug's neck, and broke both his collarbones. The mug barely had time to yelp with pain when Les head-butted him and he crashed down against the car, the baseball bat clattering on the footpath alongside him. Turning slightly, Les brought his left foot up and kicked the mug next to him straight in the balls then smashed a short, hard right into the side of his face, breaking his jaw. He hit the footpath next to his mate. Norton then just started hammering all sorts of vicious, rock-hard punches at the mug on Ponytail's right, lining him up so he'd crash into Ponytail. As he did, Les slammed a couple of quick lefts into Ponytail's face, then grabbed both of them by the hair and banged their heads together; once, then twice. Both their heads split open and they hit the footpath out cold, oozing blood across the asphalt into the gutter. The mug in the overalls was lying near the other one moaning with pain, his back against their car; the baseball bat lay where it had landed next to him. Les picked it up with one hand, brought it back, then gave him a solid, backhander with it across his bony jaw. There was a horrible, whacking sound, then his head slumped forward and blood and teeth dribbled down the front of his overalls. Les then wrapped both hands around the baseball bat and brought it over his head, then slammed it down on his thighs. While he was in the swing of things, so to speak, Les brought the baseball bat down on all of their thighs, giving each of the hoods a pair of cork legs he wouldn't forget in a hurry. Les was about to drop the baseball bat in its owner's lap then changed his mind and with one blow shattered the windscreen of their old Ford and tossed it on the front seat instead.

Satisfied everything was in order, Les went over and put his arm around Evelyn's waist and had her up the street, across the road, through the front doors of the hotel then up the stairs and inside his room before she knew it. He shut the door behind them and dropped the key on the table in the lounge room. Evelyn looked at it for a moment then looked at Les.

'Did what I see happen out there? Really happen out there?' she asked, slightly shaking her head.

'Come here.' Les took Evie by the elbow, led her into the bedroom and pulled the Holland blind back on the window. The four 'good old boys' were still lying where Norton had left them. Except for two people having a look, there was still no-one else around and they were beginning to move off. 'Look at that,' said Les. 'Just up the street from that nightclub, the pub's almost across the road, there's a police station just round the corner. And no-one saw a thing. Unbelievable.' He gave Evelyn another look then closed the blind and led her back into the loungeroom. 'Well Evie. Can I get you something?'

Evelyn blinked her eyes a little slowly. 'I don't think I need another drink.'

'Good. Cause I ain't got nothing, I'm sorry.' Les pointed to a small electric jug on a wicker stand next to a tray with a tea towel over it. 'How about a nice flat white à la jug?'

'That'll do nicely.'

'Splendid. I'll start frothing a packet of Coffee Mate.'

Norton filled the jug and turned on the heater at the same time. While he was fiddling around getting the cups and packets of coffee together he heard Evelyn's voice behind him.

'Les, I know you said you didn't have time for any panache. But did you really have to hit that guy in the face with the baseball bat?'

'Evie. I just did to another what I'm certain another

105

would have done to me.' Les turned around and, completely unsmiling, looked Evelyn right in the eyes. 'And you know where you'd be right now if those four dills had given it to me?' Evelyn just blinked. 'More than likely in the back of their car getting raped out in the bush somewhere. They were nutters. One hundred percent.'

Evelyn brought her hand up to her mouth. 'God! I never thought of that.'

'Of course Evie. If you're feeling a bit "Mother Teresaish" you can always go back over and start bandaging them up. I don't think they'll be going far. And after all, you are a nurse.'

Evelyn shook her head. 'No. I don't think I'll bother.'

'Good.'

The jug had just about boiled and while Les was pouring hot water into the cups Evelyn had a bit of a look around. 'Hey, this place is really nice. I love that old, brass double bed.'

'Yeah. You reckon it ain't comfortable.'

As Les put the two cups of coffee on the table, Evelyn slipped her arms around him and kissed him on the lips. 'Then why don't we get straight into it when we finish our coffees? I feel like a bit of a cuddle.'

Les kissed her back. 'Evie. If I get in that double bed with you. I think I'll be trying to do more than cuddle you.'

Evelyn smiled up at him. 'I don't think I'll bother fighting you off, to be honest.'

'I'll switch the electric blanket on.'

Les fixed the electric blanket and turned the

bedlamps on, then joined Evelyn on the lounge where they kicked their shoes off and sipped their instant coffee. Evelyn hadn't been telling lies about the ankle bracelet, it was still there next to the ring of dainty flowers she had tattooed around her ankle. Les gave it a flick with his fingers and her toes a bit of a tickle at the same time. Les told her he had to be down the front at eight o'clock to pick up the Mud Crabs and swap cars over. Evelyn said as long as she was back at her hotel by nine everything would be fine. Les said that was no problem. In fact, stuff the Mud Crabs and the bloke he was supposed to meet. There was no mad rush to drive back to Sydney; they could hang around out the front while she had breakfast with him, then he'd run her up to her hotel. Evelyn liked that idea and gave Les a quick peck telling him what a kind, generous bloke he was. Norton had to agree.

Les was that kind and generous a bloke he even shared his toothbrush with Evelyn and let her wear his last, clean T-shirt to bed; a black Bob Marley one. It wasn't a bad choice, because even though Evelyn crushed the front out of shape when she got it on over her massive boobs, it seemed to go with the shiny, black knickers she was wearing perfectly. The electric blanket had taken the chill off the sheets just nicely when they got under the doona and there was plenty of room in the comfortable, old brass bed. Les moved up against Evelyn and she put her arms around him.

Les knew there was something else he remembered about Evelyn from when they played together, besides her knockabout sense of humour and the tattoo round her ankle. It was the way she kissed. When Evelyn got going she was a dynamite kisser. She had a cute, round mouth, the sweetest, kissable little lips, plus a deliciously evil tongue; and tonight she was holding nothing back. Les returned her kisses with a vengeance, ran his hands over her stomach, up and down her back, through her hair, over her behind; and Evelyn moved in closer to him. Norton lifted up the front of her T-shirt, gave her boobs a gentle squeeze then kissed them and licked the nipples while he slipped his hand between her legs and started rubbing Evelyn's warm, juicy ted through her knickers. Then something inside Norton suddenly snapped. Maybe it was the warm bed, the Jack Daniels, her huge boobs, the way she kissed? But before he knew it, Mr Wobbly was screaming in his ear and he had a horn that hard you could have cracked walnuts on it; and Les had to go off. In one movement he whipped Evelyn's knickers off then got between her legs, slipped a very happy Mr Wobbly in and started going for it. Evelyn gasped a bit at first, then was rapt and started bucking and squealing under Norton. But sadly, before she even had a chance to warm up, Les emptied out with a great shudder and fell off leaving her still hanging there writhing around on the bed like an overturned Christmas beetle.

'Sorry about that, Evie,' panted Les. 'But don't go away. I'll be right back.'

'Where . . . where are you going?' gasped Evelyn.

'Nowhere.'

Les got a towel, climbed back into bed then gave Evelyn and himself a wipe and started giving her a hand job. Evelyn was rapt again. She started kissing Les and Les kissed her neck and her boobs, then let her give him a couple of tiny love bites while he let his fingers do the walking. It took Evelyn about ten minutes of moaning and wriggling before she finally let go. By then, however, Norton was that worked up watching her get her rocks off he was almost as horny as he was before. He gave Evelyn another wipe then got into it again.

The second one was better. Longer, sweeter and much, much better. Les got Evelyn's knees up near her chest and pumped away for what seemed like ages before he finally blew his bolt with a great shudder at about the same time Evelyn blew hers – with an explosion pretty much like Professor Hawkings' Big Bang theory, only louder.

While Evelyn went to the toilet, Les got up and brought them two small glasses of water. He managed to set the radio alarm next to the bed for seven-thirty and was laying under the sheets thinking of turning out the bedlamp and dozing off when he felt Evelyn slither in alongside him and start kissing him again. Mr Wobbly started to come to life a little and Norton was half-keen while Evelyn fixed all that by sliding down the bed, jamming Norton's dick in between her massive boobs and working her chest up and down. Les then spun round on top of her and started giving it to Evelyn in her giant hooters. There was nothing wrong with that either, except Les went too far with one stroke and Mr Wobbly slipped into Evelyn's mouth. Evelyn didn't seem to mind one bit. She started sucking on Norton's knob with those sweet, kissable lips, sending the big Queenslander cross-eyed. He pushed Evelyn back up the bed and got into it again, while Evelyn went for it with him like there was no tomorrow. Les knew this had to be the finale, so he got Evelyn's legs right up over her head and gave her every centimetre he could raise. Evelyn bucked and howled and the last thing Les remembered before he arched his back and emptied out was one of Evelyn's legs kicking around in the air, and the ankle bracelet he gave her nicking a piece out of his left ear lobe.

Fit and all as he was, it was getting late and the last one wrecked Norton. Evelyn felt pretty much the same. Somehow Les managed to get them another glass of water; then he turned off the light and they settled in next to each other. Norton couldn't complain one bit. Outside, the night was cold and he was in a big, warm comfortable bed with a big, warm, comfortable girl next to him. Next thing she was snoring and so was Les. His last thought was that he'd do the right thing and not tell her she snored when they had breakfast in the morning.

The radio alarm went off right on time for the seven-thirty news; Les blinked heavily at the dial and momentarily wondered where he was and what was going on? It was quite cold and still dark in the room, though a little light was hitting the end of the bed from under the holland blind. Evelyn stirred next to him, then the local news put Les firmly in the picture. First up was the arrest of the paedophile Fisher, followed by:

> Wagga police have arrested three brothers and another male in

connection with a stolen car parts racket. The men, all previously known to local police, were apprehended last night after a vicious brawl in Baylis Street in which a baseball bat was used. Police called to the scene found a number of stolen car parts and a quantity of drugs in one of the men's cars and believe it was a revenge bashing between the men and another stolen car parts gang operating between Wagga and Canberra.

Ahh, so that's what happened last night, Norton smiled to himself. And the villains are firmly in the hands of the local constabulary. Nice to see the boys in blue are right on the ball and doing their job. He reached behind him and rubbed Evelyn's backside; it felt warm and inviting. But unfortunately duty called first.

'Hey Evie. Are you awake,' he muttered.

'Mmmmrrrpppph.'

'I got to go down the front and see what's going on.'

'Mmmrrrmmmphhh.'

'Yeah, righto.'

Les swung his legs out of the bed then yawned and shivered at the floor as the news finished and INXS' 'Elegantly Wasted' cut in. Yeah, that's me all right. Only I'm not elegantly wasted. I'm completely fucked. Somehow he managed to yawn and stumble his way to the bathroom then climb into a pair of jeans, the same Mambo T-shirt he'd worn the day before, and his Levi jacket. With the keys and his hands in his pockets he walked down the stairs and out the front door of the hotel into the street.

Outside it was cold, there was virtually no-one around, and the wind whipping at his puffy eyes and grim set face soon had Norton wishing he was somewhere else. After a while he realised that the bloke he was waiting for would have to come into the hotel anyway to pick up the money, so he went back inside and stood in the foyer rubbing his hands together.

'Oh Mr Norton.' It was the fair-haired bloke behind the desk. 'There's a message here for you.'

'Yeah?' Les walked over and got handed a fax in a brown envelope. 'Thanks.' He tore open the envelope. *Les. The bus is still broken down. Stay another night. I'll see you 8.30 Friday morning. Sorry about the delay. Any problems ring Neville. If you are interested, the Mud Crabs are training at Wagga Wagga Beach 9.30 this morning. Coyne Stafford.*

Norton read the fax again then folded it up not knowing whether he had the shits or not. If he'd have known he could have stayed in bed a while longer. He was going to be stuck in Wagga Wagga for another night. On the other hand, he didn't particularly feel like driving a bus to Sydney and trying to talk to a team of swimmers who'd probably be a bunch of yobbos. Maybe it was for the best. Les told the desk clerk he'd be staying another night and was told it had already been arranged. He thanked him and took the stairs back to his room. Evelyn was standing in front of the bedroom mirror in her jeans, doing up her knitted top.

'Hey Evie. You're not going to believe this.'

'What's that Les?'

Les told her what was going on. Evelyn muttered something in reply and seemed to shrug indifferently. Les put his arms around her waist and gave her ample boobs a bit of a jiggle.

'So come on, Evie baby. Get 'em off. And let's get into it again.'

'Thanks all the same, Les,' replied Evelyn. 'But I have to be at the hotel by nine. And if I remember, you promised me breakfast.' She jabbed a finger into Norton's chest. 'Or was that just a ploy to get me into that big double bed so you could ravage my poor, innocent young body while I was drunk?'

Les put his chest out and looked admonished. 'You're absolutely right, Evelyn my treasure. Forgive me for being such an unthinking, abominable, sex-crazed, big dropkick.' He did the last button on her top up and patted it down neat. 'Breakfast it is.'

Evelyn smiled up at Les then gave him a peck on the lips. 'But Jesus. It was a funny bloody old night.'

Les returned her smile. 'Let's talk about it over breakfast.'

They talked about it over breakfast. Over steak and eggs, fried in their own delicious juices, along with lashings of cereal and toast smothered in butter and jam. It was all washed down with fresh orange juice and coffee and quite a bit of loud laughter that had the other diners, along with the staff, glancing over at their table every now and again. Eventually they'd stuffed themselves with food and it was time to leave. Les paid the bill and they went out to the Statesman. Outside, the breeze was still cool, but the morning sun had taken the chill off the day; Les had the car warmed up and Evelyn home in style before she knew it. Her hotel wasn't far from Romeros', an old grey building on a corner on the opposite side of the road; Les double parked around from the front with the engine running.

'Thanks again for everything, Les,' said Evelyn, opening the door from the inside. 'It was great.'

'That's okay, Evie. Thanks for the love bites'.

'Don't worry. There's a couple on one of my boobs I noticed.'

'You would have got them on both. But a set like that Evie, you only take them on one at a time.'

'See you, Les.'

'See you, Evie. I'll give you a call.'

Norton turned the car around and headed back down Baylis Street the way he came. At the next set of lights he glanced at his watch and yawned. Well, what'll I do now? I wouldn't mind going back to bed. But if I did, I'd probably wake up this afternoon, then I wouldn't be able to sleep tonight. I'd think I was going to work. The light turned green, Les yawned again and eased the Statesman off into the light traffic. Why don't I go down the beach and watch these Mud Crabs train? See what they're all about.

A bit further on, Les turned right at the sign pointing to Wagga Wagga Beach and followed a short street down to a car park edged in with low, pine railings and golden poplars shedding their autumn leaves. There were no other cars and no-one around. Les noticed a building saying Wagga District Highland Pipe Band and behind in the distance was an old stone church with a high bell tower. He locked the Statesman and followed a trail past a huge, concrete-covered tree stump to a long strip of coarse sand about fifteen metres wide that flanked the Murrumbidgee River. The river, flowing swiftly to Norton's left, was a shiny, olive green, shallow at the edge of the sand, deeper in the middle and with steep, tree-lined banks on the other side roughly about fifty metres away. Les crunched across the sand to the water's edge, put his hand in and pulled it straight out again. It was like ice. Bloody hell, he thought. If I wanted to liven myself up all I'd have to do is jump in there for about ten seconds. That water'd bring a week old corpse back to life. It was very peaceful though and quite a pretty country scene with lots of she oaks and weeping willows dipping their branches languidly into the green shallows at the edge of the river. The only sounds were a number of unseen birds calling to each other in the trees or the distant low of a cow moving amongst the trees on the opposite side of the river, or every now and again a leaf would spiral down in the breeze then land in the water with a gentle plop. Les closed his eyes for a few moments and found it hard to believe a small city was hustling and bustling and going about its business barely half a kilometre away. Although the sun was streaming down from a cloudless sky and it was quite calm by the river there was still a noticeable nip in the air. Les pushed his hands in his pockets and walked upstream along the beach then stopped at some trees where the sand turned into pebbles. Further on was a caravan park and at his feet a huge carp lay slowly rotting in the sun. A swarm of flies lifted off momentarily; Les watched them feasting for a few seconds then walked back the way he came and sat down on a grassy bump near a tree.

Les wasn't there very long when four old station wagons pulled up in the car park. When the doors opened a few moments later he counted seventeen people getting out; seven young blokes in red tracksuits with a silver trim, eight young girls in jeans and shiny, olive pilot jackets and two older women rugged up in woollen jumpers, pants and beanies. The boys all carried towels, one girl had a ghetto blaster, one woman had a clipboard, and the other lady carried a bag. They milled around talking amongst themselves then started walking down to the concrete-covered stump. As they got closer, Les noticed all the young people had a flag he'd never seen before sewn on the backs of their jackets. It was the Southern Cross on a blue background with a colourful rainbow serpent running up through the four, smaller white stars. Norton was impressed at both its beauty and simplicity. He was even more impressed when the boys stripped down to their Speedos and tossed their tracksuits on top of the stump. They had to be the best-looking team of young blokes he'd ever seen. Each had the perfectly chiselled build of a gymnast matched with a perfectly chiselled face and smooth, brown skin. Three were part-Aborigine, three were white, and one was Asian. They all had neat, tousled hair, bright, clear eyes and perfect white smiles that almost radiated in the sunlight. Les realised straight away why Nizegy had got them together and Warren's girl had their photo pinned up in the salon. They made The Chippendales look like a bunch of old winos waiting out the front of an early opener.

The girls on the other hand were a fairly, ordinary-looking bunch. Bland, indifferent faces, plain, straight hair cut short, backsides and necks a bit on the solid side; and when they took their jackets off there wasn't much beneath their T-shirts worth a second look either. Not that dazzling beauty meant everything to Norton. It was only that the young blokes he just saw were so good-looking, he expected they'd have all the local glamours hanging off them; and only the youngest and fairest in the land as well.

The woman with the clipboard watched them get changed then walked down to the sand and blew a whistle. The boys all jogged down and formed a straight line in front of her facing away from the river. She looked at a stopwatch then blew her whistle again and the boys started running on the spot and going for it. She'd blow her whistle again and they'd either start touching their toes, do push ups, sit ups, crunchers or some other form of vigorous exercise, then go back to running on the spot.

While the boys were getting into it, the girls walked over a little further onto the grass, did some stretches and started limbering up themselves. The other older woman stayed by the stump with a bag for the water and sponges and kept an eye on their clothes. After a while one of the girls hit a button on the ghetto blaster, then they all formed pairs and started dancing old, fifties-style, rock 'n' roll dance steps. Whoever the girls were they could sure hoof it and Les found himself smiling broadly in admiration when he stood up to get a better look. Norton was familiar with all the songs they were dancing to: Bill Haley, Eddie Cochran, Daddy Cool, The Beach Boys, etc. But one song he didn't know they kept playing over and over and that seemed to be their main routine. They'd dance like crazy to this one, twirl right out at arm's length, pull each other through their legs, toss each other over their hips or spin them across their backs, then they'd all sing out at once.

'And it's oogie, oogie, oogie. Do the Mud Crab Boogie. Mud Crab Boogie gonna rock.'

While this was going on the boys were still getting into it on the sand, with wheelbarrows followed by another set of crunchers. By now a gleaming sheen of perspiration had formed on their bodies. The woman blew her whistle and they took a break. They just had time to catch their breath and wipe some of the sand from their faces and the sweat out of their eyes when the woman blew her whistle again. The boys all turned round as one, ran as far as they could across the shallows, then dived into the frigid water and swam out into midstream. As soon as they got there they turned right and started swimming against the fast-flowing current. They'd gain a few metres then fall back, gain a few more metres then fall back again. But they never fell back past the point where they turned against the river in midstream. Norton was more than impressed. It was pure endurance and to do it in that freezing cold water made it even tougher again. The wind picked up for a moment and a shiver ran up Norton's spine just thinking about it. No one seemed to notice him standing there and, after a while, Les thought he might go over and say hello and at least let them know he'd made the effort to come down and watch them train. He walked up to the woman standing by the old tree stump. She had a happy, homely sort of face framed by a shock of greying hair tucked up under a floppy, black beanie.

'Hello there,' he smiled.

The woman gave him a brief once up and down. 'Morning,' she replied, half-returning his smile.

'I just thought I'd come over and say hello. I'm Les. I'm the bloke that's driving the boys to Sydney tomorrow. Coyne Stafford? Does that mean anything to you?'

The woman looked at Norton again. 'Oh, you're Les. Coyne told us about you. You're the fellah that's staying at the hotel.'

'Yeah. That's right,' nodded Les.

'I'm Gwen.' The woman offered her hand. 'I'm one of the boys' mothers.'

'Nice to meet you, Gwen.' Les gave her hand a quick squeeze. 'Hey, who's the woman down there with the clipboard?'

'That's Alice. She's another one of the boys' mothers.'

'Is she the team trainer?'

'Trainer?'

'Yeah.'

Gwen looked at Les for a moment. 'Hasn't Coyne told you what's going on?'

'I've never spoken to him,' answered Les. 'I wouldn't even know what he looks like. All I know is, we were supposed to leave this morning. But the bus is broken down. I'm just a friend of Neville Nixon's doing him a favour,' Les added.

'I see.' Gwen nodded and seemed to understand. 'All right. I'll tell you what's happening.'

Gwen was married to the bus driver, Alice was

119

married to the team trainer. Their husbands were driving the two reserve players back to Wantabadgery on Monday night when they hit a cow and rolled the bus. Now they were all in hospital with concussion. Not too serious. But serious enough to keep them in there for a week. They thought they might have been able to get the bus going. But it was too shot. So Coyne was going to hire one through Neville Nixon. That's what Les would be driving the boys down to Sydney in. Alice was giving the team a last training session in her husband's absence. Gwen was helping her as best she could. After that the boys were on their own.

'Right. I get the picture,' said Les. 'So the team will be going down for the grand final with no coach and no reserves.'

'I'm afraid so,' nodded Gwen.

Les turned to where the boys were still hammering away in midstream. 'Well, they train pretty hard. And they look disciplined enough. In fact what they're going through out there looks plain bloody horrible to me.'

'That's the coach's idea,' smiled Gwen. 'Make the training absolute torture, and the game feels like fun.'

'Yeah,' agreed Les. 'After swimming in that freezing cold water against a fast flowing current, then getting into a warm, swimming pool with a pair of flippers on, the boys'd all think they were dolphins.'

'That's their little secret,' said Gwen, adding a nod and a wink.

Les turned away from the river. 'So who are the eight girls, Gwen?'

'That's the cheer squad. They'll catch the train down on the weekend. Then come back in the bus on Sunday night.'

'Right.'

Les was about to ask Gwen who was driving them back on Sunday because there wasn't much chance of it being him, when someone called out over the music. He looked across and one of the girls was sitting on her behind holding an ankle.

'Oh oh,' said Gwen. 'Looks like one of the warriors has fallen. I'd better see what's going on.' She picked up the bag from next to the stump.

'Well, I might get going,' said Les. 'I got a few things to do.'

'All right. Nice talking to you Les.'

'Yeah. You too Gwen.'

Norton watched her walk off then, at the sound of a whistle blowing again, turned back to the river. The boys swam back to the sand and Alice tossed them a red and white striped grenade. She gave them about a minute then blew the whistle again and the boys swam back out into midstream and started throwing it around. Les watched them for a few moments, before walking back to the car. He was about to open the door when he heard a noise at his back. He turned around as one of the cheer squad came running up to him. She was a square-faced, brownish-blonde in a plain white T-shirt with a solid behind.

'Hey, you're the guy driving the bus aren't you,' she said.

'That's right,' nodded Les. 'Who are you?'

'I'm Angie.'

'Well I'm Les, Angie. So what can I do for you?'

'I was down at Stintsons last night and I saw what happened outside with the Mackie boys.'

Norton looked impassively at her for a second. 'Are you sure it was me? I don't remember being down that way last night.'

The girl smiled. 'No one else could dance like you and that girl in the red top. Not even us.'

Norton looked at her evenly. 'Okay,' he admitted. 'It might have been me. Have you told anybody?'

'Only the boys. So I don't think they'll be giving you any shit.'

'Okay, Angie. Whatever. Just as long as they don't think I'm some kind of silly big mug that goes around looking for fights all the time. Those idiots were waiting to give it to me and there was nothing else I could do.'

Angie gestured with her hands. 'Hey. No problems, Les. The Mackies have been skating on thin ice for ages. They're the biggest bunch of arseholes in Wagga.'

'Yes. I don't think they've got a great deal going for them,' agreed Les.

Someone called out and Angie turned around. 'I have to go. But I'll probably see you in Sydney. You'll look after the boys, won't you?'

Norton smiled. 'You can count on it.'

'See you later, Les.'

'You too, Angie.'

Les watched her run back to the others, then got in the Statesman and drove out of the car park not quite sure what to do. Why not go back to the hotel and get my camera, he thought. Take a few photos and do the tourist bit while I'm in town. There's got to be something to see in Wagga besides the Murrumbidgee River. He looked at his watch and snapped his fingers. I know one thing I'd better do. Give Kathy a ring. Norton's eyes drifted up to the rear vision mirror. Tell her how I got these love bites. She'll love that.

Back in his hotel room the woman was changing the sheets; Les could imagine what they looked like, so he mumbled a quick hello, hid his face and left her to it. He threw what he wanted into his overnight bag and walked down to the foyer, stopping beneath the stairs to use the phone. Les was about to pump some coins into the slot when he noticed somebody had left a postcard on top of the phone book. It was addressed to some one at the hotel from Anchorage Alaska; without reading the message he turned it over. On the front was a beautiful red sunset and silhouetted against it was a huge black mosquito that looked as big as a horse. Beneath that in white print was, Alaska State Bird. Very droll, thought Les, and started dropping dollar coins.

'Hello. Rose Bay Travel Service.'

'Yes. Could I speak to Ms Katherine Hannan please?'

'Just one moment. I'll put you through. May I ask who it is?'

'Yes. It's Mr Norton. I'm booking a trip to Brazil.'

There was muzak on the line for a moment or two then a familiar, voice.

'Hello, Les. How are you?'

'Pretty good thanks, Kathy. How's yourself?'

'I'm good. How was Wagga Wagga?'

'How was it? I'm still bloody here.'

'You're what?'

'I'm still here.' Les told her what happened. He also said he'd just come back from the Mud Crabs training session.

'That's a bit of an inconvenience,' said Kathy. 'So when do you think you'll be back?'

'Late Friday I'd reckon.'

'Well, that's not so bad.'

'Yeah. Anyway, how's things with you? I suppose you told Henry the truth about the other night, and that it was me who drank his beer.'

'I've been meaning to,' said Kathy.

'Christ! I was stuck there for hours listening to that bloody Rugby Union.'

'Actually, you dropped some money out of your pocket. Thirty dollars. And a piece of paper with some writing on it.'

'Yeah. All right, I'll get the piece of paper off you when I see you. Forget the money. You've probably spent that by now.'

'Oh yes. Of course I would,' replied Kathy shortly.

Norton sensed Kathy didn't think that was funny so he decided to change the subject. 'Hey, I'll tell you what, Kathy. I've found something down here that would send that rugby-mad brother of yours, Hogs Head Hannan, into hog heaven. And that other ugly big rah rah brother of yours too.'

'And just what's that Les?'

'In this hotel where I'm staying, they've got a bar called the Rugby Bar. It's full of all this grouse rugby paraphenalia. It's unreal.'

'Oh, I've heard about it. The boys have gone down there to play Riverina and they told me all about it.'

'Right. I might take a few photos before I leave.'

'The hotel itself is supposed to be rather nice too.'

'It is,' said Les. 'Except for the mosquitoes.'

'Mosquitoes?'

'Yeah. To tell you the truth, I had a few in the Rugby Bar last night and fell asleep in my room with the window open. And the bloody things attacked me.'

'Really? Oh well, don't scratch where they bit you.'

'No. But they get itchy.' Les absently ran a hand across his neck. 'Anyway. I didn't ring up to whinge about that. I'll be back Friday. Do you want to go out somewhere on Friday night.'

Kathy seemed to think for a second. 'Yes. But I won't finish work till at least seven.'

'That's all right. I should be back and have everything sorted out by then.'

'What exactly did you have in mind?'

'I don't know. Why don't we go and have a nice meal somewhere?'

'If you wish. That could be good.'

'How about you pick the restaurant.'

'I think I know just the place.'

'Good. Well, I suppose I'd better let you get back to work Kathy. What say I call round your place about eight-thirty?'

'I'll see you then. Have a safe trip back to Sydney.'

'No worries. See you, Kathy.'

'Goodbye, Les.'

Well there you go, Norton smiled to himself as he hung up. I've got another night out with Kathy when I get home. I wonder what restaurant she'll pick? Knowing her you can bet it'll be healthy and wholesome. Les dropped the postcard at the desk, picked up a tourist brochure and studied it as he walked out to the car. I think I'll make my first stop the Air Force Museum.

Les had no trouble finding a parking spot at the Air Force Museum. He got there just in time to take a photo of an old Canberra bomber and three other planes out the front, then found a sign on the door saying it was closed and wouldn't be open for another half an hour. Les had another look at his tourist brochure. Oh well. Let's check out the Murray cod hatchery.

The Murray cod hatchery was a few kilometres on the way back to town. Les turned left at a green and gold sign on a short, brick wall with a big, fat, yellow and grey Murray cod on top – only to get out of the car and find a sign on the door saying Closed For Breeding Purposes. Well there you go, thought Les, taking another look at his tourist brochure. Let's see what they've got at Lake Albert.

Lake Albert was a bit further back towards town on the left past the cemetery, and would have been delightful. Except that Wagga Wagga, like most of inland NSW, was almost in the middle of a drought. So, unfortunately, instead of a nice blue lake reflecting the clouds and the sky, it was just a couple of square kilometres more or less of pale yellow water. But it was quite still and pleasant with lots of willows and she oaks at the water's edge and plenty of nice homes built facing the lake. Les surmised that with a bit of rain the place would soon come to life and regain its natural beauty once again. He took a couple of photos and drove back to the Air Force Museum.

This time the house-sized, purple-brick building was open and a young airman in a blue uniform was sitting just inside the entrance watching Brave Heart on a small TV set.

'All right if I have a look around?' asked Les.

'Yeah. No problems mate,' was the polite reply.

The inside of the museum was like a big, old house. Les wandered from room to room checking out old books, papers, medals, photos, glass cabinets full of uniforms. There were life-like dummies in old uniforms depicting air force life during the Second World War. One room was devoted to nurses, another had a glass case full of guns on the wall with everything from a .303 to an AK-47. A bigger room out the back had the front of an old Sabre jet and an ejector seat, while along one wall were these great blow-up photos taken from a plane of bombs being dropped on Japanese ships anchored near some Pacific Island. They were that clear you almost felt you were there. Les wandered round a bit more and after checking out the exhibits and the photos again convinced himself of two things: Australian servicemen were a pretty fit-looking bunch fifty years ago, considering there were no aerobics classes and ab-rockers; they also had the daggiest-looking uniforms imaginable. Especially the women. No wonder the yanks won all the sheilas when they were out here. Les took a few photos, thanked the young airman still engrossed in Mel Gibson smashing peoples' heads in, and trudged back out to the car. Next stop on the tourist brochure was the Wagga Wagga Botanical Gardens, Zoo and Historical Museum.

This wasn't hard to find. Just a quick cruise across town, up a bit of a hill and under a bridge saying Lord Baden Powell Drive to a car park surrounded by trees and gardens and a sign saying Williams Hill Signal Box, which was the station for the model train. Another sign said the model train wasn't running that day. Oh well, looks like I won't be getting my big fat arse on the model train, thought Norton, locking the car and taking a look about. All around him was the scent of Australian fauna, flowers and huge shrubs of lavender dotted with magpies and willie wagtails hopping or strutting around the plants. Les strolled a bit further through a gate into the gardens. The first thing he noticed inside were about half-a-dozen peacocks near a sign saying Caution. Take Care. Animals And Birds Here Can Cause Injury. There were more peacocks, goats, ducks, kangaroos resting on their side in the sun, as well as wallabies, bigger ducks and more peacocks near a wombat enclosure. A couple of healthy black swans ignored him and in the trees above there would have been hundreds of birds singing and whistling to each other. It was very nice, but somehow Les couldn't quite appreciate it; his eyes felt grainy and he was just too tired. The only things that sparked him up were some Chinese silky chickens that looked like little yaks with their big, fluffy, feather-covered feet. And two soft-eyed, fluffy brown Alpacas in an enclosure. Les handed one some grass. It took the feed then walked away a little and turned its back to eat it. When it did, its cods stuck out at the back like a pair of fluffy brown coconuts. Look at that, thought Les, raising his camera. They stick out like dogs knackers. No they don't; they stick out like Alpacas knackers. Les took two photos and shook his head. What am I saying? I think I'm having a bad brain day.

Tiredly, Les roamed around the enclosure a big longer then decided to have a look at the rose gardens. On the way to the gate a tiny stream trickled through a miniature rain forest thick with ferns and staghorns and other leafy green plants. At one side was a thick patch of juicy watercress. In amongst the watercress was a plant Les recognised that used to grow by the river back home. Bahloo Berry. A skinny brown creeper with tiny blue flowers and little black berries. Its nickname was Whacko Crap. Because as well as being a mild hallucinogenic, it was also a super powerful laxative. Three berries, and eight hours later you would hallucinate for about half a minute then you would be on the can for at least thirty minutes going non-stop. You felt completely stuffed for another thirty minutes after that, then you started to come good. The trick was to try and slip a few berries into someone's food or drink without them knowing it because the victim got no warning and once the Whacko Berry hit home you shit your pants straight away and just kept on shitting. The only chance the victim got was the extremely bitter taste; if they knew what was going on they could spit them out. But it was a good trick if you could pull it off – if you were the sort of person who was into those low kind of tricks. Les knew exactly whose food or drink to slip some into. He was overweight, his name was George and he managed a casino in Kings Cross. Les pulled a hand full of Bahloo Berries up and slipped them into his pocket, then with a mischievous little smile flickering in the corners of his eyes strolled towards the gate.

The rose gardens were beautiful to the point of being spectacular. Beds of them – yellow, red, violet, white, ice-blue. Some you couldn't put two hands around and the perfume was that sweet and strong you felt like eating them. Les took some more photos and just wished he wasn't so tired and brain-dead so he could appreciate them even more. Finally, he dragged himself away to check out the museum. Les was only half-keen, if that. But he knew it wasn't far away and he knew he might not get another chance. He walked back to the car to drive the short distance and, taking a quick glance at his watch as he did up his seat belt, was surprised to find the day was almost shot.

Les walked into the brown, brick building with the green roof, said hello to an elderly man behind the counter and signed the visitors book and was told there were more exhibits out the back. The Historical Museum too was very interesting with its old shotguns, derringers, carved Chinese chairs, tele-scopes, microscopes, grandpa shirts, curling irons, little dolls and a stack of other old stuff along with an Aboriginal section. But again Les was too tired and listless to appreciate it all. He took his time wandering around the wealth of bric-a-brac then went outside to look at the old buggies, tea chests, meat safes, tractors, saws, axes and anything else you could think of from Australia's past. There was a school, a print shop, a post office. There was even an old slab hut, the Yallowin Hut, that had been saved intact from when the dam flooded the Tumut Valley. The old slab hut was something else, though. Still furnished with what passed for furniture in those days, it looked almost as if the original owners had just walked out for the moment and would soon be returning. There were some other people walking around; Les got them to take a photo of him standing out the front then walked around a bit more and decided to leave. He'd seen all he wanted and there was something he wanted to buy in town before the shops closed. He packed his camera in its case, walked back to the car and headed for Baylis Street.

Being caught out an extra day and Evelyn using his last T-shirt as a pyjama top, Les had no clean gear. He also knew he was starting to get more than a bit ripe and even after a shower didn't fancy climbing into fresh sheets in a sweat stained T-shirt and a pair of grubby jocks. He found a parking spot easily enough and followed some other shoppers down a side street into a large, brightly lit mall with a small plaza in the middle featuring several black statuettes of crows. He found an el-cheapo clothes store and bought a plain, white T-shirt, some jocks and socks then got a can of lemonade and a cabbage roll and sat down while he watched the punters. He didn't buy any music because he couldn't be bothered flicking through the CDs; he didn't even buy a newspaper because he couldn't be bothered reading it. About half way through the can of lemonade Les figured out why he was so tired. In the last two days he hadn't had a decent night's sleep; not counting all the horrendous porking he'd done, the drive down from Sydney and the piss he'd drunk. Well I'll be having an early night tonight, he thought, as he finished his lemonade. Even if Nizegy's waiting in the Rugby Bar for me with Miss fuckin' Brazil again. Good old Nizegy. I wonder what he's doing right now? It was almost dark and Les was still thinking loosely about Neville Nixon when he pulled up and parked out front of the hotel.

Back in his room Norton couldn't have cared less about Wagga and the area being in a drought. He hung in the shower and let the steaming water almost wash him away. It felt that good he could have slept there. He didn't though. He just wasted more water than he should have, wasted more while he shaved then got changed into his clean T-shirt, jeans and Levi jacket and walked down to the Rugby Bar.

There was hardly anybody in there; one or two couples and a few in the bar opposite playing pool. Les was dog tired as it was, but he knew if he had a few beers and a big meal that would finish the job completely. He got a middy of sparkling VB, sat down at the same spot as the night before and gazed out the window. By middy number three he was starting to think about Neville Nixon again. Nizegy was okay all right. But he just seemed overly-trusting, giving him four hundred grand in the boot of a car to take down to Wagga like it was a box of oranges. What was to stop Les from saying he got robbed on the way? Not that he would. But people have done a lot worse for a lot less. On the other hand, he never mentioned anything about delivering money to Les first up. What was to stop someone robbing Les? Norton knew plenty of people who would put a bullet in him if they knew he was driving around with that sort of money on him. They could form a queue outside the Kelly Club four deep and it would go round the block twice.

And did Nizegy know about all this rattle with the bus getting overturned before he offered Les the job? Now the ace promoter was sending one team into a grand final with no coach and no reserves. And from what Les had seen so far, as well as being a bad handicap, the Mud Crabs looked liked schoolboys compared to the Sydney Sea Snakes. Super-fit, super-handsome schoolboys, but still schoolboys. Les sipped his beer, shook his head and gazed out the window. Yeah, Nizegy was all right he supposed. It was just that for a big wheeler and dealer he somehow seemed a bit vague. The sort of bloke who would organise a round Australia rally then find he'd locked the keys in the car when it was time to go. Penny-wise and pound-foolish could be another way of putting it. Like that stupid business with the bet. He snips Les for a thousand dollars then hands him four hundred thousand bucks in two overnight bags. Oh well, yawned Les, just as long as my two hundred K falls in on Sunday. I guess that's all I have to worry about.

Middy number four went down and by now Norton's eyelids were starting to roll down too. It was time to eat then hit the sack. He stared absently at his empty middy glass for a moment or two, then got up and drifted slowly into the hotel restaurant. This time Les chose the chicken and pineapple kebab for an entree, the same as Evelyn had. And Veal Medallions topped with ham, Italian tomato sauce and melted Mozarella cheese for a main. Again the food was sensational only now Les didn't feel like shaking his tail feathers anywhere. In fact if they'd thrown a pillow and a blanket on the restaurant floor he would have slept there. Somehow he managed to find the strength to sign the bill and take the stairs to his room.

Les switched the electric blanket on and while it warmed the bed, watched half of some documentary on SBS about the Middle East. As soon as it was over he switched the TV off and crawled into the sack. The fresh sheets, his clean T-shirt and the big, warm bed were heaven. Les barely had time to set the radio alarm for seven in the morning and switch off the bedlamp before he was sawing wood. Plenty of it and heavily.

It was a new Les Norton who woke up two minutes before the radio alarm went off at seven. The graininess was gone from his eyes, his head was clear, and he knew straightaway what he had to do. He yawned, wriggled around and stretched on the bed while he listened to the news; pleased there was nothing more about the fight, he got up, opened the window and looked out on a clear but cold day. A brisk run would be good now thought Norton. But it would take too much time and he didn't have his trainers. Instead Les did a few stretches and gulped in some good, clean Wagga air while Joe Camilleri's 'New Craze' bopped out on the radio, then headed for the bathroom. A few minutes later he was taking the stairs to the restaurant in his jeans, the T-shirt he slept in and his Levi jacket. He had plenty of time before he had to meet Coyne Stafford and pick up the Mud Crabs. With the smell of yesterday morning's steak and eggs still in his nostrils, Les got a complimentary paper from the counter, sat down and ordered. After leisurely stuffing himself with food plus an extra cappucino, Les paid the bill then walked back to his room and packed his bags. By eight twenty-five he had it all together and went downstairs to sign the tab. He left his bags in the foyer and walked out the front.

He wasn't there long when a white minibus with a dark green stripe along the side came round the corner and lurched to a stop, double parking a little down from the Statesman. The team was in the back all straining across to check out Norton; Les looked at them for a moment then turned away as the driver came round the front. He was taller and heavier than Les, wearing a shiny, black tracksuit and a cap with the same unusual flag on the front. His shoulders had a confident roll when he walked and he had a beefy, happy face with a broken nose and scar tissue over a pair of brown eyes that emanated a mischievous glint something like a cheeky kid who's just pulled an innocent prank.

'G'day mate,' he said, with a cheery drawl.

'G'day,' replied Norton. 'You must be Coyne?'

'That's right. How are you, Les?'

'Good thanks, Coyne.'

They shook hands and each man give the other a quick once up and down. Going by his manner and appearance, Les had a feeling Coyne would be able to handle himself more than adequately in a sticky situation and for some strange reason found himself warming to him.

'So what's the story Coyne, old mate?' said Les, nodding towards the hire car. 'You're picking up the Statesman plus the four hundred K. Then I'm off to the old steak and kidney in the uncle Gus with the mighty Mud Crabs.'

'That's about the size of it Les, me old currant bun.' Coyne nodded towards the bus. 'You ever driven one before?' Les shook his head. 'Well don't worry. It's a piece of piss.'

'If you say so, Coyne. And you've got to be one of the most honest-looking blokes I ever met.'

'Thanks Les. That's very nice of you. Now where's the chops?'

'In the safe. This way.' Norton led them back to the front desk, got the two bags of money and handed them to Coyne. 'Nizegy said this is to pay the other teams with.'

'That's right.'

'You're gonna have a fair bit of running around to do.'

Coyne shook his head. 'I'm meeting all the managers in Cowra. Save a lot of rooting about. I should be back in Sydney early tonight.'

'Oh.'

'In fact I have to see you late Saturday. There's something else Nizegy wants you to do. Is that all right?'

'I suppose so,' shrugged Les. 'You got my number?'

Coyne nodded. 'Nizegy gave it to me.'

'Okey doke then. No worries.'

'He also said to give you this.' Coyne handed Les a thousand in cash. 'That's for petrol and to feed the boys.'

'Fair enough.' Les put the money in his jeans.

Coyne looked at Norton evenly for a moment. 'Anyway Les, I have to get my finger out. And you've got to get to Sydney. How about I see you on Saturday?'

'Righto Coyne. Give me a ring first.'

Les picked up his bags and followed the big man out the front, then watched him throw the money in the boot, get behind the wheel and expertly squeeze the Statesman out from between the car in front and the bus. There was a quick toot of the horn and he was gone. Sensing the Mud Crabs watching him, Les walked round, climbed in the front of the bus and threw his bags on the nearest empty seat. The team was seated haphazardly around the bus in their grey tracksuits and black caps same as Coyne's, with the Asian boy on the back window sprawled casually amongst the teams luggage and overnight bags. They stoped talking when Les came in and suddenly became very subdued, looking up at him in awe almost. Les surmised that when Angie told them about the fight outside Stintsons she would have given them a complete blow by blow description, plus whipped cream with a cherry on top. Les thought he might as well play along with it.

'G'day fellahs,' he said, with a curt nod of his head. 'I'm Les. I'm your new driver and I'm looking after you on this magical mystery tour till next Sunday.' The boys mumbled something and exchanged awkward glances. 'Anyway, without me having to run around shaking all your hands, what's your names?'

The team exchanged more awkward glances then the Koori boys spoke first.

'I'm Felix.'

'Raymond.'

'I'm Clarence.'

Les looked at the white boys.

'Rodney.'

'I'm Garrick.'

'I'm Jamieson.'

Les raised his eyes to the Asian boy sprawled along the rear window seat.

'Rinh.'

Rinh seemed a little self-conscious and when he quietly answered his name the others made low barking or snarling sounds amongst themselves.

'Okay,' said Les. 'Pleased to meet you. Now I've never driven one of these things before. So why don't you just go on talking amongst yourselves while I turn the radio down and sort this thing out.' There was a mumbled chorus of, 'Sure, Les. Anything you say, Les. Yo de man, Les.' Norton gave them a tight smile then strapped himself in and turned off the radio while he sorted out which buttons did what.

It wasn't too difficult at all. The bus was an automatic with power steering; you sat up high and had a good sight of the road with a big, rear view mirror and big mirrors on the side. Pretty much like Coyne said – a piece of piss. Les hit the starter, slipped the bus into drive and without too much trouble was able to drive to the end of the street, make a U-turn then come back and take a left into Baylis. The morning traffic wasn't heavy and before Norton knew it he'd swung easily onto Hammond Avenue, heading out of town for the highway.

Wagga Wagga soon disappeared behind them and now it was rolling, olive hills, skinny creeks and trees going by. His confidence gained and in a way almost starting to enjoy himself, Les turned the radio back on to some pop music and watched the boys in the rear vision mirror. They appeared to be in high spirits, joking amongst themselves and poking fun at each other in an educated sort of way; although a lot of the gags were going in Rinh's direction, he seemed to cop it sweet, giving back as good as he got. The boys also seemed to refer to each other by nicknames. Felix was Cats. Raymond was shortened to Razza and Clarence naturally got called Clarry. They called Rodney Rat, Jamieson was Jam Tin and somehow Garrick got called Harry. But the one that had Les completely flummoxed was why they kept calling Rinh Dogs. The kilometres rolled by and the radio started getting a bit scratchy. Les was thinking of putting on a cassette when Rinh came down and took a seat on Norton's left to watch the road approaching through the windscreen. Les turned and caught his eye.

'So how's it going there, Rinh?'

'Pretty good thanks, Les.' Rinh's voice was soft and polite with a broad outback Australian accent.

'If you don't mind me asking,' said Les. 'Where's your family from Rinh? You don't look Chinese.'

'Laos.'

'Laotian eh? I've never been there, but I know where it is.' Les brought the bus in a little as a giant semi-trailer ground past. 'There's something else I want to ask you too, Rinh.'

'What's that, Les?'

'How come they call you Dogs? You don't eat the bloody things, do you?'

'No,' laughed Rinh. 'My full name is Rinh Tinh Trinh.'

Norton shook his head. 'Say no more, Rinh.'

'Yeah. Well I got Rin Tin Tin from the word go. And that ended up getting changed to good old plain Dogs.'

'What about Rodney?'

'The Rat? We used to call him Rotten Rodney. Or Rodent. But Rat suits him better.'

'Fair enough,' said Les. 'What about Garrick?'

'Harry? Well every time Garrick meets a sheila, she always ends up calling him Gary. And it gives him the shits. So we always tell them his name's Harry. And that shits him even worse again.'

'What are you saying about me, Dogs?' came a voice from behind.

'Yeah. What's going on down there, Dogs?' came another voice.

'Nothing,' replied Dogs. 'Me and Reg are just talking.'

'Reg?' said Norton. 'What's with the fuckin' Reg?'

'That's the nickname we've decided to give you,' smiled Dogs. 'You know. Reg Varney. "On The Buses".'

Les shook his head trying not to smile himself. 'You blokes have got to be kidding.'

Garrick moved down and sat behind Les, followed closely by Rodney. Then the rest moved down the front of the bus as if Rinh was onto something and they were missing out. Norton sensed as soon as he stepped on the bus that after what Angie had told them the boys weren't too sure how to handle him and were a little trepidatious. But now, by the looks on their faces in the rear vision mirror, it was as if they'd suddenly taken a liking to him and wanted to get to know him. Which was probably why, in a back handed display of friendship, they'd given him that innocent, if stupid, nickname. Whatever the situation, Les didn't mind one bit. Because even though he'd deliberately been a bit gruff at first, he now found himself taking an instant liking to the Mud Crabs. They were much different to what he was expecting.

'Listen fellahs,' he said. 'Where did you get the flag on your caps and the backs of your jackets from? I've never seen one like that before.'

'The rainbow serpent flag,' said Felix. 'We all go to Sturt University and a couple of students from Armidale uni stayed with us for a while. They entered it in a new Australian flag competition up there and we borrowed it as our team flag. Looks neat Reg. What do you reckon?' Felix turned the back of his jacket slightly to Les.

'Neat?' answered Les. 'It looks super sensational. Better than that poor old butcher's apron shoved in the corner of the one we got now.'

'Agreed,' said Raymond. 'And it also sums up the whole scene Reg.'

'How's that Razza?' said Norton.

'Well, according to the blackfellahs, Australia has always been Gondwanaland. Land of the Rainbow Serpent. Yingarna the mother. Ngalyod the father. Right Reg?'

'Yeah,' agreed Les. 'I know about that.'

'And when the whitefellahs came. They called it Australia. Land of the Southern Cross.'

'That's right, Razza,' nodded Les.

'Well,' said Raymond. 'This flag says it all. We're the land of the Rainbow Serpent. And we're also the land of the Southern Cross. And Les, if you look just under the top star where the Rainbow Serpent's eye is, it forms the Aboriginal flag.'

Rinh being the closest leant over and tapped the flag on the front of his cap. 'See Reg?'

Norton took his eyes off the road for a moment and studied it. 'Well I'll be, Dogs. It does too.'

'You wait till the grand final on Sunday,' said Jamieson. 'When we come out waving our Rainbow Serpent flag. The crowd's going to go ape.'

'Oogie, oogie oogie. They'll all be doing the Mud Crab boogie,' said Clarence.

'You better believe it,' added Garrick, enthusiastically.

'Hey, that's something I want to ask you,' said Les. 'When I was watching you train yesterday, your cheer squad kept playing that song. What's it called?'

'Our cheer squad. The Murrumbidgee Mud Crabettes,' said Rodney. 'It's off a CD. Carl Perkins and John Fogarty singing "All Mama's Children". We just changed the words around and made it our team song. And the Crabettes did the rest.'

'Well, it certainly works boys. It certainly works,' said Norton. A highway patrol car appeared out of nowhere and sped past. But with the speedo set on a steady 100 kmh Les relaxed and watched it disappear into the distance. 'Hey Dogs,' he said. 'Do us a favour will you? Hand me a tape out of that small bag there. Any one'll do.'

'Yeah, all right.' Dogs did as he was asked and watched as Les looked at the number written on the front before he slipped it into the cassette player.

'So what sort of music do you blokes like?'

The boys exchanged glances for a moment. 'I dunno,' said Clarry. 'Anything but house music and Celine Dion.'

'Rock 'n' roll's cool, Reg,' said Jamieson.

'Yeah, well I don't know what you like. But you're getting this.' Les turned the volume up a little and 'Home and Broken Hearted' by Cold Chisel started hoofing out of the speakers.

'Hey, this is all right,' said Clarry.

'Reg. Killer DJ,' said Cats.

'Thank you music lovers' acknowledged Les. Cold Chisel slipped into 'Weed Life', from Rahsun and Skeeta Ranks. The kilometres started slipping easily by, more tracks played and Les began engaging the seven young Mud Crabs in a bit of question and answer.

They were each aged nineteen and university students. Felix, Raymond and Clarence were doing agricultural science. Jamieson was doing commerce and marketing research, while Rodney and Garrick were doing business administration to take up careers in the public service. Rinh was doing biology and fish farming. Their parents were all battlers without much money; Rinh's family had a small restaurant that lost as much money as it made. They didn't have any girlfriends and a just about non-existent sex life. Between their studies and training, they didn't have the time to get involved with girls or the money to take them out. Getting their degrees was paramount. They were all good swimmers and played water polo at uni for something to do, when Neville Nixon swept into town and hustled them into signing six month contracts to play Extreme Polo on pay TV at two hundred dollars a win and one hundred dollars a loss. Not bad money when you're practically broke, with the big pot of gold, Nizegy offering them two hundred thousand cash if they won the grand final against the Sea Snakes in Sydney.

The Mud Crabs had played the Snakes twice before for a win and a loss, with the Sydney team always playing rough and dirty when they met, always seeming to have it in for the Mud Crabs. All the games were tough and they tried to explain some of the rules to Les, but all Les could remember was Rinh was team captain and goalkeeper, Rodney, Garrick and Jamieson were the forwards, Raymond and Clarence were backs and Felix was the lock. But they trained hard and were pretty quick in the water and somehow managed to win more games than they lost, though a couple of the boys conceded they appeared to have luck on their side on more than one occasion. Which to Norton's suspicious mind washed up that Nizegy might have pulled a few games now and again to get the dream team into the grand final. The garage at Coogee was Nizegy's idea and although it seemed a bit dodgey at first, suited them. They didn't like and didn't trust Sydney and this way they could all be together and keep an eye on their gear. Plus Neville said he might pay them a bonus later seeing he was saving money from not having to put them all up in a hotel. So forty-eight hours stuck in a garage wasn't all that bad, as then they could get their money and get back home to the Riverina. But even though the boys weren't all that keen on Extreme Polo and doubted if they'd back up again next year, it was all a good buzz and they were keen to win the grand final; the prize money would put them through their studies in comfort with maybe a bit left over to buy a half-decent car each. Though they also admitted that their chance of winning had decreased when the coach and their reserves got hurt in the bus crash – under all the joking and cameraderie they were a bit despondent.

Apart from Les, they were on their own. But even though he was only their driver, he seemed a little different and maybe they could depend on him to look after them in Sydney. Les promised he'd do his best. When Les asked about Coyne Stafford, the boys said they didn't know him all that well. He once worked for ATSIC and used to run a martial arts gymnasium in Queensland before he started working for Nizegy. Les now realised he was right when he thought Coyne was a fighter and that's where all the scar tissue had come from. Then the boys started asking Les a few questions about himself. So Les told them a bit about Warren, the Kelly Club, Billy and Price, and his trip to America; and yes that was him who'd flattened the Mackie boys on Wednesday night; and that he'd appreciate it if the boys kept that to themselves. That was cool by the Mud Crabs.

'Drug Train' by The Cramps was rattling and banging out of the speakers when they pulled into an all-nighter just outside of Goulburn for some petrol and food. Les hoped the boys needed their carbohydrates because that's what they got: greasy hamburgers, chips and gravy plus milkshakes and whatever. Seeing he was going out for dinner that night Les didn't bother getting stuck into the junk food with them, settling instead for a packet of

145

Dorritos and an orange and mango mineral water. They got back on the bus and a little further on 'The Lights Coming Over The Hill' by Slim Dusty and James Blundell, started twanging through the speakers as they climbed a slight hill and headed non-stop now for Sydney. Les told the boys a bit more about himself and how Nizegy had once lined him up with Miss Brazil. He also offered to take the boys training on Saturday and he'd probably bring his mate Billy Dunne with him. The Mud Crabs liked the idea of that.

Soon the sun was setting and the traffic started to increase. 'Dirty Rotten Shame' from Dallas County Line honky-tonked into 'Bullfrog Blues' and that cut out with Dave Hole ringing the neck off his guitar as they went past Camden and began winding through the Western suburbs towards Parramatta Road. The boys went back to their seats and were much quieter now, staring out the windows at the homes, shops, cars and people going past as if it was some strange, alien world out there. Les tuned the radio to an AM talkback station for the news and traffic reports and, even after all the tape playing, he could feel the added apprehension in the bus as well as see it on the Mud Crab's faces in the rear-vision mirror. The boys from Wagga Wagga definitely didn't like the big city one bit. As they pulled up for a set of lights in a cloud of exhaust fumes and honking cars Les flashed back to the trees and birds alongside that peaceful, little beach where the Murrumbidgee River wound through their home town and didn't blame them in the slightest. Sydney was exciting and certainly had its good side, but it could be very daunting as well. He got onto

Anzac Parade then finally came down the hills behind Randwick Junction; it was well and truly dark when he pulled the bus up alongside Coogee Oval and across the road from the garage.

'Well, here it is fellahs,' he said, switching off the engine. 'The Presidential Suite at the Coogee Hilton.'

The boys got their bags and followed Les off the bus stopping for a moment to let a couple of cars go past and glance at some football players training under lights on the oval. Les walked across to the driveway, opened the small door on the garage and stepped inside. Somewhere in the gloom he managed to make out a square of white plastic on a wall and found a light switch.

The garage went back a bit further than he had expected and looked as if at one time someone had used it as a flatette. There was a shower and toilet in one corner, a sink, a fridge, a toaster, heater, TV and frypan. Across from these were five double bunks with identical, grey, sleeping bags and white pillow cases. Les switched on another light while the team filed in and looked around.

'Very nice,' said Les, opening and closing the empty fridge. 'You've done well.'

'It could be heaps worse,' said Felix.

'Yeah heaps,' agreed Jamieson.

'There's a couple of spare bunks,' said Les. 'I might even move in myself.' Around him the boys started picking which bunk they wanted, dumping their bags on the spare ones. 'So what are you going to do now?' asked Norton, glancing up at a crack running across the unpainted concrete ceiling.

'Probably read,' said Rodney.

'Study for a while,' said Clarence.

'Catch up on a few notes,' said Rinh.

'Yeah? Well that's good.' Les was impressed to find that as well as being intelligent the boys had plenty of self-discipline as well. He looked at his watch. 'All right. Well, I might leave you to it. I've got things to do. But if you need me, Dogs has got a mobile and you know my number.' Les dropped two fiftys and a spare key to the garage on one of the bunks. 'That's for whatever. And I'll be around here at nine in the morning to take you training.'

There was a general chorus of, 'Okay Reg. Thanks Reg. Unreal. See you in the morning, the Varns.'

'See you tomorrow fellahs.'

Les stepped out of the garage closing the door behind him, got his bags out of the bus, locked it, then walked down to the corner and hailed a taxi to take him to Chez Norton.

How do the words to that song go? It's so nice to go travelling. But it's oh so nice to come home. Reckon. Les threw his bags in his room and started climbing out of his dirty clothes. Whenever he left the house, even if only for a couple of days, it always seemed longer. There was one message on the answering service – from Warren seeing if he was there and saying he'd be home later. Les rang Billy, got his answering service and left a message saying he was back and did Billy want to go training in the morning? He'd ring back then. Les switched on the kettle in the kitchen and got some FM going on the stereo in the lounge, then got under the shower and mulled things over while he soaped away the two days out of town. Everything in the garden seemed rosy. The Mud Crabs were tucked away safe and sound, the trip had turned out okay and he was home safe and sound; and now he had a delightful dinner date with the equally delightful Katherine Hannan. There were a couple of loose ends he wasn't sure of; but nothing to worry about. The only cloud on the horizon was Nizegy wanting him to do something Saturday night. Les thought he already was doing something. Looking after the Mud Crabs. Nizegy didn't say anything about any other chores. Maybe he expected a bit more for his two hundred thousand. Still, it was a lot of money for just a few days graft. Les had a shave then covered the love bites on his neck with Pinke Zinke and picked the nick on his ear till it started bleeding again then daubed it with a cotton bud dipped in iodine. He gave his face a splash of Island Lyme then slipped into a pair of white 501's, a denim Shooters with topaz leather trim and the vest Jimmy Rosewater gave him. Les then stood in front of his bedroom mirror, gave himself a once up and down and shook his head. I can't believe it's not butter. He was standing in the kitchen sipping a cup of coffee while he sorted out his keys, cash and credit cards when the front door opened and in walked Warren in a pair of jeans and a black leather jacket.

'Hello Woz,' said Les. 'I'm back. You miss me darling?'

Warren stared at Les. 'What happened? What's going on? You were supposed to be back yesterday.'

'There was a drama with the bus. I had to wait for another one.'

'But the Mud Crabs are here? You got the team

back all right didn't you? The Mud Crabs are okay? Debbie's been worried sick. Why didn't you ring?'

Warren sounded like he was more interested in the Mud Crabs then whether anything had happened to Les. 'There was no phone in my room.'

'Well why don't you buy yourself a mobile? You miserable big prick.'

'I will Woz. Next week. I promise.'

Warren helped himself to a cup of coffee while Les gave him a quick debriefing about the trip. Warren was absolutely stoked and he knew Debbie would be too. He was working all day tomorrow, but he'd make sure he went and met the Mud Crabs before they left. Les told Warren where they were staying and promised he'd arrange for Warren to go over and meet the team or whatever.

'So that's the story, Woz. There's more, but right now I have to get cracking. I'm taking Ms Hannan out for dinner. She's picking the restaurant and I don't know where I'll finish. Back here I hope,' Les added.

'Half your luck. She's grouse.'

'Yes, she's not half bad,' nodded Norton. 'So what's your play homeboy?'

'Pretty much the same as yours. Dinner somewhere. Only I might stay at Debbie's and go to work from there.'

'Fair enough, mate. Well, I'll probably see you tomorrow night.'

'Okay. Have a good one, Les.'

'Oogie, oogie, oogie. Do the Mud Crab boogie,' smiled Les, then walked out the front and fired up the mighty Datty. Shortly after he was knocking on the door of Kathy's unit in Hewlett Street, Bronte.

'Hello, Les. How are you?' Katherine was wearing a black, leather mini and black stockings that made her long, sexy legs look about ten feet longer than they normally were and a tangerine, woollen top sashed in the middle that showed just the right amount of cleavage to get plenty of second and even third looks. Despite Kathy's hot outfit she seemed a little cool in her attitude. Norton was the complete opposite.

'Pretty good thanks, Kathy,' he replied happily. 'How's yourself?'

'I'm fine. Come in.'

Les expected maybe a peck on the cheek, instead Kathy closed the door and so he followed her down the hallway. He'd been in the unit before and apart from a bigger TV set, nothing had changed. Good leather furniture, thick ochre carpet, chrome lamps, paintings, an expensive stereo. Kathy and her brother Steve never went without.

'Where's Grorlak the Repulsive?' said Les, looking around for Steve to suddenly appear and eyeball Les like he was just about to rape his sister on the floor. 'Out robbing graves?'

'No. He's up on Henry's property in the Hunter Valley. All the family's up there for a christening. I'm going straight up to join them after work tomorrow.'

'Hoo-ee! So all the Hannans are agonna be up on brer Hawg's farm eh? Yo'all takin' yo banjos?'

'Very funny Ralph. Actually it's three hundred hectares with a vineyard and two rivers going through it.'

'You'd need nine hundred hectares to get away from Henry's snoring.'

Kathy ignored Norton's crude remarks about her

brother and gave him a lingering once up and down. Les was expecting maybe a comment about his vest or how he looked. Instead, Kathy moved her gaze to the side of his face and said, 'What happened to your ear?'

'That's one of those mosquitoe bites I was telling you about,' replied Les. 'I started scratching at it coming back in the bus. It's not bleeding again is it?'

Kathy shook her head. 'No. But I wouldn't scratch it anymore.'

'I won't.' Les looked at her for a moment. 'So what's the story? Where are we going?'

'Somewhere rather decent.'

'Okay. Sounds good to me.'

'I suppose you want a beer or something before you go?' said Kathy, her tone of voice sounding a little condescending.

Les shook his head. 'No thanks. To tell you the truth Kathy. I wouldn't mind getting going. I'm starving. I haven't eaten since we left Wagga.'

'Suits me too. I missed lunch myself today. If we have to, we can talk going over in the car.'

'Okay. Then let's hit the toe.'

Kathy got her keys and locked up the unit; Les followed her down the stairs, his eyes not leaving her backside squeezed into the leather mini for a second. Outside, they walked over and stood in front of Norton's car.

'Yeah, all right. It's a dog, I know. But they stole my other one and it's all I got at the moment. Do you want to catch a taxi?'

Kathy looked at Les for a moment. 'Why don't we take my car.'

'It's up to you.' Les made a gesture with his hands. 'I'll pay for the petrol.'

Les followed Kathy to a double garage in the units, where she pressed a button on her remote and the door rolled up to reveal a small, shiny, blue BMW. Inside was all soft leather upholstery, orange dash lights, a good stereo and air-conditioned luxury. She quickly reversed out, hit the remote again and headed back down Hewlett Street towards Tamarama and Bondi.

'Nice car,' said Les.

'Yes. They go well,' replied Kathy shortly.

Tamarama went past. 'Am I still not allowed to know where we're going?'

'You'll find out soon enough.'

Norton stared ahead for a moment. 'Yeah, righto.'

It wasn't long and they were through Bondi heading down O'Sullivan Road towards Rose Bay. Kathy scarcely said a word on the way over. If anything she seemed quite testy, preferring to listen to her car radio set at some FM station playing the usual, easy-listening schmaltz. Les felt this might have been because she brushed the Datty and had to take her car. Then, it might have been because he had bagged her two brothers. But that was only in fun. And shit! Even though he'd never quite seen Henry, Steve was bloody ugly, and he'd never gone out of his way to be friendly or even civil to Les for that matter the few brief times they'd met. Les knew Kathy was a more serious type of person than him, but she and the night never seemed to click right from the word go – even if she did look like a million dollars when she opened the door. Les wasn't expecting her to roll out the red carpet for him when he arrived, but he did feel they'd had a lot of fun on Tuesday night mainly at his expense. And she sounded as good as gold over the phone. So what brought this on? Maybe she'd sprung the love bites. No. With the Pinke Zinke and his collar up, Les was flat out noticing them himself. It had to be something else. No matter what, Kathy's moodiness towards Les didn't faze his feelings towards her. Next thing Les knew, Kathy had turned the BMW into Lyne Park, Rose Bay and pulled up nose first to the water just down from the Sunderland Restaurant near where the old flying boats used to land in Sydney Harbour years ago.

'Here we are,' she said, switching off the motor and opening her door almost in one motion.

'T'rific,' answered Les. He got out and followed her past a plain, white wall facing the park to the entrance.

Norton had heard about the Sunderland; as much as being a place to eat, it was also the place to be seen. Media supernovas loved to dine there along with the usual social cockroaches and glow worms around Sydney; and outside was a jetty where advertising moguls and others with more money than taste liked to pull up in seaplanes and cruisers.

A dark-haired woman in a grey, check, dress suit opened the door for them. 'Good evening,' she said, with practised politeness. 'Do you have a reservation?'

'Yes, Hannan. For two,' replied Kathy.

The woman consulted a book at the reception desk. 'Certainly. This way please.'

Inside it was fairly spacious with a smaller, non-smoking section. But very plain. Stark white walls, a polished wooden floor, chrome and plastic chairs at the tables, tall windows facing the harbour, a wooden wall at one end, a bar at the other and that was about it. Les couldn't see any paintings or indoor plants, just starched white tablecloths that almost shone in the backlights. The place would certainly have had a beautiful view across the harbour in the daytime. But at night, all you could see were distant pin pricks of light in the darkness and as far as Les was concerned you could have been eating in a wharfies canteen. The only thing worth looking at was the other punters. The woman sat them down in the non-smoking section where Les had a magnificent view of the wooden wall behind Kathy. A waiter in white came over and placed a wine list on the table.

Les shook his head. 'Just a mineral water thanks. Ice 'n' slice.'

'I'll have a glass of chardonnay,' said Kathy.

'Certainly.' The waiter gave a quick bow and scrape and headed towards the bar.

Les checked out what punters he could see, who in turn seemed to be checking Kathy and him out, then turned to Kathy. 'Nice,' he said, trying to sound like he meant it.

'Yes. I like it here,' replied Kathy.

'I have to admit, though, I like sort of smaller restaurants.'

'To each their own.'

'Yeah.' Les began studying the menu.

Kathy's wine arrived along with Les's mineral water. She took a sip, took a look at the other diners then opened her purse. 'Oh by the way, Les,' she said. 'Here's that piece of paper fell out of your pocket the other night.'

'Thanks.' Les tucked the piece of paper in the fob pocket of his jeans.

'And here's your money.' Kathy seemed to raise her voice and make a show of handing Les his thirty dollars.

'Thanks,' repeated Les tightly, conscious of the other diners watching him accept what appeared to be his girlfriend putting in for the bill.

'That's quite all right,' smiled Kathy.

Les felt a touch of scarlet creep into his cheeks. 'Kathy, if you're trying to embarrass me or something, you're doing a pretty good job.'

'Embarrass you?' replied Kathy innocently. 'I haven't the foggiest idea what you're talking about.'

'Yeah, not much,' said Les. 'What's your next trick? Pull your pants down and fart in front of everyone?'

'Les. Do you mind!?'

Norton was about to say something. But he changed his mind and just shook his head.

Les went for a dozen oysters with spicy, green, coconut milk, and a snapper fillet with potato and garlic puree and lemon and caper butter sauce. Kathy also went for the oysters plus vitello tonato: veal fillet with potato and rocket salad. While they waited, Les picked at a fresh bread roll and tried to make some sort of small talk. But the small talk seemed to get smaller all the time and the bread roll, along with the night so far, seemed to take the edge off his appetite. Les for the life of him couldn't seem to fathom out why Kathy had such a rat up her knickers.

The oysters arrived and were pretty good. But halfway through his snapper fillet Les felt the chef could have taken the skin off. Kathy said her oysters were delicious and so was her veal. So there. She even went for sweets. Pudding with coffee-flavoured ice cream and rich caramel sauce. Les had a taste and found it just a tad too sweet. Before long, however, there wasn't much left on the table except stains on the tablecloth and a few crumbs. Les looked at Kathy. Kathy looked at Les. They both looked at each other.

'So what do you want to do now?' asked Les. He felt a bit better after the meal and was even starting to see a funny side of things. So he decided to be cool and accept Kathy's strange mood swing. He was even sorry for the crack he made about her pulling her pants down and farting.

'Well, I've got no intentions of having a late one,' answered Kathy. 'I do have to work tomorrow.'

'Yeah, same here. I promised the Mud Crabs I'd take them training in the morning.' Les looked at her for a second. 'Do you want to come back to my place and have a cup of coffee?'

Kathy's eyes narrowed. 'What was that?'

'I said, would you like to come back to my place and have a cup of coffee.'

'Come back to your place and have a cup of coffee,' she said, slowly and deliberately and very ice-like.

'Yeah,' shrugged Les. 'Coffee, tea, Bonox. A banana smoothie. Anything you want.'

This seemed to be the catalyst Kathy was waiting for, while at the same time Norton felt he knew what was bugging her. Katherine Hannan had been porked by someone beneath her station and had inadvertently liked it. It wasn't only Les's car that wasn't good enough for her. Kathy had thought things over since he'd rung and Les wasn't good enough either. He wasn't part of the rah-rah establishment like her two ugly big brothers. Les was a semi-autonomous gangster from the wrong side of the tracks. Les wasn't in the old school tie Mafia. And somehow or despicably other, he'd managed to remove Lady Hannan's knickers and give her a bit of what for. And even more despicable again, Lady Hannan had backed up for more. Now, as well as being filthy on Les, she was filthy on herself as well. Les had a sinking feeling that this was going to be the end of what should have been a beautiful relationship. Les also felt a little bit angry, because apart from having a bit of a joke about her brothers he had not done one wrong thing. Such being the case then, if he was going to go out, he may as well go out in style.

'Now you listen to me . . . Les Norton,' said Kathy.

'I'm one big ear . . . Katherine Hannan,' replied Les.

'Just because of what happened the other night, doesn't mean you can take me out somewhere for a quick feed, then tell me as soon as we've finished we can whip straight back to your place and get into another great sex session.'

Les looked at Kathy for a second. 'I said that?'

'You know what you said. Blokes like you are all the same. All you think of is your stomach and what hangs off it.'

'We do?'

'Of course you do,' huffed Kathy. 'I know your type. You've got a girl for every night of the week.

Out you go. Lay on the charm. And there it is. All the crumpet you want.'

'What?' Norton couldn't believe what he was hearing. 'Are you fair dinkum? I wish it was like that.'

'Of course it is. Don't come on to me you . . . you . . . fast-talking, Kings Cross Lothario.'

Norton stared at Kathy. 'Lothario? I don't believe it. Why don't you just call me a pimp and be done with it. You wombat.' Les didn't know whether to laugh or cry. Instead he decided to let it all hang out. 'Okay Freda Drunge,' he said, looking directly at Kathy. 'And I'm going to be both rude and blunt here. Explain this to me: say you're out somewhere, you're a bit pissy and a bit fruity. You see some bloke you fancy, so you go up to him and say, "G'day handsome. I feel like taking you home and fucking you." What would happen?'

Kathy blanched and her jaw dropped slightly as if she couldn't believe what she'd just heard. 'I . . .'

'I'll tell you what would happen. The bloke would either laugh. Or say. Righto, you want to go now, or will I finish my drink first.' Norton rivetted Kathy with a gimlet-like stare. 'Now, what would happen if I was some bloke out somewhere and I went up to you and said, "How's it going there, sexy. You look all right. I wouldn't mind taking you back to my place and fucking the arse off you?" What would happen?'

'What would happen?' Kathy's face reddened and a couple of diners turned towards their table. 'I'll tell you what would happen. You'd get a swift kick right where it hurts. And your drink would be in your face.'

'Exactly,' answered Les. 'Then you get the bouncers to throw me out for being a foul-mouthed, drunken mug. And quite rightly too, I might add. But explain that one to me?'

'Well. I . . . I see your point.'

'Laid on my arse,' said Les. 'And as for, "All I think of is my stomach and what hangs off it", what about the bloke who said a woman is an animal that micturates once a day, defecates once a week, menstruates once a month, parturates once a year and copulates whenever she has the opportunity. How does that grab you baby?'

'Les, do you mind. That's . . .'

'You hoity toity peanut,' cut in Norton. 'You go on as if I barged into your place the other night, chloroformed you, then raped you on the floor. It takes two to tango sister, and you started the ball rolling. And the second time round I'm lucky Hogs Head, or whatever you call the silly big goose, didn't come in and try and kill me.'

A look of complete insouciance painted Kathy's face. 'Well, I . . .'

'All right. I admit I'm not madly bloody in love with you. After one night out with you I'd be telling lies if I said I was. But if I was given the chance I could love you. Christ! I've fancied you for long enough. I do have feelings you know. And fair enough, I'm a bit lacking in social graces. But I've always treated you with respect.'

'Oh Les. I . . .'

Norton tapped his finger on the table. 'Even if you got up now, Kathy, and walked straight out to your car and left me here and said you never wanted to see me again, I'd still say I had a terrific night. Just because I was with you for a little while.'

'Oh Les. I'm sorry. I didn't really mean anything. I just wasn't thinking.'

'Wasn't thinking.' Les could feel he'd won. And won well. But he had to put the boot in. He cocked his head to one side, stared at Kathy and gave her the full-on, little boy lost look – with more than a touch of added lost. 'You sure know how to hurt someone's feelings.'

'Oh, Les. I didn't know you felt that way.' Kathy reached across the table and placed her hand on Les's. 'And if I've hurt your feelings I'm sorry. I really am.'

Les managed to give her just a bit more little boy lost. 'That's all right. I've had my emotions shattered by harder women than you, Katherine Hannan.'

'Oh . . . shattered emotions.'

Norton took his hand away. 'See, there you go. Now wound me with your scorn. You're merciless, woman.'

'Merciless? Oh for God's sake! All right then. Let's go back to your place and have a cup of coffee. Hemlock, cheap gin, anything.'

'Yeah?'

'Sure. Why not? Actually, I've never seen where you live.'

'Chez Norton,' smiled Les. 'You'll love it.'

Les didn't quite have heart palpitations when he paid the bill. But driving back to Bondi in the BMW he figured that for what it cost for a plate of oysters, some fish and potatoes, a glass of water and a bread roll he could have got something he could keep a bit longer; like a couple of good shirts or a stack of CDs. However, Kathy seemed a lot happier now that she'd been fed and got whatever it was off her superbly conditioned chest. She still wasn't staying long. Just one cup of coffee, a look around and then home. That was okay by Les. A quick cuppa, then he'd come with her and pick up his car. When he told her this, Les wasn't sure whether Kathy's reply was serious or she'd cracked it for a quick one-liner.

'Yes, I'd rather you picked it up tonight. If you left it there during the day it could ruin the property values.' Kathy parked out the front of Chez Norton and they went inside.

A soft light was on in the lounge and the stereo was still playing when they walked down the hallway. Les switched the main light on and went into the kitchen. Kathy checked out all the good furniture Les had got at the right price, the prints and posters on the walls, the expensive stereo and TV, their extensive CD collection. The house was nice and tidy because Warren had organised a cleaning lady to come in every Monday morning for two hours and give Chez Norton the once over. The kitchen lacked for nothing either. Norton was still tight, but he didn't mind splurging some of the black money he had buried on any mod cons that were needed in the preparation of food.

'Hey, how about we have a mug of Ovaltine?' he said, getting some milk from the fridge.

'Okay. That sounds like a good idea.' A minute or two later Kathy wandered into the kitchen and had another look around. 'So you own this,' she said.

'Yep,' answered Les, from between the microwave oven and the mugs. 'Chez Norton. She's all mine. I used to own a block of flats at Randwick. But they got blown up in a gas leak explosion about the same time the council reclaimed the land. Now I'm stuck in a Catch 22 between the council and the insurance company waiting for a settlement.'

'Really?' Kathy's eyebrows rose a little. Maybe Les wasn't such a peasant after all. He definitely wasn't old school tie, but he did own some valuable real estate. 'It's funny Les. I still don't know all that much about you. You come from Queensland and you work for . . . how should I say it? Well-known racing identity Price Galese.'

'That's about it, Kathy, said Les. 'I just help him run a gambling house up the Cross. But it's cool. There's no real dramas. To be honest, it's a bit of bludge.' He gave Kathy a smile as the microwave pinged. 'And I can always wangle a night off if you want to come out with me again.'

'Of course I want to come out with you again.'

'Good. And with a bit of luck I should have a better car next time. Do you like those Nissan Cedrics like the one on *Club Buggery*?'

'Mmmhh. Try and get one with zebra skin upholstery.'

Les handed Kathy her mug of Ovaltine. 'Why don't we sit in the lounge and I might throw a CD on or something.'

'Okay.'

Les stepped back to let Kathy go first. She didn't notice the corner of the kitchen table and bumped it hard enough to tilt her mug and spill most of her hot Ovaltine all over Norton's white jeans.

'Oh Les,' she exclaimed. 'What have I done? I'm sorry.'

'That's okay,' grimmaced Les, as the hot drink

soaked into his groin then down to both knees of his jeans. 'It's only milk. I just copped the lot, that's all.'

'I am sorry,' said Kathy, still holding her empty mug. 'Oh dear, have a look at you.'

Les put his mug on the kitchen table. 'Look, why don't you make yourself a fresh mug while I get changed?'

'Okay. Sorry Les.'

'Don't worry about it.'

Les went to his room and tossed his jeans into the dirty clothes basket, hung the rest up then changed into a dark blue New Balance tracksuit and a pair of black Courtsters. He walked back into the kitchen where Kathy was stirring a fresh mug of Ovaltine. She gave Les a once up and down and put her spoon in the sink.

'I don't care if you spill that one on me too, Kathy,' said Les. 'But just try not to get any in my eyes, will you.'

'I'll do my best. I promise.'

They went into the lounge room and Kathy sat down on the lounge while Les fiddled with the stereo. He wasn't sure about Kathy's taste in music, but he thought he'd better not put on anything too frantic. He found a laid back tape, slipped it in and with 'Heart's Desire' by Lee Roy Parnell warbling nicely through the speakers sat down next to Kathy on her right. They sipped their Ovaltines and chatted away with Les doing most of the talking and Kathy happy doing the listening. He told her about the Mud Crabs, how good-looking they were, how hard they trained, where they were staying and how they nicknamed him Reg Varney. Kathy said she would have loved to have met them, but she'd definitely be watching the grand final up at Henry's farm on Sunday night along with the rest of the family. Kathy somehow managed to move a little closer to Les; as she did, the woollen sash on her top loosened revealing quite a bit of good quality tit covered by a delicate, white lace bra so flimsy it was almost invisible. She made no attempt to cover herself up or say anything to Les when she noticed his eyes bulge. Les looked at Kathy looking at him looking at her boobs and thought, what the hell. He reached over, put his hand around the left one and gave it a gentle squeeze.

Kathy looked at Norton's hand on her tit then looked up at him. 'Are you having a good time there, Les?'

'Yeah,' answered Les. 'As a matter of fact I am. In fact it's that good, I was thinking of slipping my hand under that poor excuse for a bra you're almost wearing and giving them both a squeeze.'

'Well, I mean, don't let me stop you.'

Les took his hand away and put it gently on her shoulder. 'You can if you want me to.'

Kathy shook her head and a sweep of shiny brown hair danced magically across her shoulders. 'No. As a matter of fact I kind of like what you're doing. Even if you are a complete and utter bastard for doing it.'

Les shook his head also. 'See what I mean? I'm dammed if I do. And dammed if I don't. You can't win.'

Kathy gave Les a smile that was both lovely and enigmatic. 'Les. Be honest,' she said. 'When were you ever meant to?'

Kathy's face tilted up and Les brought his down as Jimmy Buffett's "School Boy Heart" started tingling away on the stereo and they had a long, lingering, very tender kiss. The next kiss was just as tender, but a lot deeper. Then things on the lounge began getting quite steamy and very soon hands, arms and tongues were going everywhere.

Les thought he might leave Jimmy to it. He took Kathy by the hand and led her into his bedroom and by the soft light coming in from the hallway they got undressed then got into bed and started making love to each other. No-one else. Just each other. And as far as Les was concerned this time it was even better again, if that was possible. No big brother to have to worry about, no having to sneak out in the dark, no having to hold back. He was home, relaxed, the house was his and he was very happy. Katherine didn't seem to be complaining either. When they'd finished, Les was laying back with Kathy's head on his chest thinking he was somewhere in between a dream and reality. Before long the night, the meal and the long drive back from Wagga started to creep over him.

'Hey Kathy,' he said very quietly.

'Yes Les,' she answered softly.

'I'm just going to close my eyes for a minute. Let me know when you're ready to go home, will you?'

'All right.' Kathy nestled up a little closer.

'This time Les didn't hear Kathy leave, nor did he feel it when she tucked the blankets up around him. Though he did mumble something incoherent yet nice when she kissed him goodbye.

Norton blinked his eyes open around seven-thirty, took a quick glance to his left then a smile lit up his face as the night filtered back to him. What a sweetheart. She let me sleep. He looked at his watch then got up, drew back the curtain and stared out the front window. It wasn't too bad a day; a few clouds around and what appeared to be a light westerly drifting across Cox Avenue. A good day to do the things a man's got to do. Like, among other things, retrieve a certain black car before it ruined the property values of a certain young lady's valuable home unit overlooking Bronte Beach. But to do this he was going to need a lift. Les hit the bathroom, climbed into his old grey tracksuit and trainers, turned the kettle on in the kitchen then got on the blower. His lift was home.

'How are you mate? You got my message?'

'Yeah,' replied Billy Dunne. 'So what's doing? You got back from Wagga Wagga all right?'

'Yep. Everything's sweet and I got tales to tell. You still want to come training with me and the mighty Mud Crabs?'

'Bloody oath! In fact I was just about to ring you myself and see what's going on.'

'I only just got up. All right. Well, why don't you come over my joint and I'll give you the whole John Dory.'

'Righto. I'll see you in about ten minutes.'

'I'll have a coffee waiting for you.'

Les put the phone down, filled the plunger in the kitchen, tossed a towel and his gear into an overnight bag then went back to the bathroom and said goodbye to a couple of old friends. By the time he'd done this

Billy was knocking on the front door wearing an old pair of blue shorts, an equally old black T-shirt with a grey sweatshirt over the top, and his trainers. He feinted a quick left rip to Norton's ribs as they exchanged greetings then walked down the hallway to the kitchen.

'So what's the story, Les baby?' asked Billy, pulling up a chair as Norton shoved the plunger into the coffee. 'You sounded pretty chipper over the phone.'

'Mate. Mate,' replied Les. 'You reckon I haven't been up to some nice capers the last couple of days.'

Les poured two coffees then gave Billy a quick, blow by blow description of what had happened since Tuesday. Kathy, Evelyn, the fight in Wagga Wagga. Giving Coyne the four hundred thousand dollars, the Mud Crabs and the trip back in the bus. By the time he'd finished Billy was on his second cup of coffee, laughing his head off one minute and absolutely fascinated the next.

'So you've had a bit of a quiet one, Les,' said Billy, giving his head a slight shake.

'Yes, you could say that,' smiled Les.

'And you managed to worm your way into Tae Kwon Do Kate's pants too eh?'

'I think she wormed her way into mine,' smiled Les. 'Though I had to tap dance pretty quick last night.' Les looked evenly at Billy over his coffee. 'But I have to admit Billy, I do fancy her.'

Billy made an open-handed gesture. 'I don't blame you. She's a good style.'

'Yeah,' nodded Les. 'She's not bad. Not bad at all.'

Billy looked at Les for a moment. 'What about

Nizegy? Does all this rattle sound kosher to you? Christ! He doesn't mind throwing a bit of cash around.'

'Yeah,' admitted Les, with a slight shrug. 'But it all seems pretty sweet. He just reckons he owes me a big favour. And I'm not going to argue with him. Not for two hundred large. There are a couple of things I'm sort of . . .'

Les was about to say more when the phone rang. He cocked an ear towards the lounge, heard a familiar voice on the machine then walked over and picked up the phone.

'G'day Neville. How's things?'

'Hello Les. How are you, mate? You got back safe and sound.'

'Yeah. Coyne got the chops. And the boys are tucked away in the garage like seven little silkworms.'

'I know. I rang them this morning. Rinh said you're taking them training around nine.'

'Yeah. They seem like a pretty good team of blokes. So I thought I'd give them a bit of a hand while I'm doing nothing.'

'That's terrific, Les. Where are you thinking of taking them?'

'Just for a bit of a jog round Tamarama. Then a swim in Bronte pool.'

'Okay. That's perfect. Because I've lined up some media coverage.'

'Yeah?'

Nizegy nodded at the other end of the line. 'I'll organise it for Neil Brooks and Channel 7 to meet you down Bronte pool at ten thirty. And maybe the Telegraph.'

'Neil Brooks from the Mean Machine?' said Les. 'He's my idol.'

'Yeah Brooksie's all right. He'll look after you. And at four o'clock, SBS'll be out at the garage to interview them about the team's racial mix. Can you handle it? Say you're the trainer or something? I can't get there.'

'Ohh yeah,' replied Les. 'I don't see why not.'

'Good stuff,' beamed Nizegy. 'You'll kill 'em on TV, Les.'

'Billy'll be with me.'

'Oh! That's even better. Hey Les, I'm sorry about all that Elliot with the bus and you had to spend an extra night in Wagga. I didn't know how bad it was wrecked. I would have got in touch, but I've been flat out getting all this shit together. It's a fuckin' nightmare at times.'

'Fair enough,' answered Les. 'So what's all this business with Coyne tonight?'

'Coyne'll tell you about it when he sees you. It won't take you long. About an hour at the most.'

'Yeah? It's all ... you know. Osher-kah, Neville old mate?'

'Of course. Why? What makes you say that?'

'Ohh nothing. Just asking, that's all.'

'You just got to pick a bloke up, and ... look after him a bit. That's all.'

'Look after him?'

'Yeah. Coyne'll fill you in. It's nothing.' Nizegy gave a bit of chuckle down the line. 'I think you've been hanging around with too many gangsters, Les.'

'Possibly. And not the Saturday afternoon variety either Neville.'

'Don't worry, Les. Everything's sweet. Anyway, I

have to get going. I got a million things to do. If you don't hear from me, I'll see you at the grand final tomorrow. You got my number if you want me.'

'All right, Neville. I'll see you when I see you.'

'You too, Les. Take care mate.'

Norton put the phone down, stared at it for a moment then went back to the kitchen. 'That was the man himself?'

'I figured that' said Billy. 'What's the story?'

'He'll see me at the grand final.' Les looked at his work mate for a second or two. 'How would you like to be a TV star William?'

'How would I like to be a what?' answered Billy.

'A TV star.' In a light-hearted way Les told Billy about Nizegy's one day media blitz.

Billy listened intently and his face lit up. 'Okay,' he said, in an even more light-hearted way. 'I'll be in that. You can be the team's trainer. I'll be their manager. I'll have to brush the SBS one. But we'll give Brooksie the in-depth, sporting interview of the decade.'

'You give it to him,' corrected Les. 'I'll just stay a shadowy and mysterious figure in the background.'

'Suit yourself. So where are we taking the mighty Mud Crabs for their gruelling training session?'

'Bronte pool. But we'll kick off with a run.'

'Okay. Where to?'

'Well. One of the boys is called Garrick, William,' replied Les.

Billy nodded knowingly. 'Say no more, Les. Say no more.'

Les looked at his watch. 'Anyway, we'd better make a move. I said I'd be there at nine.'

'All right. Let's hit the toe.'

Les locked the house up then they got into Billy's dark blue Commodore station-wagon and headed for Coogee, with Les deciding to pick the Datty up on the way back. He also decided not to mention having to meet Coyne that night or anything else he had on his mind about Nizegy for the time being. Instead he just told Billy a bit more about what happened in Wagga Wagga. The traffic was the usual Saturday morning grind getting out of Bondi. But eventually, with Norton giving directions, Billy nosed the station-wagon up onto the driveway in front of the Mud Crab's garage.

'So this is it?' said Billy, peering round through the windscreen.

'Yep. This is it,' answered Les, unclipping his seat belt and opening the door.

The small door to the garage was slightly open. Les gave a quick rap on the roller and they stepped inside. It was still a little gloomy despite both lights being on, with a few shafts of sunlight from a window above the shower picking up the dust at the back. The boys were sprawled across their bunks studying; some were munching pieces of fruit from a plastic bag of apples and other fruit on the table.

'Good morning, girls,' said Les cheerfully. 'We're your Avon ladies. Can we interest you in our new range of cosmetics?'

'Hey. It's the Varns,' said Garrick.

'Reg,' said Clarence. 'What's happening big daddy?'

'Fellahs. This is my mate I was telling you about, Billy Dunne. Billy, these are the Mud Crabs.' Les pointed the team out to Billy by their nicknames.

Billy nodded and smiled. 'Hello fellahs. Pleased to meet you.' He gave the garage a quick perusal. 'Glad to see you're enjoying your stay in Sydney.'

'So how's it all going boys?' asked Les. 'Everything okay? The boogie man didn't get you last night?'

'No. He couldn't get in here for the cockroaches,' said Rinh.

'Hey, Dogs. A home isn't a home in the Eastern suburbs without a few Bondi butterflies.'

'Terrific.'

'We've been up about an hour,' said Raymond. 'A couple of us went down and got some fruit. And we just been sitting around, reading and waiting for our ace DJ, driver and trainer to get here.'

'Well, he's here as promised,' acknowledged Les, making an open gesture with his hands. 'And I've brought my second ace conditioner and your new manager with me.'

'So what have you got lined up for us, Reg?' asked Felix.

'A run around Tamarama followed by a swim at Bronte pool. Then breakfast,' replied Les.

'A run around where?' queried Garrick.

'Tamarama,' said Billy, smiling at him. 'And you're going to love it, Harry.'

Les caught the look in Billy's eye and clapped his hands. 'Well come on girls. Let's make a move. The day ain't getting any younger.'

There was a general chorus of agreement as the boys threw their fruit peel in the bin and picked up their bags. Les made sure the garage was locked securely, then the team all followed him and Billy over to the bus and they headed for Bronte.

Les tuned the car radio to the nearest FM station and kept it down low while he told the boys about the film crew coming to do a story on them at Bronte; he also told them Billy would be acting as their manager and to go along with the gag. When the SBS mob came over to film them at the garage they could do or say what they liked. The boys said that was cool and were looking forward to meeting Neil Brooks. Billy and the Mud Crabs seemed to click immediately in the back; they told him about the flag on the backs of their tracksuits and he told them about his boxing career. A few pop songs played, the traffic eased a little and they were bumping down McPherson Street, past where Les first met Neville Nixon, towards Bronte Road. As they took the bend past Tipper Avenue the boys couldn't help but be impressed by the view – from the cliffs over the green of Bronte Park to the long lines of blue swells rolling in from the Pacific all the way past Bronte and Tamarama right up to Bondi.

'Hey, this looks all right,' said Jamieson.

'Yeah. Unreal,' chimed in Raymond. 'Look at those waves.'

Les couldn't remember the last time he was at Bronte. But it had certainly changed. Where it was once just old flats facing the park with a row of daggy little shops below offering not much at all, now it was cheek by jowl with boutique cafes spread out along the footpath, serving everything from homous to herbal tea; a face at every window and a bum on every seat. Going by the people and the cars around, Les knew he had more chance of finding a gold watch than a parking spot. So he gunned the bus past the shops and up the hill, swung a tyre-screaming U-turn in front of a Saab convertible full of yuppies coming down, and screeched to a halt on a no parking zone alongside the white railing facing the park above the bus stop.

'Yeah! Go the Varns!' said Clarence as they all rocked back into their seats.

'Reg. Top gun,' said Rodney. 'The man is on!'

Billy was still shaking his head. 'Christ! Where did you learn to drive you cunt.'

'If we get a ticket, Nizegy can sort it out,' grunted Norton, blowing the yuppies a kiss as they hissed past in a torrent of abuse and blaring car horns. 'Righto girls,' he said, switching off the motor. 'This is it. Beautiful, downtown Bronte.'

They got their bags, climbed out of the bus and began following the path down to where the pool nestled beneath the cliffs at the southern end of the beach. The wind had turned slightly on shore, but there was plenty of blue sky and bluer ocean, the park was that green it almost shone and the water in the pool was beautifully, crystal clear with a lazy wash frothing gently over the rocks and stairs leading into the sea below.

'Wow! I like this,' said Rinh.

'Yeah. It's a nice spot all right,' agreed Billy.

Les was looking around for a safe place to leave their bags when he spotted a familiar face amongst a team of old timers sitting in the sun on the benches next to the shower block. One-legged Jack and his son two-legged Jimmy. Jack was a huge, retired barrowman who lived in his Speedos and was as brown as a berry from sitting on his arse in the sun

175

all day. He had a rumbling, growl of a voice as deep as his stomach was big and was famous for his dry sense of humour and razor sharp repartee. His son Jimmy was also a big lump of a bloke who worked at another game in Double Bay. Seeing as Jack only had one leg he naturally got called one-legged Jack. But seeing his son was normal he somehow got called two-legged Jimmy. Like a lot of other old knock-abouts from around Bondi Baths, Jack retreated to Bronte pool after Les and the major did them all a big favour when they blew the baths and the Bondi Icebergs up round the moons of Jupiter. Jimmy was walking towards the cafes and Les was about to approach Jack when another hanger from the baths came walking up from the pool. Taxi Pat. Pat was no spring chicken, loved a drink, was always in a sour mood – and looked it walking past in a pair of baggy white shorts, a beanie, and an old Souths football jumper. She spotted one-legged Jack and decided to have a go at him.

'G'day Jack,' she snarled. 'I heard you had your prostate done, you fat heap of shit. How is it now?'

'A lot smaller than it used to be, Taxi,' growled Jack. 'Pity they can't say the same thing about your rotten ted.' Pat muttered something filthy under her breath and kept going. Jack spotted Norton and in almost the same breath said, 'G'day Les. How are you mate?'

'Pretty good thanks, Jack,' replied Norton. 'Hey mate? Could you do us a favour?'

'Sure, Les. What is it?'

'If we leave our bags here, will you keep an eye on them for us?'

'Sure, Les. No trouble at all.'

'Good on you, mate. Thanks a lot.'

'G'day, Billy. How are you?'

'I'm good thanks, Jack.'

Les told the Mud Crabs to stack their stuff just up from one-legged Jack, then he and Billy led them over to the wooden railings near the promenade for a few stretches.

'Hey, before we go too far, Reg,' said Jamieson. 'We're not into running marathons on concrete.'

'Yeah, we're swimmers, Reg,' said Felix. 'You know. Like, water, pools, Speedos, goggles.'

'Sprints are cool,' added Rodney.

'All right. Don't shit your pants,' replied Norton. 'We're just going to do a couple of slow kilometres. Maybe a couple of little sprints for your wind. Then you can come back and flop around in the pool till you go blue in the face.'

'All right,' nodded Garrick. 'So where are we going?'

'Just follow your new manager,' said Les.

'That's me,' winked Billy. 'And like I said, you're going to love this, Garrick.'

Les waited until he was convinced they'd done enough stretches.

'All right, Billy,' he said. 'Let's move 'em up. And head 'em out.'

'Righto.' Billy looked at his watch and pointed North. 'Mud Crabs. Hooohhhhh!' With the ocean on his right and the others behind him, Billy led them off at an easy pace towards Tamarama.

The Mud Crabs certainly looked a picture as they jogged along Marine Drive in the sunshine with their snappy, red tracksuits and striking good looks. Leading the way, Les and Billy looked just as fit, except in their old training clobber they looked more like a couple of garbos who'd forgotten it was their day off. Billy was hardly setting any pace, barely passing two fat women in sweaty tracksuits puffing and panting their ample behinds off. The Mud Crabs were looking at each other, half-sniggering and thinking this was a doddle; but happy enough to go along with it and have a look about them at some pleasant surroundings. They got to the bus stop at the bend when Billy stopped and held up his arm. He waited for a break in the traffic then waved them on.

'Righto boys,' he said. 'Over the road into the park.'

They jogged across Tamarama Park and up the concrete path to where the brutally steep steps zig-zag up to the corner of Cross and Birrell Streets. Les had told Billy about how Major Lewis ran him ragged up and down those steps backwards and forwards, so they started going there till they could get on top of it. They weren't anywhere near as nimble and quick as the major, but they weren't bad and could run rings around anyone who wasn't used to them. As soon as Les said one of the Mud Crabs names was Garrick, Billy twigged straight away and planned a small surprise for the boys from Wagga Wagga. They got to the bottom of the steps and Billy stopped again.

'Okay boys,' he said, getting ready to suck in a deep breath. 'This way up.'

Les and Billy hit the steps at a gallop; not flat out, but a lot quicker than the pace they'd been jogging. The Mud Crabs were taken aback a little at first. But they were young and fit and had trained hard themselves, so they were only about six or so steps behind when they got to Les and Billy waiting on the grass at the top. Felix and Rodney were first up.

'Bit of a sneaky one there, the manager,' said Felix.

'Not so bad,' shrugged Rodney.

Billy ignored them and waited till the others arrived, then he and Les stood facing them on the top step.

'Righto boys,' said Billy. 'Now we go down. Backwards.'

There was a great, disbelieving chorus of 'Wwhhaaatttt!!?'

'Backwards,' repeated Billy. 'And if I see one face on the way down, I'll put a fist in it.'

'You heard the man, ladies,' smiled Les. 'Let's go.'

Without waiting Les and Billy started scrabbling back down the steps. Above them the disconcerted Mud Crabs were a complete mess, slipping and slithering all over the place. By the time Jamieson arrived, with the others spread out and spun out behind him, Les and Billy were waiting at the bottom fully recuperated.

'What's that old expression Billy?' said Les. 'Coming in like Brown's cows?'

Billy shook his head. 'No. I think it's coming in like Murrumbidgee Mud Crabs.' Billy looked at the entire team puffing and panting for a few seconds. 'Righto girls,' he said. 'Let's try it again. Yay team!'

Billy led the charge once more and before the Mud Crabs knew it, he and Les were waiting at the top for them again. Clarence was the first one up this time.

'You got to be kiddin' haven't you?' he puffed.

'You're off your head,' spluttered Garrick.

Les gave him a smile. 'He told you you'd like it, Garrick.'

Billy waited till they were all there, then went back to the top step. 'Okay girls,' he said. 'A one and a two, and a you-know-what-to-do.'

Les and Billy started back down the stairs again, with the Mud Crabs above and behind doing their best to stay on their feet let alone catch up. Once more Billy and Les were waiting at the bottom, cool calm and breathing easy. This time Rinh was the first to arrive.

'This is wrong, man,' he said, shaking his head. 'Wrong.'

'What did he say?' asked Billy. 'Wong?'

Les shook his head also. 'Buggered if I know. I don't speak Chinese.'

Billy waited for them all to arrive then gave them a disinterested once over. 'Come on. Let's go back to Bronte. I'd like to do another eighteen sets of those. But if we got to wait for you, we'll be here all fuckin' day.'

With the team behind him, Billy led them out of the park and back along Marine Drive, only at a little steadier pace this time. The boys had got their act together, but they were still puffing noticeably when they got back to the wooden railing above the pool.

'So how did you like your warm up, fellahs?' said Billy, as the team grouped around him and Les.

There was a bit of murmuring and muttering at first, then the boys started to smile at having one put over them by a couple of older and craftier heads from the city.

'Yeah. Nice one, manager,' said Raymond. 'You got us.'

Garrick nodded grudgingly. 'Chalk one up for Oswald and Louis.'

'Oswald and Louis,' repeated Billy. 'I think I like that, Les. Maybe these boys are really cool dudes after all.'

'Just give me a second,' said Les. 'And I'll switch on the part of my brain that cares.'

'Yeah,' said Billy. 'But don't get too close to them. We might catch a bad dose of the stupids.'

'All right. You win,' said Garrick. 'So what's on now?'

'Now,' said Les. 'You're on your own. Just get in the pool and do your own thing. We'll stay up here and keep an eye on you. And sort out the TV thing.'

'Yeah. We're middle distance street fighters,' said Billy. 'Not swimmers.'

Rinh nodded. 'I think we get the picture.'

'And when you're finished,' added Norton, 'we'll go and have some breakfast.'

Les and Billy gave the boys a bit of a pat on the back and they went over to their bags, changed down to just their Speedos and got the grenade. After training in the freezing cold water of the river back home, the water in Bronte pool felt like Great Keppel Island; it wasn't long before the boys were splashing and swimming around, tossing the grenade to each other and practising plays or whatever. It also wasn't long before a crowd began to gather – included some Japanese tourists armed to the teeth with cameras and video recorders and an increasing number of girls ogling at the seven spunks in black Speedos. Les and

Billy were leaning against the railing enjoying the perv when a cheerful face, head and shoulders above the rest, wearing a blue, Channel 7 jacket, came walking through the crowd followed by a two man, film crew also wearing blue, Channel 7 jackets. Neil Brooks stopped near Les and Billy, put a hand over his eyes and looked around.

'Righto, Billy,' said Les. 'I think this is your big chance. Go get 'em tiger.'

Billy caught Brooksie's eye and waved. 'Hey Neil. Are you here to interview the Mud Crabs?'

'That's right,' said Neil, walking over. 'Are you Les Norton?'

Billy shook his head. 'No, that's him. I'm the manager.'

'That's right, Neil,' said Les. 'He's the man. Anything you want to know, see him.'

'All right,' said Brooksie. 'So, ah ... what's your name?'

Billy offered his hand. 'Scravortis. Fitzy Scravortis. But everybody calls me 'Scrarv, Neil.'

'Okay Scrarv.' Brooksie shook Billy's hand and wrote the name down on a clipboard. 'Righto Scrarv. All we want to do is ask you a few questions about the Mud Crabs and get some film of them in the water.'

'No trouble at all, Neil,' replied Billy. 'In fact the boys are just down there in the pool finishing their workout now.'

'Oh good.'

'In fact, if you want to Neil, why not shoot the questions now while I'm standing here against the railing. Get it out of the road. Look good too with the ocean in the background and all that.'

Brooksie looked at his film crew who shrugged back an affirmative. 'Okay. Why not?' said Brooksie. 'We can edit the rest in back at the studio.'

The cameraman hoisted his TV camera up onto his shoulder while the soundman checked his levels. It suited them. The sooner they got it shot, the sooner they could get to the next shoot then home.

'Film ready when you are Neil.'

'Sound is good.'

'Okay. Let's shoot it.' Brooksie straightened his jacket and cleared his throat. 'Mud Crabs interview. Take one.' He gave it a beat then smiled into the camera. 'I'm here at Bronte Beach with Fitzy Scravortis, manager of the Murrumbidgee Mud Crabs. The young, dynamic team everybody's talking about, who might just manage to upset the Sydney Sea Snakes in the grand final of Extreme Polo at the Homebush Aquatic Centre on Sunday night. And for those who have never seen it, Extreme Polo is the new game sweeping Australia, a game where men do walk on water.' Brooksie turned to Billy. 'Scrarv. What's the main reason you think the Mud Crabs will win the grand final tomorrow?'

Billy looked into the camera like an old pro. 'Because they're rotten, lying, cheating, no good little bastards. Just the kind of team you'd like to play in, Neil.'

'Thanks ... Scrarv. Ahh, I believe the team not only trains in the freezing cold water of the Murrumbidgee River, they also have a revolutionary, secret training method. Is that right?'

'That's right, Neil. Would you like to know it?'

'Sure. Yeah.'

'Well, I'm sorry, I can't tell you. It's a secret.'

'Oh.'

'But I can tell you this, Neil,' said Billy. 'The mighty Mud Crabs are red-hot specials to win the grand final tomorrow. Because not only do they train like Spartans. They have a special drink they take. A secret, herb tonic. I can tell you what that is, though.'

'You can?'

'Sure, Brooksie. No worries, mate. It's an ancient, blackfellahs medicine. It consists of a unique moss that grows only on the banks of the Murrumbidgee River. Plus a special tree bark gathered for us in secret by the Aboriginal elders of the local tribe. The boys boil this in their own urine and drink it. Heaps of it.'

'They what?'

'They drink their own urine.' Billy's face suddenly turned very sage. 'Which is where I would like to say, Neil, that I was badly misquoted by both Channel 7 and the press recently.'

'You were? I didn't . . .'

'A number of sports journalists said that I encouraged both bad behaviour and team drinking. I did no such thing, Neil.'

'You didn't?'

'No. All I said was, I liked to see the boys getting stuck into the piss all the time. It was good for them.'

'I'm sorry you were taken out of context, Scrarv.'

'That's okay, Brooksie. Better than having it taken out of my wages.'

'Right. Well I don't think we need add much to that. Thank you Fitzy Scravortis, manager of the Murrumbidgee Mud Crabs, for a rare insight into the team's training methods. And good luck in the grand final.'

184

'My pleasure, Neil. And may I just leave you and the fans with those famous words the Earl of Roseberry said when he addressed the Commonwealth of Nations in Adelaide in 1884.'

'What was that Scrarv?'

'Oogie, oogie, oogie. Do the mud crab boogie.'

'We'll leave it there.' Brooksie moved a finger across his throat. 'And cut.'

'Looked good to me,' said the cameraman.

'Sounded perfect.'

'You happy with that, Neil?' asked Billy.

Brooksie shook his head. 'It was flabbergasting.'

'So what's on now, Neil?' asked Les.

Brooksie nodded to the pool below. 'We'll take a few shots of the boys. Then we're off to Ryde pool to interview the Sea Snakes.'

'Yeah?' said Billy. 'Give them a message for me. When the Mud Crabs are finished with them, they'll be jellied eels.'

Brooksie shook both their hands and thanked Billy again, then he and his film crew went down to the pool to do some more filming.

'Jees! You can't help but like Brooksie, can you,' said Les.

'Yeah,' agreed Billy. 'Shit! He's a big bloke. I didn't know he was so tall.'

'Yep. And you had him in the palm of your hand, Scrarv. That interview'll go down in sporting history.'

Billy peered down into the pool where they'd started filming again. 'I don't think I ruined it too much.'

'About the only thing you didn't ruin is my appetite. I'm fuckin' starving.'

'Yeah. Me too. I'll be glad when Brooksie's finished so we can go and get something to eat.'

'Reckon.'

'Why don't we go and have a swim while we're waiting?'

'Yeah. Good idea.'

They left their gear on top of the rest, Les gave one-legged Jack his wallet to mind, then he and Billy jogged down to the water and jumped in near the rock pool. The water wasn't freezing cold, but it was certainly bracing. They didn't bother about doing any laps; just ducked under a few waves, splashed around, freshened up and got out. By the time they'd showered and dried off Brooksie was finished down at the pool. He gave them a big friendly wave as he and the crew walked past, the boys waved back and few minutes later the Mud Crabs came up the steps.

'So how was Brooksie?' asked Les.

There was a general chorus of 'Excellent. Unreal. A really cool guy ...' The Mud Crabs were pretty stoked at meeting Neil Brooks; being an Olympic gold medallist, he was obviously an inspiration to them.

'He reckons our manager might have a bit of water in his petrol pump, though,' said Rinh.

'Neil said that?' Billy seemed mildly surprised. 'I can't understand why.'

'But don't worry. We said you were choice, Scrarv,' chuckled Raymond.

'Thanks. Now why don't you get under the shower and we'll go and get something to eat. Managing you cheeky little pricks is hard work.'

The Mud Crabs didn't need to be told twice; the brisk training session had put an edge on their

186

appetites also. They showered and got back into their tracksuits, laughing amongst themselves and almost completely oblivious to the young and not-so-young women watching them intently – and indeed the platoon of Japanese tourists shooting more film at them than *Gone With The Wind*. Les thanked Jack again for his trouble, then they carried their bags back to the bus. Les got his camera and they went in search of a restaurant.

The breakfast crowd had temporarily thinned and they were able to find two tables and enough chairs on the footpath beneath the blue and white awning of Cafe Z. Les had never eaten there before, but it looked nice and bright with its lime washed walls, blackboard lunch menu inside, and paintings and mirrors; and the chairs were comfortable. Les picked up the breakfast menu and decided on a Bronte Booster: muesli with fruit, eggs benedict with smoked salmon and a flat white. Billy went for a New York smoothie, muesli, toast, a big breakfast with extra mushrooms and a Moroccan fresh mint tea. The boys ordered just about everything on the menu. Fruit frappes, iced chocolates with strawberry and whipped cream, muesli, muffins, baguettes, eggs, bacon, sausages, anything they could see. A young blonde waitress with a kiwi accent, wearing a long-sleeved T-shirt and a short butcher's apron took their orders. While they were waiting, Les bit Billy for some change and walked across to the phone booth just out the front.

'Hello. Rose Bay Travel Service,' came a pleasant voice.

'Yes. Could I speak to Katherine Hannan please.'

'I'm sorry. Katherine is out of the office at the moment.'

'Okay. Will you tell her Les rang. I'm busy and I'll ring her on Monday.'

'I'll see that she gets the message.'

'Thanks.' Les walked back and sat down.

'How was Tae Kwon Do Kate?' asked Billy.

'Out of the office,' replied Norton.

'Oh well. She'll probably come back sooner or later. You think you'll be all right?'

Les drummed his fingers on the table and looked at Billy. 'I'll probably have to force my breakfast down.'

The food and beverages arrived; lots of it and all delicious. Les took some photos then got the waitress to take a couple with him in them. Amongst the passers by and other people eating were several newsreaders from SBS and the ABC, some actors out of the soapies, a well-known female lawyer and other people in the public eye. When the waitress went to take their photo she had to step back to let Paul Barry, the host of Witness, walk past. Five minutes later the reporter from the Telegraph arrived. He was about thirty, with sandy hair, and wearing a badly matched shirt, tie and pants. The photographer was a girl about twenty-five with dark, straight hair, wearing a pair of black stretch pants and a green Balinese top. They didn't seem all that interested and everybody was more interested in eating than talking to them. So it wasn't long before they got the copy they needed, along with the photos they wanted and Billy despatched them fairly smartly and everyone continued eating. The Mud Crabs were already chuffed at meeting Neil Brooks, now they felt they were part of a mini-Hollywood scene as well. They might not have liked Sydney, but there was nothing wrong with Saturday morning at Bronte Beach.

Eventually it was time to go. Billy had things to do at home and it had started to cloud over. Les paid the bill, slipped the waitress a lazy twenty and they walked back to the bus. There was more joke-cracking and yahooing on the trip back to Coogee; in fact, the way they were all carrying on you would have thought they'd just come back from a giant piss-up instead of a training session. Les nosed the bus up against the railing at a bit of an angle this time and then they all got out and walked over to the garage.

'Well, I'm going home for a while,' said Les, as Rinh opened the smaller door. 'But I'll be back at four to sort this SBS thing out. What are you blokes going to do?'

'Study and take it easy,' said Jamieson.

'I thought you might.'

Billy shook every team member's hand and although he couldn't get to the grand final he wished them all the best and said he and his family would be watching and cheering for them on TV. The boys were rapt. Les repeated he'd see them later then jumped in the station-wagon next to Billy and they headed for Hewlett Street.

'So what are you going to call yourself when the SBS team gets there?' asked Billy.

'I don't know, Fitzy,' replied Les. 'Something suavely ethnic I suppose. How about Con the fruiterer?'

'You know whatever you say or do they're still going to call you a racist, don't you?'

'Oh of course,' said Les. 'Though you'd wonder how when I'm minding three abos and a chow. Who I've sworn to guard with my life.'

'Makes no difference. What about the three aussies?'

'I'll hide them in the bus.'

'Then they'll call you a subliminal racist.'

'How about I settle for being just a plain neo-Nazi?'

'They'll see your neo-Nazi and raise you a crypto-fascist.'

'Yeah, you're right,' said Les. 'Don't forget xenophobic too. I may as well turn up in a white sheet with a burning cross.'

'Hey, why don't you? They'd probably love that. That'd keep them in documentaries for the next six months.'

'I ought to. Don't worry though Billy. I'll think of something to stir these whingeing wogs up.'

'I'll be extremely disappointed if you don't mate.'

Before long they were in Hewlett Street and Billy stopped the car just down from Kathy's home unit. Billy told Les he had things to do in the afternoon and one of his boys was playing soccer that night so the family was going out to cheer him on. But he'd be in touch. Les thanked him for the lift then climbed into the mighty Datty. It gave a few whines and wheezes before spluttering into life; Les gave it a few moments to get over the shock then drove home.

There was one message on the machine. From Warren, saying he had to work back – they were behind. He'd be home about seven-thirty. How were the Mud Crabs? Les stood in the lounge room staring at the phone and then into space wondering what he should do for the next couple of hours. He was about to get a drink of water when the phone rang. It was Debbie looking for Warren.

'Hello Zanna. How's things in the Volterra Nebula? The Betazoids haven't got you?'

'Hello Kahless. How are they hanging? Long and loose and full of juice? I'm trying to find Warren. His mobile's off. Is he home?'

'No. There was a message. They're behind at work. He'll be home around seven-thirty.'

'That late eh?'

'That was the message.'

'I see. So what are you doing?'

'Me?' Les decided not to tell Debbie about SBS wanting to do an interview with him and the team. She'd probably want to tag along and drive everybody mad with her Star Trek gibberish. In fact, he wouldn't even mention the Mud Crabs. 'Just hanging at home all day, Debbie. I got a few things to do round the house. Then I'm going out for a drink with a couple of blokes tonight.'

'You are eh?'

'Yeah. What's doing with you?'

'Oh, working Les. Work. We're quite busy actually.'

'That's good, Debbie. Keep the old till ringing.'

'Like a Barzanian temple bell.'

'Okay. Well I'd better let you get back to it. When I see Warren I'll tell him you rang.'

'Thanks. See you, Les.'

'See you, Debbie.'

Well that's Star Fleet Command's First Hairdryer Squadron out of the road. Now, what was I going to do? Outside it looked as good a day as any to do nothing. Les moved his eyes to the TV set and snapped his fingers. Talking about SBS, that's what I'll do, seeing there's no-one home. There was a documentary on Brian Wilson of The Beach Boys Les had got Warren to tape for him while he was at work one night. Les got a glass of mineral water from the fridge, found the tape, kicked off his trainers and settled back in front of the box with the sound coming through the stereo. The doco was pure excellence. The music was great, the black and white photography was sensational and Brian Wilson was as happy as a clam – proving once and for all that reality is only for people who can't handle drugs. Good old SBS, smiled Les, as he tucked the tape away for safekeeping. Most of the time it's shit with subtitles. But now and again they come up with an absolute ripper. Les was still whistling and singing old Beach Boys tunes when he got out of his tracksuit and changed into a white shirt, and a pair of black trousers and matching black vest he used to wear at the club before they went casual, plus his old, black Julius Marlows. In Warren's room was a hatrack full of caps and hats he'd souvenired from different film shoots. Les helped himself to a black fedora, with a black band that was a size too big for Warren, but fitted Norton's big, red head perfectly. Leaving his vest hanging open, he adjusted it in front of his bedroom mirror then tied a couple of black bootlaces to his black leather belt. Yes, thought Les, giving the hat another dip, I could definitely pass for a good Jewish boy observing the sabbath. Okay. Maybe I'm not completely orthodox, but I am a member of Hakoah Club, yet . . . already . . .

He locked the house then fired up the mighty Datty and crawled towards Coogee, muttering 'shut up, shut up, shut up, shut up' at the other cars bipping their horns – and hoping no ultra orthodox Jews spotted him driving his car on Saturday and began stoning him. He nosed the Datty in behind where he'd angled the bus almost hiding it from view, got out and adjusted his hat again. He was surprised to see the garage door closed and Dogs out the front, one foot against the wall, eating an apple. Rinh looked twice when he saw Les coming across the street.

'Dogs, what are you doing out here on your own?'

'Just getting a bit of air, Reg.'

'Right,' nodded Les, going to open the door. 'All the boys inside?'

'I . . . wouldn't go in there if I were you, Les.'

'Wouldn't go in there?' Norton's brow furrowed. 'Why not?'

'The boys have got a chop-up going.'

'What!?' Les couldn't believe his ears. 'You mean to tell me those clean-cut, country boys have got a bun in there?'

''Fraid so, Reg.'

'You're kiddin'. There's a fuckin' film crew arriving here any bloody minute. Jesus Christ!'

'You can't blame the boys,' pleaded Rinh. 'We were just sitting inside on our bunks studying. And she burst through the door wearing all this crazy gear and attacked the whole team.'

'Attacked you? Ohh bullshit!'

'She did, Les. Fair dinkum. She burst in the door raving on with all this space talk and started pulling her clothes off. Then ran around the garage pulling everybody else's gear off and started giving us all head. Then she jumped on the nearest bunk, spread her legs apart and told us to go for our lives. Felix jumped on first. Then they were all into it. And that's the truth, Les. It was unbelievable.'

'Unbelievable all right.' Norton shook his head not knowing whether to laugh or cry then looked at Rinh again. 'So how come you're not in there getting amongst the festivities, Dogs?'

Rinh shook his head also. 'No thanks. I copped a quick blow job. But as well as being nuts, she's a beast. She looks like a cross between Mimi and the creature from outer space.'

Norton's eyes narrowed. 'That's the second time you've mentioned space, Dogs. I think I'd better see this.' Cautiously Les opened the door a little and peered in. Whoever it was had blonde hair and her back to Les, going up and down on Raymond while she was sucking Garrick's knob. On the other side of the bunk Clarence was shoving it up under her armpit. Standing around in the half-light the others were all stropping themselves waiting their turn or whatever. Les stared in disbelief for a moment or two more then quietly closed the door. 'Dogs,' he said softly. 'How did she get here?'

'I don't know for sure. In that car across the road I think.'

Norton's eyes followed Rinh's outstretched arm to a purple Mustang convertible slightly hidden in front of the bus. He gave a double blink then closed his eyes. It was her. It was Debbie. The boys were in their bunning Warren's girl. When he opened his eyes again, 'Shit!' was all he said to Rinh.

Les was wondering what he should do when a plain, beige station-wagon with SBS on the door pulled up near the Datty and another three person film crew got out. A dumpy, black-haired woman in a blue and white dress suit who could have been Greek, a sound man in a grey jacket and jeans with shiny black hair and dark skin who had to be Indian, and a sour-faced cameraman with a bull neck and a buzz cut of curly, black stubble across his head who looked like a Hezbolah suicide bomber.

'Leave this to me and don't say a word, Dogs.'

The woman approached Les and smiled. 'Good afternoon,' she said. 'Are you Mr Les Norton, the manager?'

Les looked at her for a moment then started waving his arms around. 'Do I look like a Les Norton, the manager?' he wailed. 'I'm Solomon Shalomovitz, the owner.'

'Oh. I'm sorry.'

'And who are you voman? And vot's vit the cameras? The fire's not till next veek.'

'We're here to interview the swimming team,' said the woman.

'Schwimming team? Ve don't got no schwimming team here. Ve got footballers. You got the wrong address.'

The woman checked her clipboard. 'Not according to our information.'

195

'Information. Schinformation. Believe me. I know footballers. And they're footballers.'

The soundman shook his head. 'No, no. You are wrong, suh. They are swimmers.'

'Vot! Vot! Vot!' Les started dancing around like the fiddler on the roof. 'You're telling me I don't know footballers?'

'Please,' said the woman. 'There's no need to get excited.'

'Excited? Excited? A heart attack is what I should get standing here arguing with you. Where's the police?'

The cameraman's face turned to stone. 'Oh, be silent you fool.'

The soundman adjusted his headphones. 'We are here now. Why not we are walking in and vox popping them?'

'That's an idea,' said the woman.

'Yes,' cried Norton. 'Vox pop them. Schmox pop them. Do vot you vant. Trample all over my property. Nazis!'

'Let's go,' said the cameraman hoisting his TV camera onto his shoulder. 'Ignore the fool.'

'Anti-semitic is what you are.' Les gave them the Yiddish finger then got out of sight in the passageway next to the garage.

He wasn't there long when a bloodcurdling shriek almost blew the garage door off its hingest and a blonde apparition, half in and half out of Third Season Star Fleet uniform, came howling out of the garage and down the drive. It zoomed across the street, almost going under a Camry full of bowlers, then leapt straight into the purple Mustang and got behind the wheel. In a nanosecond the Mustang roared into life and fishtailed away from the garage in a scream of smoking rubber towards Randwick Junction. Les came back up from the passageway and caught Rinh's eye.

'Wow! What a burn off,' said Rinh.

'Stay here Dogs, while I get rid of that film crew.'

Les walked in the door and looked around. The Mud Crabs were running around everywhere putting their Speedos and tracksuits back on while the cameraman was still trying to get shots of them; next to him the soundman had his headphones off rubbing at the pain in his ears from when Zanna's scream nearly deafened him. The woman was standing next to the table with her clipboard, half gob-smacked and half-perving on all the trim young bodies and grouse big dicks being covered up and tucked away.

'Righto. That's it,' said Norton. 'Come on. Out mit you. Out mit you. Ve don't vant this shenanagans. I run a respectable block of flats.' He put his hand over the lens and pushed the camera away.

'You don't touch the camera,' snarled the cameraman.

Les put his face a few inches from the cameraman's. 'I'll wrap it round your fat fuckin' neck in a minute Abdul, if you don't piss off. Now get. You too, Nana Mouskouri. Put your eyes back in your head and hit the road. 'Come on, Gunga Din. You heard me. What are you, deaf or something?'

'I think we've got all we need here,' said the woman. Like the rest of the crew she sensed all the fun in the garage had suddenly disappeared along with Norton's Yiddish accent.

'You've got more than enough,' said Les. 'Now on your multicultural bike. The lot of you. Out.' Les pushed the door open and ushered them towards it. They had a last, quick look around the garage then started filing out; the woman going first. Les followed them halfway down the drive and stopped just as the woman turned around and caught his eye. 'Back to your own country, you should go,' he said, half-slipping back into his Yiddish accent. 'And take your salami with you. Wogs.' Les watched them get in their car and do a U-turn back towards Coogee then turned to Rinh. 'Righto Dogs. Inside. You're part of this too.'

Norton let Rinh into the garage first then closed the door behind him. Inside, the boys had just about got all their clothes back on and were witting on their bunks doing up their shoelaces. The looks on their faces ran from guilt, to humour to complete shock and Les surmised that as well as taking the Mud Crabs by surprise, Debbie might have taken a couple of cherrys while she was at it. But even though it was definitely a complete hoot, he was going to have to put some sort of lid on it or the whole thing might get out of hand.

Les stood in front of them, gave it a moment or two and tried to look stern. 'Well, isn't this lovely. I leave you little schwinehunds alone for five minutes and you're in here having a bloody sex orgy. Terrific.'

'I tried to tell him what happened,' pleaded Rinh.

'Yeah. What were we supposed to do?' said Felix. 'Shit! I never seen nothing like that in my life.'

The other team members all started to talk at once.

'Yeah. It was insane Reg.'

'I was raped.'

'Ohh yeah. I'm glad I wasn't.'

'I wonder if she'll come back after the grand final.'

Les raised a hand. 'Hey. It doesn't make any difference. You should have resisted. You should have shown moral courage.'

'Ohh yeah, for sure Reg,' said Rodney. 'What would you have done if some scozza come up and undid your fly and started going the rat?'

Les stared at the faces in front of him then caught Rinh's eye. 'Well, I s'pose I probably would have copped a quick polish. But what you just did, that's disgusting. Be nice if news of this ever got back to Wagga Wagga.' The boys shuffled looks amongst themselves then dropped their eyes. 'In fact if I were you, I wouldn't say anything to anyone about this. You never know who that ratbag was. She might have a nutty boyfriend or brother and say you raped her. What if she's a Fatal Attractionist and comes back and blows the place up or something? You're in the big city now, boys. Think New York. Crazies. Knives. Guns.'

'Yeah. Shit!' Raymond's eyes lit up. 'Remember when she told us if we said anything, she'd come back with a phaser and vaporise us.'

Clarence nodded in agreement. 'Yeah. She was off her melon all right.'

'See what I mean? Now you're getting the picture.' Les looked the boys over. 'All right, I'll concede you're not entirely to blame for this afternoon's sordid events. But for being such mugs, I'm still going to have to penalise you.'

'What?'

'Ohh, you're kiddin'.'

Les pointed a very stern finger. 'You're all going down the beach for a nice swim and a wash under the showers with plenty of soap. How do you know the space lady wasn't swarming with strange creepy crawlies from another planet? You wouldn't want your first to be your last now, would you?'

Jamieson swallowed hard. 'Shit! That's a thought.'

'Then let's go.'

The boys tossed some towels and gear into their overnight bags, Les locked the garage and herded them towards the north end of Coogee Beach. On the way, he pointed out where the old Coogee Aquarium used to be and told them a bit about the famous shark arm murder case. He also told them how Coogee was once the scene of a grizzly shark attack; pretty much on an overcast day like this and about the same time. He also pointed out Wedding Cake Island to them and how it was made famous in an instrumental by Midnight Oil. Although they could have done it easy, the boys had no intention of swimming out to Wedding Cake Island and back. After all the talk about sharks they barely went in over their heads and even then they were looking at every movement in the water, strange shadow, or piece of seaweed within fifty metres of them. They got under the open air showers and started soaping and scrubbing away, not missing a spot. There was a steady afternoon crowd walking past and again it wasn't long before a smattering of girls plus several slim, young men with moustaches had gathered for a bit of a look. After the boys had towelled off, Les got them some corn chips and drinks and stuff at one of the shops on the way back to the garage and gave Rinh some more money for their dinner that night; at the same time he told them to get an early one as they had a big day on tomorrow. He had to go out that night by himself for awhile, but he might call in after to check up on them. That was when Rinh said the Mud Crabettes would be in town before long. Neville Nixon had done a deal with the resort just up the road and got them two rooms to share, so they'd probably call in later on to say hello. To this, Les replied that he probably would call round later on now and make sure there was no hanky panky or carrying on with the home town dancing girls. The boys were adamant there wouldn't be. Les didn't bother going back into the garage with the team. But if he wasn't there later he'd be round at nine to take them for breakfast – then a team talk and maybe a few stretches and that before he drove them out to the grand final.

'See you later, Les,' said Felix. 'And thanks for everything.'

'Yeah, thanks heaps,' added Garrick. 'Unreal Reg.'

'Yeah reckon,' said Rinh. 'Shit! I'm glad we met you.'

Les didn't quite know what to say after that. 'And I'm glad I met you too. I'll see you later, fellahs.'

Les climbed in the mighty Datty and started wheezing and gasping back up Mount Street towards Bondi. For some reason he felt good inside. They were hard doers the Mud Crabs. But they were his hard doers. They were his team. His mates. He now felt he had an interest in this that went beyond just looking after them. Those kids needed him and appreciated having him around. And by hook or by crook, he was going to do whatever it took to see that his team won the grand final tomorrow, short of jumping into the pool with a set of webbs and flippers on himself.

Les was still feeling happy when he climbed out of the shower back at Chez Norton and even happier when he got into his blue tracksuit and detected a whiff of Kathy's perfume still clinging to it. What a nice nutty day, he smiled to himself. Wait till I tell Billy when I see him. What I wouldn't mind now is a drink. A good one. Except I might start to get the taste and I still don't know what I'm doing tonight. Les looked at his watch. I wonder if that'll make tonight's news on SBS. I'll have a look later. In the meantime, I might just lay on the bed, relax and read a bit more of that book Billy gave me. Les was on his back with a couple of pillows behind him getting into Jack Kerouac's *On The Road* when the phone rang at six. It was Coyne.

'Hello mate,' came the usual, cheerful drawl.

'G'day, Coyne. How's things?'

'Pretty good. So how was your day? The media thing go over all right?'

'Yeah. Billy handled Channel 7 and the Telegraph. The mob from SBS were only at the garage a few minutes and then they pissed off.'

'And the boys are all happy? You had a good breakfast?'

'Yeah. They were wrapped in meeting Neil Brooks.'

'I thought they might have been.'

'So what's the story tonight, Coyne old mate?'

'I'll be round your place at seven-thirty. I have to give you something.'

'Flowers and a box of chocolates?'

'No. Not quite. How about I see you at your place?'

'I'll see you when you get here.'

So he wants to give me something, mused Les. I wonder what? Les was still musing when he settled back with a cup of coffee to watch the news on SBS. There was nothing about the bun from outer space. Maybe they were saving it up for a Sunday special or something. They liked that sort of thing on SBS. He'd have to keep an eye out for it though, and very discreetly make sure Warren was there; preferably with Zanna the friendly Eymorg. Les sipped his coffee and began watching Gourmet Ireland. About halfway through the salmon with leeks and black potatoes Warren arrived home, his jeans and a brown suede jacket all over him, looking like Dean Moriarty when he drove into San Francisco with Jack Kerouac after a week on Benzedrine.

'Good evening, Warren,' said Les pleasantly. 'How was your day at the pickle factory?'

'Fucked!' Warren stormed into the kitchen, grabbed a long neck from the fridge, poured half down his throat then stood at the entrance to the lounge room and burped. 'Twelve fuckin' hours, to shoot two dopey sheilas and a Brad Pitt lookalike eat a fuckin' bar of chocolate and say five words. You wouldn't fuckin' believe it.'

'Maybe they were enjoying it, Woz. I like to take my time when I'm eating a bar of chocolate myself.'

'Bloody hell! Where does the agency find these boneheads?'

'Same place they find the idiots that work there, I'd reckon. That island in the middle of the Hawkesbury

River with all the big walls and barbed wire round it. You fuckin' peanut.'

Warren glared at Les. 'Why bother talking to you? What would you know about shooting TV commercials?'

'I know they pay all right. How about throwing me into one?'

Warren muttered something, took another swallow of beer then sat down on a lounge chair and closed his eyes.'

'Debbie rang,' said Les. 'She was looking for you. Your phone was off.'

'Yeah? What time was this?'

'About two.'

'She say anything else?'

'No. She was busy at work.'

'The till ringing eh?'

'Yeah. That wasn't the only thing she had ringing later on either Warren.'

'What?'

'I said, I reckon she'll ring you later on Warren.'

'Yeah.' Warren muttered something about having a shower and took his beer into the bathroom. He was still in there showering away a hard day in the advertising game when Coyne arrived right on seven thirty.

'Punctuality,' smiled Les, opening the front door. 'I like that in a man.'

Coyne almost filled the hallway in his black leather jacket, black trousers and black Deadly Sounds T-shirt. 'That's the way it should be all the time, Les,' he said, returning Norton's smile. He followed Les into the lounge room and had a look around. 'Nice place you got here, Les. That's a good stereo.'

'Thanks.' Les hit the mute button on the remote. 'Can I get you something?'

Coyne shook his head. 'No. I'm right thanks.'

'Okay. Then grab a seat and let's cut to the chase.'

They sat opposite each other; Coyne took a chunky envelope from his jacket and placed it on the coffee table. 'That's the key to a motel in Curlewis Street plus some money. And everything you need to know written down on a piece of paper.'

Les picked the envelope up and shook it. 'I'll open it in a minute. In the meantime, like the lady said, please explain.'

'Okay. You've got to go down to Walsh Bay at nine-thirty and pick up a seaman who's going to jump ship. Take him to that motel, give him the money and see that he's okay. Then put him in a taxi at nine tomorrow morning and send him out to Ryde. It's all written down anyway. You can't go wrong.'

Les looked at Coyne for a moment. 'Who is he? A member of some Chinese Triad on the run for murder?'

'No. He's a Russian defector. His name's Vadim Shatkov.'

'What? Hey, hang on. He's not a fuckin' spy is he? I'm not getting involved in any government shit. Fuck that. Nizegy can stick his money.'

'No. Nothing like that, Les. He's an Olympic gold medalist and used to captain the Russian water polo team. He's going to play with the Sea Snakes in the grand final tomorrow. Then we're getting him political asylum.'

'What? In other words, he's a ring-in.'

Coyne shrugged. 'Something like that.'

'Ohh terrific. What about the poor bloody Mud Crabs?'

'Les. There's a bundle riding on the Sea Snakes at even money. This just gives the punters a little more odds. That's all. Hey, it's not as if we're rigging the game.'

'Ohh no. You wouldn't dream of it.' Les looked directly at Coyne. 'I'll bet you've rigged a few in the past though, haven't you?'

Coyne made an expansive gesture with his hands. 'Well, I admit, like in the kick boxing, I rehearsed a bit of choreography in the dressing rooms now and again. Same with Extreme Polo. We've had to organise a bit of synchronised swimming on odd occasions.'

'Yeah. To get the Mud Crabs in the grand final because they look good. Now you're going to dump on them.'

'Hey. They can still win it. It's not like a complete fix.'

'Bullshit! They're just a bunch of kids going to university. I've only seen photos of the Sea Snakes. But they're monsters. And with this big Russian in the side they'll be unbeatable. It'll be a slaughter.'

A thin smile flickered in Coyne's eyes. 'No-one's unbeatable, Les.' Coyne looked evenly at Les then at the envelope on the coffee table. 'Anyway, that's the story, Les. What do you want me to tell Nizegy to do with his money?'

Les stared at the envelope as well and felt the bile rise in his chest. He shook his head in disgust. 'Yeah all right. I'll go and get him. How come you can't?'

Coyne gestured with his hands again. 'I got a million other things to do.'

'Yeah, I'll just bet you have.' Les stared impassively

at the big man in the black leather jacket. 'You know, for a while there, I was starting to think you and Nizegy weren't bad blokes.'

Coyne made another gesture with his hands. 'No-one's perfect, Les. And you know why? Because it's not a perfect world out there.' Coyne got to his feet. 'But I'll see you after the game tomorrow and you'll get your money, rain, hail or shine. That's the main thing.' He smiled down at Les. 'In the meantime, I'll see my way out. And see you tomorrow.'

Les didn't bother to look up. 'Yeah, all right,' he said tightly. 'I'll see you then.'

Coyne left Norton staring at the coffee table and exited about the same time Warren came out of the shower with a towel around him.

'Did I just hear the front door?'

'Yeah. It was a mate of Nizegy's. I have to go out for a while later.'

'Oh.'

'What are you doing? You going out?'

Warren shook his head. 'No. I'm having an early one. I'm fucked.'

Les smiled mirthlessly. 'Yeah. Aren't we all?'

Warren went to his room and Les flicked through the envelope Coyne had given him. It was all there. Everything he needed to know plus a thousand dollars. Les went through it all again then put the envelope in his jacket and brooded at the silent TV screen. Les Norton, he smiled sourly to himself. Judas Norton would be more like it. Only instead of thirty pieces of silver, I've sold my friends out for two hundred thousand dollars. Still, it is a lot of money, and I imagine I'll enjoy spending every cent of it. Les looked at the carpet on the lounge. If it hadn't been his he would have spat on it. Warren came out of his bedroom wearing a maroon and blue, Brooks tracksuit and got another beer from the kitchen.

'What do you want to watch on TV?' he asked.

'I don't give a fuck,' grunted Les.

'There's a show on Channel 7 about Mars. I was going to tape it.'

'Go for your life.'

Warren slipped a tape in the VCR then turned up the volume and they settled back to watch computer graphics of rockets orbiting Mars, rockets landing on Mars and what life on Mars, if there was any, might look like. Whatever it looks like, thought Les, it couldn't look as low an arsehole as what I do. He stared blankly at the TV screen till a news break came on at eight-thirty. Seeing Channel 7 were showing the Extreme Polo grand final, they were giving it extra time on their sports segments. Neil Brooks flashed up on the screen with part of Billy Dunne's interview at Bronte. A shadowy figure leaning against the railing in the background was Les.

Warren sat up in his lounge chair. 'It's the Mud Crabs. And that's Billy Dunne. Hey, you're in there too.' He turned to Les. 'What's all this about?'

'They interviewed the team at Bronte Pool this morning. I meant to tell you.'

'Shit! I'm glad I got it on tape.'

'Yeah. T'rific.'

There were shots of the team training in the pool and shots of girls in the crowd ogling them like they were male models. Billy's interview was a sound bite of him saying the team were red-hot specials to win the grand final and the type of team Neil Brooks would like to play in, followed by Brooksie quoting Billy's line about how the Sea Snakes would be jellied eels after the grand final. Then it cut to Ryde Pool and, compared to the Mud Crabs, the Sydney Sea Snakes looked like professional wrestlers. Muscles bulged everywhere from under their black lycra outfits as they churned up the water with their sinister-looking helmets jammed onto seven, bull like necks. Les almost had to look away. And what did Coyne say? They could still win it. Yeah, bullshit! Even without the Russian champion it'd still be a slaughter. They were just too big. It finished with their manager, who was just as big and horrible in a tight-fitting grey suit, saying forget jellied eels. After the grand final there wouldn't be enough left of the pretty boy Mud Crabs to make a plate of Thai fish cakes. Norton's heart sank further.

'Yeah? That's what you think. You fat heap.' Warren sneered at the TV screen. 'The Mud Crabs'll make minute steak out of you, in seconds.'

Les looked impassively at Warren. 'Do you really think the Mud Crabs have got a chance against those gorillas, Woz?'

'Of course they have. They're liquid lightning. Oogie, oogie, oogie. Do the Mud Crab boogie.' Warren took a mouthful of beer and stared at Les. 'Well come on, sing boy. They're your fuckin' team. Christ! What's the matter with you? You miserable big prick. You look like you just bit into a bad oyster.'

'Yeah,' replied Les, turning away.

Les was stuck for an answer because ironically

Warren was right. That was exactly how he felt. Like he'd been left with a rotten taste in his mouth. They settled back to watch some more about the red planet. A Martian dust storm blew over and Les stood up at the next commercial break.

'Okay Woz. I gotta go. I might be back about ten-thirty.'

'I'll be snoring my head off by then,' replied Warren.

'Fair enough.'

'I'll come over to Coogee in the morning and meet the boys. Take some photos.'

'Sure. Take as many as you like.'

'I'll probably bring Debbie.'

'Yeah, do that Woz. I'm sure the boys'd like to meet her. See you in the morning.'

'See you, Les.'

Les fired up the engine then nosed the car round towards the city and tried to put the bad side of things out of his mind. Now, what have I got to do again? he mused, as the mighty Datty hit the rise of Old South Head Road and shuddered back into first. Go to Walsh Bay, wait at loading dock 9. The Russian would find me, then take him to the Sands Motor Inn in Curlewis Street. I wonder what this goose'll look like? Big and ugly I imagine, like his new team mates. Norton's eyes narrowed as he absently stared at the tail lights of the car in front of him. Maybe I could sabotage the cunt? Break his ankle or something so he can't swim. Run up the arse of some car and hope he hits his head on the dashboard. The seat belts in this thing are fucked like everything else. Les shook his head. No. Knowing my luck, I'd be the one that gets hurt, Nizegy'd smell a rat and I'd end up with no chops as well as a face full of stitches. Buggered if I know. And what about the boys? Should I tell them what's going on?

Les ground remorselessly towards the city, along past the gaudy, neon lights of Oxford Street and the 'Strip' and through the usual sprawl of people and traffic going down Liverpool Street and spreading into Chinatown. He turned right towards the Harbour Bridge, then swung left past Darling Harbour and up the Northern Sydney turn off.

A bit further along on his left, Les found the checkpoint gate he was looking for and drove in, slowing down for the speed hump. The light was on, but the office seemed deserted so Les drove straight through into a bitumen-paved parking area, at least five hundred metres long and wide enough for the biggest truck to turn round in. On his left the northern distributor ran past the city skyline and on his right was a massive grey warehouse with a concrete loading dock running along the front, split in the middle by a driveway also big enough for trucks. High above the loading dock, the warehouse roof angled out and in the spooky glow of its magnesium lights Les could make out the number nine where the loading dock ended at a cyclone wire gate. There were hardly any other cars about so Les drove slowly down and brought the Datty around in front of the loading dock, just as a small, white ferry with Darling Harbour Rocket on the side chugged past in the short distance behind the cyclone wire. Facing him from behind the loading dock were three brown doors. The first had windows on either side and TIME KEEPER

SUPERVISOR on it, the second door was double and locked, the third was half-open with GENTS across the front. Les dimmed the headlights and waited. Within seconds a figure appeared outside the gents wearing a blue, double-breasted sailor's jacket, jeans and a black woollen cap; over one shoulder was a blue tote bag. Les flicked the lights, the figure had a quick look around then jumped off the loading dock and walked over to the driver's side window.

'You are Les Norton?' he said, with a typical Russian accent.

'That's me, comrade,' replied Les. 'Jump in.'

The Russian went round and opened the front door, tossing his bag on the back seat as he did. When he squeezed his frame into the bucket seat he almost filled the front of the car and inadvertently pushed Norton against the window. He was easily as tall as Neil Brooks only with wider shoulders and a thicker neck. A pleasant, if slightly jowly sort of face said he was around thirty and beneath the seaman's cap were a few tufts of thick, brown hair and a pair of warm, hazel eyes. He turned to Les and offered his hand.

'I am Vadim.'

'Les. How's it going, Vadim?' Vadim appeared friendly, without being pushy and his handshake was warm and strong.

'Thank you for coming, Les,' he said, a sincere tone in his voice.

'That's okay,' replied Norton indifferently. 'Any time.'

Les eased the Datty back towards the checkpoint, deciding to cut across Sussex, then down towards Central and miss the Oxford Street traffic by heading back to Bondi via Moore Park Road past the SFS. Vadim seemed happy in an apprehensive sort of way, staring out his darkened window at a freighter being pushed into mid-stream by two bustling little tug boats. A ship's horn echoed across the water as they went through the checkpoint and Vadim turned his face to the windscreen. Norton imagined Vadim would have some kind of mixed emotions at the moment, but he didn't give a stuff for the Russian's feelings. Les was more interested in his jacket. It was a ripper. All neat and crisp with a row of shiny, brass buttons down the front. It would have been sensational in the winter.

Vadim had a quick look round the Datty and turned to Les. 'Is your car, Les?'

'Yeah,' answered Norton. 'Made the last payment yesterday.'

'Is nice car.'

Les stared at Vadim wondering if the big Russian was fair dinkum or just trying to be polite. Probably they only drove old bombs in his part of Russia. 'You like it do you?'

'Yes. Sure, I like it.'

'All right. I'll swap you it for your jacket.'

Vadim ran his eyes down his chest. 'This?'

'Yeah. You want to swap?'

'You like jacket?'

'Yeah,' nodded Les. 'It's the grouse.'

'Okay. Is yours.'

Vadim undid his seat belt and started squeezing his huge bulk awkwardly out of his jacket. He got it off, folded it and placed it on the back seat. Underneath he was wearing a blue denim shirt that looked like it had been round the world a few times. 'I don't need such jacket no more,' he said, putting his seat belt back on. 'Weather is warm here and soon I buy Australian clothes.' He smiled at Les. 'And you don't worry about car. I buy car myself. Soon I have money.'

Norton had only been joking, but thought what the hell. 'Okay. Thanks Vadim.'

'Is pleasure, Les.' Vadim clapped his hands together as if getting rid of his jacket was like getting rid of his past. 'Oh Les, I am so glad to be in Australia.'

'Yeah. They all say that.'

'No. I mean this, Les. Always I have wanted to come to Australia. I meet Australian swimmers and rowers at Olympic Games. They always good ... good blokes. Laugh. Drink. Have good time.'

'I'm glad you got on so well.' Les swung the Datty to the left as a taxi cut him off near a set of lights. 'So what's your story Vadim? You're not really a defector are you? All that shit finished when the wall came down, didn't it?'

The big Russian looked evenly at Norton. 'What do you know of me, Les?'

Norton looked evenly at the big Russian. 'Not a great deal. You're a champion swimmer and they've got you in the grand final tomorrow. You're what we call a ring-in. The whole thing's a bit ...' Les made a gesture with one hand, 'shifty.'

Vadim slowly nodded. 'Okay. I tell you some things, Les. But not all.'

'Please yourself,' said Les, as another taxi cut him off.

214

'I am on run, Les. From Russian Mafia.'

'Mafia?'

'Yes. In Moscow I was security guard. Is big business now in Moscow. All security business run by ex-KGB. One night in park I see ex-KGB security boss talking with Mafia boss. They think I follow them. So they try kill me. But I too fast. I shoot them. Bang! Bang! Dead. Plus one other. Now I am to be killed. For revenge from Mafia.'

'How long ago was this?' asked Les.

'Maybe one year.' Vadim gestured with his hands. 'So I get new papers. Become seaman. Disappear. I am on ship in Australia. Mackay, Queensland. You know this one, Les!'

'Yeah, I know it. Near Bowen.'

'Yes. Is right. I meet this peoples. Australian sailors with yacht.'

'A yacht?' Something made the light bulb above Norton's head switch on for a second. 'You don't remember the name of it do you?'

Vadim gestured again. 'Good news? Good times? Something like this. It was before summer. They say to me. Swim one game in Sydney. Plenty money. Then can stay in Australia. I say for sure I do.' Vadim stared at Les. 'Why not, Les. In my country I don't last long. Then I am dead man.'

'It sure seems that way.'

'Is truth, Les. I am not gangster. I hate gangster. I am honest man. I swim for my country. I fight for my country in war. Now this happening to me, Les. Is very awful.'

'Yeah. Shit certainly happens.' Les stared through the windscreen at the traffic ahead thinking how funny it was the way things could suddenly change. On the way in he was hating the Russian and wanting to give it to him somehow. Now he turns out to be a good bloke. Bad luck about the Mud Crabs. But he was only doing what Les was doing. Taking the opportunity for an earn coming his way. Besides that, he was six-feet-four, an ex-soldier, ex-security guard and if it came to a pinch he wasn't worried about putting a few bullets into someone. Vadim had to be a good bloke. 'So what about your family, Vadim. What happens to them now?'

'There is only mother and sister. They are safe in tiny village long way from Moscow. Mafia don't trouble them.'

'No wife, Vadim?' asked Les. 'No girlfriend?'

'I had girlfriend,' replied Vadim. 'Beautiful. But stinking Mafia try to kill her one night. She go back to Siberia.'

'Shit! Oh well, you never know. Once you settle in here you might be able to bring your mother and sister out.'

Vadim's eyes lit up. 'Oh Les. That would be so good. They would love it here. And hey, Les. You would like my sister. She is tall. Red hair. Very beautiful too.'

'Yeah? What's her name?'

'Natalia.'

'Nice name.'

Vadim closed his eyes for a moment or two and seemed a little more relaxed after talking to Les and getting part of his story off his chest. Norton's mind, on the other hand, was tap-dancing to a completely different beat altogether. That yacht in Mackay had to be the one Nizegy never told Les about and also the one he never had time to go sailing on. The one that Patooties and her girlfriend were scrubbing down at the marina. Nizegy and Bain must have been organising this Extreme Polo sting for months. And not a bad little sting either if they pulled it off; which they were odds-on favourites to do. Yes, there certainly turned out to be more to Extreme Polo than first met the eye. Or swimming goggle.

Before Les knew it, he'd gone down Old South Head Road, turned right at O'Brien and was cruising along Curlewis Street. The Sands was on the right about half-way between Glenayr Avenue and the Bondi Hotel. A brown brick, two-storey building. Office out the front, rooms behind and above with a parking area and swimming pool out the back. Les drove straight in and pulled up in front of a row of white doors and windows with blue curtains.

'Well, here we are mate,' he said, pulling the envelope from his pocket and handing it to Vadim. 'There's the key to your room and some money they said to give you. A thousand bucks. You want to count it?'

'No. Is all right,' replied Vadim, taking the envelope. 'Thank you, Les.'

'So what'll you do now? You don't need me to hold your hand do you?'

Vadim shook his head. 'I go straight to bed. Maybe watch TV. Read book. I am tired. Also little bit nervous still. Yes?'

'Fair enough. Well, I'll see you in the morning at eight-thirty.'

'Okay. Maybe we have breakfast. And I am

shouting. I have money.' Vadim got his bag from the back seat and opened the door. 'Thank you again, Les,' he said, offering his hand once more.

Les shook it. 'No worries. I'll see you in the morning Vadim.'

Les reversed the car around, then drove to the front of the motel and tapped his fingers on the steering wheel; while he waited for a break in the traffic, he tried to figure out what he should do. For some reason he was feeling a bit tired and an early one wouldn't have been a bad idea. On the other hand, it wouldn't be a bad idea to tell the boys what was going on; better than springing it on them first thing in the morning. At least this way they'd get a chance to sleep on it. Or maybe not sleep much at all. Norton shook his head. It was like he told Kathy – you're damned if you do and damned if you don't. Les hit the blinker and turned right down Curlewis, joining up with the usual crush of Saturday night traffic and people swarming along Campbell Parade. He managed to get around it then headed left down Sandridge towards Tamarama and Bronte; Les was still deep in thought and didn't even notice Kathy's unit on the left as he flogged the Datty up the steep part of Hewlett Street then onto the steeper hills heading into Coogee. The roller door was closed as usual, but there was a thin crack of light coming from behind the smaller one when Les pulled up in front of the garage. He knocked a couple of times and let himself in. The boys were seated around the TV watching some old movie; they turned around as Les came in the door.

'Hello. What's going on here?' said Les, nodding towards the TV. 'Aren't we neglecting our studies?'

'Hey. It's the Varns,' said Raymond, amidst a chorus of greetings from the other Mud Crabs.

'Hang on a minute.' Les took a quick look around the bunks and the garage. 'There's someone missing.'

'Yeah. Jamtin, Rat and Felix went up to get something to eat,' said Rinh.

'Eat? Where?'

'McDonalds. Whatever.'

Several furrows appeared on Norton's brow. 'Christ! They want to be careful wandering around Coogee on Saturday night. It's a shit fight. How long have they been gone?'

'About half an hour,' shrugged Garrick. 'It's okay though, the girls are with them.'

'The girls are with them?' Norton's voice rose. 'What do you mean, the fuckin' girls are with them?'

'The Crabettes called round bout an hour ago to say hello,' said Clarry. 'When they left to go back to their hotel, the boys went with them to get a quick bite. It's all cool, Les.'

'Ohh yeah. Real cool,' said Les. 'I got three young hillbillies wandering around out there who wouldn't know shit from shortbread. And eight bimbos with them whose IQ's are probably the same as their shoe size. Great.'

Garrick and the others seemed to find Norton's concerned attitude amusing. 'Les, you've got it all wrong,' he said. 'Nothing's going to happen.'

'Yeah, chill out dude,' weighed in Clarence. 'Kick back and grab some tube with us. This movie's doing it.'

'You're a bit of a worry, Reg,' said Rinh.

Les ignored them. 'Stay here and don't move,' he

said. 'I'll be back.' He left the garage, closing the door shut behind him.

Maybe it was his guilt complex over Vadim adding to things. But Les couldn't help a rising uneasiness coming from the pit of his stomach. Bloody young dills, he scowled to himself. They'll stick out like dogs knackers in those red tracksuits. And you can bet your life those sheilas'll drag them into the pub for a drink. Fuckin' idiots. I told them to stay home and have an early one. Shaking his head with worried disbelief, Les picked up the pace and headed towards the Coogee Bay Hotel.

He trotted down a set of steps across the road from the garage that led onto a path running around Coogee Oval. He followed that around coming out at another shorter path hemmed with shrubs and mini palm trees that led into the car park; McDonalds was on the next corner. Like Bondi, there was another rolling maul of traffic and people crowding the streets and shops. McDonalds was no exception. Les looked through the window and was about to go inside when a glimpse of red tracksuit amongst the people across the road caught his eye. Directly opposite McDonalds was a row of cream and brown buildings; two looked like kiosks with the shutters down and in the middle was a bus shelter. Left of the bus shelter were two phones and a row of wooden pillars leading towards the beach that separated the buildings. Standing in front of the phone booths were the boys in their red tracksuits and spread along the footpath near the bus shelter you couldn't miss the eight Crabettes in their bomber jackets, jeans and Country Road boots. Between the girls and the buildings were five blokes around thirty wearing jeans and jumpers or hang-out shirts; they didn't look like hoods, more like a bunch of drunks out to get into some trouble. One tall, dark-haired bloke in a blue shirt was trying to get at Felix who appeared to be standing his ground. Angie was between them pushing Felix away. The other four blokes were egging their mate on, taking very little notice of the Crabettes casually standing around them with their hands in the pockets of their bomber jackets. Rather than charge straight in and start sorting things out, Les waited for a break in the traffic then crossed the road to the park and positioned himself between a table and a small pine tree a few metres behind Jamieson, Rodney and Felix.

'Come on. Don't take any notice of him,' said Angie, still pushing Felix away. 'Just get out of here.'

Felix glared at the bloke in the blue shirt. 'You're an idiot, mate. You need your head read.'

Angie pushing Felix away made Blue Shirt even keener. 'Come on you little cunt. You and me. Don't hide behind your ugly fuckin' girlfriend.'

'Yeah. You're a real big man, aren't you,' said Felix.

'Why don't you find out? You little dickhead.'

'Ignore him,' said Angie. 'He's a goose.'

Les wasn't sure what it was all about, but he could see Blue Shirt was determined to get at Felix. As usual a number of onlookers had started to gather and Les was thinking of making a move before Felix and the girls got themselves into trouble, when he noticed Angie slip her watch off and put it in her jacket pocket. Blue Shirt was too busy concentrating on Felix, so convinced he was going to have an easy victory that he didn't notice Angie step in a little and let go a sizzling, short right over the top. It was one of the best king hits Les had ever seen and caught Blue Shirt flush on the jaw, wrenching it over the other side of his face. His mouth fell open with shock and pain as Angie followed up with a left hook, splattering his nose; he was almost out on his feet when Angie stepped back and sunk the toe of her boot into his sternum hard enough to crack it like a plate. Blue Shirt had barely hit the footpath to the gasps of the crowd when the rest of the Crabettes, along with Angie, went into action like a well-oiled machine. Six of the girls swarmed all over Blue Shirt's four mates bashing them with short, hard punches, kicks and knees, while the other two girls slipped amongst the blows and pulled their jumpers and shirts down over their heads.

It was a slaughter. The four blokes didn't know what hit them and when they did they couldn't untangle their arms to defend themselves; they were just human punching bags. In barely minutes they were all on the footpath, then the Crabettes swarmed in again and gave the crowd probably the best display of Balmain folk dancing they'd ever seen. With tigerish ferocity the girls just about kicked the five blokes' heads almost off their shoulders. Blood was oozing everywhere and even over the gasps and screams from the crowd and the noise of the traffic you could hear the bones crunching and flesh ripping as the boots connected. It was a revolting, horrible sight and many people in the crowd had to turn away in disgust. Les certainly got the surprise of his life, but on the other hand didn't think it was too bad at all.

222

Felix, Jamieson and Rodney didn't bother to help and simply stood out of the road with their hands in their tracksuit pockets, passing brief comments amongst themselves as if they'd seen it all before.

Then almost as quickly as it had started, it stopped. The crowd stood gasping while the five blokes lay on the footpath moaning with pain, their chests and stomachs heaving, trying to get some air into their lungs through their shirts and jumpers still pulled up over their faces soaking up what blood wasn't running onto the footpath. Angie looked across at Felix and was surprised to see Les now standing behind Felix and the two others. She knew what to do though. Les caught her eye and abruptly pointed in the direction of where they were staying. Just as abruptly, she nodded back.

'Come on,' she said to the other girls.

They didn't need to be told twice. In seconds they melted into the crowd and disappeared towards the Coogee Bay Hotel. The boys turned around and got a surprise to see Norton standing there.

'Come on you three,' he said. 'Follow me.'

Without looking around him, Les led the three Mud Crabs into the park and, swiftly and quietly and without running, took them the same way he'd just come, back to the garage. With a quick look behind him to make sure no-one had seen them, he opened the door and got the boys inside. The others were still watching TV. They glanced up and from the looks on Les and the other boys' faces realised something must have happened.

'What's up?' asked Rinh.

'What's up?' echoed Les. 'Your dancing girls just

gave five poor mugs one of the worst kickings I've ever seen. Bloody hell!'

Garrick gave his shoulders a brief shrug. 'We told you not to worry.'

Les stared at him and the others watching TV. 'All right. But that's not the point.' He stared at Felix, Jamieson and Rodney, who were seated on their bunks. 'What were you doing down there anyway? I told you to stay home. And what was all that about?' Les held up a hand. 'You do the talking, Cats.'

'Okay,' said Felix. 'The girls were going back to the hotel. So we walked up with them to get something to eat. We were just finishing some satay sticks near the bus shed when that goose in the blue shirt said I bumped into him and he got peanut sauce on his shirt. I didn't. But I still said I was sorry. Then he went on and on, trying to pick a fight with me. Next thing they started slagging the girls. They were drunk and looking for trouble. One thing led to another and the girls sorted it out.' Felix shrugged. 'That's about it.'

Les shook his head almost imperceptibly. 'That was about it all right.' The boys looked at him evenly. 'Anyway, at least we all got home without anyone seeing us.' Les looked back at the boys for a moment. 'Okay. Where did they learn to fight like that? They're pretty good on their feet, and with them too.'

Rodney went to talk. But Felix felt he was still the spokesman. 'They're all in the Air Force Reserve back home. Perimeter guards. They do some sort of unarmed combat out there. And two of the girls fathers used to be boxers. So they get into that as well as dancing.' Felix smiled. 'They've sorted heaps of

224

blokes out back home. They go a bit mad sometimes but.'

'And they don't mind a fight either,' added Rodney.

'Evidently.' Les leaned against a wall and looked at the boys not quite knowing what to say. There wasn't much he could say.

'So you came up to make sure we were all right, did you Les?' asked Felix. 'Gee you're a good bloke. Thanks mate.'

'Yeah, you sure are,' said Rodney. 'But we knew it was all cool. And we wouldn't have done the wrong thing by you, Les.'

'No. No way.' Clarence shook his head sincerely.

'Yeah, I know you wouldn't,' said Les. 'I was just a bit worried. That's all.'

'None of us would do the wrong thing by you, Les,' said Rinh. 'Because we all know you wouldn't do the wrong thing by us.'

'Believe it, Les,' said Raymond. 'You're our number one China.'

'Yeah, you're right.' Les swallowed and wished a hole in the floor would open and swallow him too. He noticed a couple of boys starting to yawn. 'Anyway, it's getting late. Why don't we put all today's madness behind us and get a good night's sleep? And I'll see you about nine tomorrow and we'll go and have breakfast. Where do you want to go for breakfast?'

'What about that place we went to at Bronte?' said Garrick. 'That was choice.'

Les was hoping they'd say that. After tonight's slaughter down the road he didn't fancy the boys parading around Coogee in their Mud Crab tracksuits. Just in case. 'Okay. Suits me. And what time have we got to be out at Homebush tomorrow? Nizegy hasn't told me any fuckin' thing.'

'Four o'clock,' said Rinh. 'And we have to be out there at least two hours before then.'

'Okay. Breakfast at nine. And we'll leave here about one. The girls going to come with us?'

'Yeah,' nodded Rinh.

'Okay.' Les smiled round the faces looking at him. 'Well, get a good night's sleep. And I'll see you in the morning.'

There was a chorus of 'Goodnight Les. See you the Varns. Onya Reg ...' Les closed the garage door behind him and climbed into the Datty.

Yeah, that's me all right, thought Norton, as the Datty levelled off after the climb out of Coogee past the turn off to Clovelly. I'm your mate. A real China plate. Still, it's not as if I completely dumped on them. I just did what I more or less had to do. Les was still making excuses for himself and thinking about the night when he pulled up outside Chez Norton behind Warren's metallic gold Celica.

The lamp in the lounge room was still on, but the boarder was sound asleep when Les walked quietly down the hall and switched on his bedroom light. Before he did anything else he tried on the jacket Vadim had given him and checked it out. It was an East German naval officer's jacket and just about a perfect fit; a little loose maybe, but it would be super-comfortable and warm in the winter with a denim shirt underneath. Les admired the double-breasted row of brass buttons in the mirror for a moment then hung it in his wardrobe. He went to the bathroom and cleaned his teeth, got undressed and climbed into bed. Tomorrow was another day, he yawned, and stared up at the ceiling in the darkness for a few moments. Not such a good day if you were a Mud Crab though. Yes. With a bit of luck they might have been a chance against the Sea Snakes. But with Vadim in the team, they'd need more than luck. They'd need the Crabettes in full battle cry. Les shook his head and closed his eyes. He was almost snoring when the light bulb above his head flickered on for a moment à la Wylie Coyote. What time did Rinh say the game started? Four o'clock. An odd smile suddenly tugged at the sides of Norton's mouth. It stayed there for a little while then flickered out along with the light bulb above his head. Next thing Norton knew, he was snoring like a baby.

Les blinked his eyes open around eight the next morning, a bit later than he'd intended. He swung his legs over the bed and stared into space for a moment. Today was the day. Grand final time for the Mud Crabs, with the odds a hiding to nothing. Maybe not. Maybe the boys from Wagga might find a bit of luck in their corner. A fairly big maybe though. Les tossed his slept-in T-shirt into a rapidly filling dirty clothes basket and changed into a white, Hahns beer one and the same tracksuit. After today he'd be able to hire a maid to do his washing. Les allowed himself a mirthless smile as he got himself together in the bathroom, then wandered into the kitchen; Warren was there sipping coffee in a pair of jeans and a hang-out, check shirt while he listened to the news finishing on the kitchen radio.

'Hello, Woz. How's things?'

'All right, after a good night's sleep. You want a cup of coffee?'

Les shook his head and got some orange juice from the fridge. 'I haven't got time. I'm having breakfast with the Mud Crabs.'

'Yeah. What's the story there Les? I'm still dying to meet them.'

'Well, why don't you come and have breakfast with us at Bronte.'

'The grand final breakfast. Unreal. I'll give Debbie a ring. Okay if she comes?'

'No sweat. And you can do me a small favour while you're at it.' Les explained that he had to see a bloke down the road about something and he was going to walk down. It wouldn't take long. Warren could pick him up outside Bondi Beach Public School at quarter to nine. They'd go over to Coogee in Warren's car, then they'd all go over to Bronte in the team bus. 'That okay by you, Woz?'

'No problems at all, Les. Hey, there was a bad brawl at Coogee last night. I just heard it on the news.'

'There was?' Les sipped his orange juice and did his best to look nonchalant. 'What happened?'

'A bunch of hoods bashed up some blokes from Wollongong. Three of them are in intensive care.'

'Fair dinkum. Well I doubt if it was the Mud Crabs, Woz. Fighters they ain't.'

'Whoever it was, they almost killed three of these blokes.'

'Yeah, it's getting more like a jungle out there every day. I'm glad I work up the Cross where it's safe.' Les rinsed his glass and put the orange juice back in the fridge. 'I'll see you outside the school at quarter to nine.'

'Righto. See you then.'

Les went to his room and stared into space again. Shit! That's all I need. More fuckin' dramas. Those stupid, bloody sheilas. He shook his head in disbelief. Oh well, I suppose it couldn't be helped. He got whatever he needed from his dressing table, tossed it in a small overnight bag and walked out the front.

Outside it wasn't too bad a day; a few clouds around and the same light southerly keeping the temperature down. Les walked to the end of his street then skipped across Six Ways almost getting run over by a Volvo outside the Jewish grocery store. It was gone before he had a chance to abuse the driver, so he just kept walking down Glenayr Avenue with his hands in his jacket pocket and if not deep in thought, at least well up past his waist. When Les knocked on the motel door, the big Russian was dressed in the same clothes as the night before, his bag packed and sitting on the bed, a tray of empty plates and cups on the table.

'Hello, Les. Is good to see you again,' he beamed, pumping Norton's hand again as he closed the door.

'G'day, Vadim,' said Les. 'How are you?'

'I am . . . very terrific. Thank you.'

'That's good.' Les nodded towards the tray on the table. 'I see you've had breakast.'

'Yes. Was nice. But . . .' Vadim tried to smile. 'They don't give you so much.'

'You still hungry are you?'

'Yes. I still little hungry.'

'Big bloke like you,' said Les, 'why wouldn't you

be? Well come on. We'll go and get a snack, then I'll put you in a taxi.'

'We go.' Vadim got his bag from the bed as Les opened the door.

There was no-one in the office. So Les told Vadim just to leave the key on the counter, Nizegy would fix it all up, and they set off down Curlewis Street towards the beachfront. In the daylight, Vadim appeared bigger again marching happily along the footpath, and Les had to step fairly lively to keep up. As they strode along about six cars went past full of people that knew Les: Joe Heets from Redwoods in his Rolls Royce; a couple of expensive hookers Les knew driving a BMW convertible; punters from the game; a sports writer. They all bipped their car horns and Les would smile and wave back.

'You know many peoples, Les,' said Vadim. 'You are popular man.'

'Yeah, that's me Vadim,' replied Les. 'Everybody's mate.'

Opposite the TAB, Les steered Vadim left, crossing over to Gould Street then right down Beach Road onto Campbell Parade. On the corner was a liquor store, next to that a mobile phone shop, then the last shop before Bondi Beach school – a Japanese Yakitori grill, the Toriyoshi. A friend of Warren's owned it, a surfer and part-time actor called the Gull because of his surfing style. Les led Vadim through the crowd swarming along the street, either searching for food or peeling off to visit the Sunday markets in the school grounds, and stopped outside the Toriyoshi.

Les nodded to the Hokusai painting of a wave and

Mount Fuji on the window. 'You like Yakitori, Vadim?'

Vadim shrugged. 'I never try before.'

'You like your food a bit spicey?'

'Yes. Spice is good.'

'No River Murrays, Vadim.'

'Is what?'

'No worries. That's something else you're going to have to learn while you're in Australia, Vadim,' smiled Les. 'How to speak English properly.'

'Oh.'

Les stepped inside the Toriyoshi amongst the other customers. He couldn't see the Gull, but the staff in their grey, Yakitori T-shirts and garish Japanese headbands appeared to be handling proceedings adequately without him. Les ordered four Torimi sticks, paid the girl and went to the self-serve, spice bar. Vadim was waiting patiently out the front watching the passers by; mainly the girls in their tight shorts or raggy jeans and midriff-showing tops. Les spread the Torimi sticks liberally with wasabi, ginger, seven chilli powder and whatever else, then went out and offered Vadim his choice. The big Russian took the two from Norton's left hand. Les nibbled a small portion from one of his and was about to ask Vadim what he thought, seeing the big Russian had wolfed his first one down in about four seconds flat.

Vadim screwed his face up and blinked his eyes. 'By golly, Les. Is for sure spicey.'

'Yeah, I put plenty on,' admitted Les, chewing politely and almost like a woman, compared to the big Russian.

Vadim wolfed the second one down and screwed

up his face again; only worse. 'Phew! I not so sure I like these ones, Les. Is hot yes. But bitter.' Vadim picked at his lips. 'And what is little seeds?'

'They're pickled caper berries,' answered Les. 'A bit of an acquired taste. Oh well. Sorry you didn't like them, mate. Maybe next time.'

'Yes. Maybe next time.' Vadim made another face then wiped his mouth with a paper napkin.

Les nodded behind Vadim. 'Anyway, here comes a taxi. You may as well grab it.'

Les whistled the taxi and it pulled up out front of the Toriyoshi. As Vadim went to get in the back seat he offered Norton his hand once more. Les went to shake it and clumsily dropped one of his Torimi sticks on the road.

'Oh Les. I am sorry,' apologised Vadim.

'That's okay mate. I can get another one.' Les pumped the big Russian's hand again. 'Anyway. Good luck Vadim. Maybe after the game we can all get together and have a drink or something.'

'Yes. I would like for that very much.' Vadim stood at the back door of the taxi and looked at Norton for a moment. 'Hey, Les. What is you do? They say you are just driver. But ...' Vadim smiled and gestured with one hand. 'Maybe I don't know so much.'

Les returned Vadim's smile and winked. 'That's me. I'm just a driver. I'll see you after the game.'

'I see you then, Les. And thank you again.'

'Any time.'

Les waved Vadim off into the traffic. He was about to pick up his dropped Torimi stick when a skinny, black dog with a white face appeared out of nowhere, scooped it up in its mouth and ran off into the school

232

grounds. Les stared after the dog slightly taken back at how quick it was when he heard a horn beep almost next to him. It was Warren arriving a few minutes early. Les dumped his other Torimi in the nearest bin and climbed in the front seat.

'You know where to go, Woz?' asked Les, doing up his seat belt.

'Yeah. You told me.'

'Okay then.' Les settled back in comfort and looked around him. After the Datty, Warren's brand new Celica was like a little rocket ship and just as fast.

Warren seemed to read Norton's mind as he took the next roundabout to go back up Campbell Parade. 'When are you going to buy a decent car, you miserable big prick? And get rid of that two hundred dollar heap of shit you're getting around in.'

'The same day I get a mobile phone, Woz. I promise. So what's happening with Debbie?'

'I left a message and said I'd see her at Coogee. I think she's still in bed.'

'She sounded like she'd been working fairly hard when I spoke to her yesterday,' said Les.

'Yeah. She puts in long hours at the salon sometimes. I know she's dying to see the boys though.' Warren turned to Les. 'Maybe I should call up and get her? Her place isn't far from Coogee.'

'Why don't we have breakfast first?' suggested Les.

'Righto.'

Warren turned left at Sandridge and headed towards Bronte. On the way to Coogee he talked incessantly about the grand final and as well as being excited at meeting the Mud Crabs he was chock-full of confidence they'd take out the big one.

233

'So you still reckon they'll win, Woz?' said Les.

'Win?' Warren stared at Les for a moment. 'Are you kidding, Les? They'll shit it in.'

Norton stared ahead and gave a grudging nod of approval. 'Yeah. You never know, Woz. You could be right.'

Shortly after they pulled up in the driveway. Les knocked on the garage door and they stepped inside. The boys were seated around on their bunks wearing their tracksuits; some appeared to be studying, others were staring at the floor or into space. There was no cheeky banter when Les walked in; if anything, the boys were noticeably subdued. A few quiet 'hellos' and 'how are yous' and that was it. They didn't even seem to notice Warren.

'G'day fellahs,' said Les. 'How's things? All right?'

Rinh looked at Warren for a second then Norton. 'Yeah. Fine Les.'

'That's good. Anyway fellahs, this is Warren Edwards. The other bloke I was telling you about.'

Warren's eyes lit up. 'G'day fellahs,' he said, enthusiastically. 'How's it going?' Les introduced Warren to the boys and he pumped all their hands like he was meeting seven Elvises. 'You guys don't mind if I take a few photos later, do you?' The boys nodded and shrugged an indifferent reply that said it was okay.

'You'll have to excuse the boys, Woz,' said Les. 'They're all a bit edgy. Today's a big day for them.'

Warren held up his hands. 'Hey, I can understand that. This is the grand final. I'd be feeling the same way too.'

'Exactly,' said Les. He clapped his hands together

and smiled around the garage. 'Anyway, why don't we go and have our grand final breakfast?'

'Okay,' said Felix.

'Yeah, why not?' shrugged Jamieson.

'Then let's make a move.' Les opened the door and ushered everyone out; Warren went first. As they were filing through the narrow door, Rinh took Norton aside.

'Les. You know that fight last night? The police have been around.'

'I tipped that's what was going on,' said Les. 'What happened?'

'There was a message at the desk for one of the girls. And when she went down to get it, two detectives were there asking questions. They know whoever was in the fight is staying at the hotel.'

'Go on.'

'So the girls are going to check out of the hotel and stay here for the time being. I gave Angie the spare key when she came round to tell us.'

'Fair enough. They should be pretty sweet here. Have you heard from Neville Nixon?'

Rinh shook his head. 'Should I ring him?'

'No. Not for the time being.' Les looked evenly at Rinh. 'Look, tell the boys not to worry. I doubt if the cops'll do anything till tomorrow, and by then you'll be back home.'

'You think so?'

'Yeah.' Les gave Rinh a reassuring pat on the shoulder. 'Come on, Dogs. Let's go and have some breakfast.'

'Okay then.'

They locked the garage door then everybody filed

into the bus. Les hit the engine and they started climbing out of Coogee, while Warren shifted around the bus taking photos and yabbering away to his Mud Crab heroes. Behind Warren's back Rinh was spreading the word that Les said not to worry too much, the girls would be okay and they'd all be home safe and sound before long. As they got near McPherson Street, Les had to admit to himself he'd only been half-honest with Rinh about the police. The constabulary took a very dim view about people getting kicked half to death by gangs of thugs; girls or whatever. It all depended on how busy they were and how long it took before they got a phone call from a concerned citizen noting all the comings and goings at the garage by the boys in the red tracksuits before they dropped by; especially now that the boys had what looked like a bunch of groupies staying there. Les was involved now as well. He might not have been in the fight, but he knew the parties concerned and didn't report it. And what if the police should just happen to swoop when he had his two hundred thousand dollars. If they were anything like the cops he knew up the Cross, they'd keep the money, charge him with something and tell him to do his best. Les gobbed sourly out the window. This Extreme Polo thing was starting to turn into a bit of a shit fight. Then there were the boys themselves. As well as Vadim, they didn't need all this aggro before the big game. They still had to win. He mightn't have been their coach, but he had to give them some sort of a pep talk before the game. How could he warn them about the big Russian without coming across as a complete dropkick? Yes, it was a turning out to be a shit fight all right.

Les caught Rinh's eyes and motioned for him to come and join him. 'So how's it going, Dogs? How are the boys feeling now?'

'All right,' replied Rinh. 'I told them what you said. Gee your mate can talk though.'

'Yeah. He's not bad when he gets a roll on.' Les swung the bus into McPherson Street and they headed down to Bronte. 'How do you reckon you'll go this afternoon? You confident of winning?'

'Yeah. We're in with a chance. They're big boys and they belted us the first time. But we beat them by four points the second time.'

'When we were driving up from Wagga Wagga, you said something about how the replacement rule evened things up. What did you mean by that again, Dogs?'

'Because we've got no replacements, they can't use any either. In other words, it stops them from bringing in fresh players towards the end of the game.'

'What about if someone gets injured?'

'Makes no difference.'

Les nodded slowly. 'Right. Well at least that's something I suppose.'

Rinh gave Les a quizzical, half-smile. 'Les, what's up? You sound as if you're expecting us to get slaughtered. We're not bad in the water you know. How do you think we got to the grand final?'

'Oh, I didn't mean it like that,' answered Les. 'It's just ... I was just hoping this drama with the girls hasn't thrown you out a bit. That's all.' Les gave Rinh a wink. 'Christ! I've seen you blokes train in that freezing cold water back home. You're unbelievable.'

'That's right.' Rinh leant across and gave Les a pat on the shoulder. 'And with you on the case, the big Varns, we can't go wrong.'

'Exactly Dogs. Exactly.'

Les did pretty much the same with the bus as the last time they were in Bronte. Only this time he swung in front of a white BMW convertible full of yuppies and got abused by Warren when he pulled up above the bus stop.

'Bloody hell!' he howled. 'Who do you think you are, Maxwell fuckin' Smart?'

'Shut up, Warren,' said Les. 'Get too smart yourself and you might end up paying for breakfast.'

When they crossed the road all the little restaurants were packed with diners as usual, and it looked like the grand final breakfast might be take-away. But as luck might have it, a family got up from a table out front of Cafe Z, and by scrounging up some extra seats they were able to spread themselves around the footpath pretty much like the day before. They got the same kiwi waitress who seemed extra friendly this time, even knowing who they were.

'Hello,' she said. 'And how are the Mud Crebs today?'

'We're sumply fentestuck,' answered Les. 'How did you know it was us?'

The waitress pointed to a cutting out of the Sunday Telegraph that the owner had pinned on the wall behind them. With all the other media rattle that had happened the day before, Les had completely forgotten about it.

'Hey boys,' he said. 'Looks like we got our picture in the paper.'

There was a reasonable photo of the team plus Billy and Les all stuffing themselves with food, and a bit of a blurb about them. There was also a photo of the Sydney Sea Snakes looking big and mean in their snake outfits and a bigger blurb about them.

'Jesus! They are big bastards, aren't they?' said Warren.

'Yeah,' agreed Les. 'But you know the old saying, Woz?'

'What's that?'

'The bigger they are, the quicker they sink.'

'Hey, can you stop at a paper shop later,' said Rodney. 'So we can get a copy?'

'Sure,' replied Les. 'I'll get you one each.'

This time Warren went for the eggs benedict; Les chose a Z omelette and a Bronte Lagoon, plus coffee and toast. Again the boys ordered just about everything on the menu, along with seven serves of French toast with banana and ice-cream. Again the food was delicious and despite the bit of drama the boys were all keeping from Warren, the grand final breakfast went down a treat. Warren took some more photos and tried to ring Debbie on his mobile. A couple of little kids came up and asked the boys for their autographs. The boys were only too happy to oblige, then sat back feeling like seven rock stars. Before long they were down to coffees and a pile of dirty plates. Warren looked around the table and raised his caffe latte.

'Well I'd like to propose a toast,' he said.

'I'll be in that,' said Les.

'To the mighty Mud Crabs. Here's to them winning the grand final.'

'My bloody oath,' agreed Les, clinking Warren's glass along with whatever the boys were all drinking. 'To the mighty Mud Crabs. Oogie, oogie, oogie. Do the Mud Crab fuckin' boogie.'

'Hear hear,' said Warren.

'Thanks Les.'

'Yeah. Thanks heaps.'

'You too, Warren.'

'Yeah. Thanks Woz.'

'Unreal Les. Thanks Warren.'

Les waited till the boys put their drinks down then looked evenly around the table. 'Listen fellahs,' he said. 'I'm not your coach and I know fuck all about Extreme Polo, but I reckon you should try this in the big game – and you're talking to a man who's played in a grand final, with the Dirranbandi Devils under-fifteens.'

'Wow! Heavy dude,' said Warren.

Les tried to be as sincere as he could without giving away what he knew. 'I reckon in the first two thirds you should concentrate on defence. One of you hang back with the goalie, even if it means leaving yourself a man short at times up front. Score if you get the chance by all means, but concentrate on defence. Then, if it all goes to plan and there's only a few points difference in the final third – go for it! Attack like mad and give it everything you've got.'

There was silence round the table for a moment until Warren spoke. 'And what's your theory behind this genius game plan, Les Norton super coach?'

Les ran a finger round the top of his coffee cup. 'I

saw the Sea Snakes on TV. They're big blokes all right. But I got a feeling they're going to get tired in the last third and feel like a quick breather. But because of the reserve player rule they can't. And it might just stuff them up. And if, if by some lucky chance one of them had to go off tired, or hurt, you might just finish up a man in front during the final third.' Les ran his eyes round the table. 'They're just my thoughts boys. That's all.'

There was another silence for a second or two then Rinh nodded in agreement. 'Actually, that's not a bad idea,' he said. 'We'll keep it in mind.'

'Yeah,' agreed Clarence.

'Makes a lot of sense,' said Garrick.

Felix's eyes seemed to light up. 'Shit! We're the fastest team in the comp. And we know we're the fittest. We can do that all right.' He looked about him to a chorus of agreement around the table.

'Well, there you are,' gestured Les. 'Why not try it?'

It would have been nice to stay there a little longer sipping coffee or whatever. But the boys had to get their gear packed and Les had to get home himself and, just to be on the safe side, get rid of Warren before he stumbled across the Mud Crabettes. They finished the last of what they were drinking and Les paid the bill. Warren made out he was having a mild heart attack when he saw Les produce the readies, then started making choking sounds when he saw Les slip the kiwi waitress a rock lobster. They bundled back into the team bus and headed for Coogee; stopping once outside a fruit shop in McPherson Street to get several copies of the Sunday Telegraph.

Next thing Les slewed the bus once more alongside Coogee Oval. Warren took a last team photo outside the garage and shook hands with his idols, wishing them all the best again and telling them he and his girlfriend would be barracking for them on TV; then he climbed behind the wheel of the Celica.

'All right, fellas. I'll see you back here in about an hour,' said Les, getting in the other side.

'See you then, Les.' Rinh opened the garage door and they all went inside.

'Shit! I wonder where Debbie is?' said Warren, starting the engine. 'She'll be filthy not meeting the boys before they leave.'

'Yeah. I imagine she will be,' agreed Les.

'Maybe I should go up and get her while I'm here?'

'How about running me home first, mate? I got to get our heroes to the grand final on time.'

'Yeah, you're right.'

Warren reversed back down the driveway then turned towards Bondi, doing his best to avoid the Sunday gridlock by cutting back down behind the Royal Hotel across Edward Street. When he got to Chez Norton he didn't bother going inside, opting instead to go straight over to Debbie's unit at Kensington and see if he could find her.

'I'll see you tonight when you get back from Homebush,' said Warren. 'Good luck at the grand final.'

'Thanks Woz,' replied Les, closing the car door. 'Say hello to Zanna for me.'

'I will.'

Warren zoomed off towards Randwick and Les went inside. There was nothing on the answering service although it appeared someone had rung without leaving a message. Funny there's no word from Nizegy, mused Les, taking a quick glance at his watch. Still, between organising this and his betting scam, I imagine he'd be flat out. I'll see him at the grand final and Rinh knows what to do and where to go. Now what will I wear to the grand final? This tracksuit's starting to hum just a little. Les decided to schmick up for the occasion. He changed into a pair of clean jeans, tan Colorados, a cream, single-breasted jacket and a light blue shirt, topping it all off with a genuine 1940, maroon design tie he bought for a dollar at an op-shop. Standing in front of his mirror he looked like a crooked cop in a Mexican soap opera. While he was in his bedroom Les thought it might be an idea if he got out a large overnight bag and put the same tracksuit in it, plus his trainers, socks, a towel and everything else he felt he'd need because he had a feeling that whether the Mud Crabs won or not there was a good chance he'd finish up in the pool. He had a last look around, a think for a moment or two then picked up his keys, went outside and got behind the wheel of the mighty Datty.

Warren's right, thought Les, as the Datty whined and gasped its way up Denham Street towards the Royal Hotel. I definitely have to get another car. As well as a maid, the two hundred grand should get me a nice car too. A brand new Judasmobile. With a personalised numberplate. DROPKICK 1. Les was still wondering what sort of car he should buy when he pulled up in front of the garage.

The boys were seated, scattered around the bunks; the girls were seated near them, with a couple at the kitchen table wearing the same bomber jackets and jeans only they'd swapped their boots for trainers. The boys had their bags packed near the door, the girls had a pile of bulky, overnight bags, a rolled-up Rainbow Serpent flag, plus a rack of what looked like colourful suits and dresses in protective wrappers. Up close the girls were a solid, homely-looking lot, with no make-up and thick, brown hair cut in an old rock 'n' roll style like Gene Vincent or Eddie Cochran. From a short distance they could easily have passed for men, but looking at them Les felt certain they weren't lesbians. Just hard, maybe a bit old-fashioned, country girls.

Angie was leaning against the fridge nonchalantly chewing on an apple. 'Hello Les,' she said. 'Nice to see you again. How are you?'

'I'm fine, Angie,' replied Les, easily. 'How's yourself?'

'Good.' She turned to the Crabettes. 'Girls, this is Les. The fellah I was telling you about.'

The girls all smiled up at Les. Les smiled back and gave them a quick once over. 'Hello ladies,' he said, with pleasant sarcasm. 'Lovely to meet you. There's no need to tell me all your names. I think at this stage of the game, the less I know about you the better.' He turned to Angie. 'So it looks like you and the warriors are on the run from the local cops, Angie.'

Angie tossed her apple core in the bin. 'Yeah. I guess it looks that way, Les.'

'You don't blame them. That wasn't a bad serve you gave those blokes. Do you think you might've gone just a bit overboard?'

'Hey, you needn't talk,' said Angie.

'Yeah. But I was on my own fighting for survival. Not the other way round.'

'Hey, we're just a team of poor defenceless women,' said one of the girls on the bunks.

'Ohh yeah,' said Les. 'So is a pack of tiger sharks.'

'Ahh, fuck that prick in the blue shirt,' said Angie, contemptuously. 'Wanting to bash up my mate Felix for no reason.'

'Yeah, fair enough I suppose,' conceded Les. 'But now we got to get you out of Coogee and out of Sydney.' He looked at Rinh first then the others. 'I'm not going to be driving you back to Wagga, fellahs.'

'We kind of figured that,' said Clarence.

'You got a driver's licence, Angie?' asked Les.

'Yeah.'

'All right. You're the new Varns.'

'No sweat.'

'I wouldn't mind a lift part of the way home after the game,' said Les. 'Then you can get straight onto the highway from Parramatta Road. I'll catch a cab back. Or a train. I don't give a stuff.'

'We thought of that, Les,' replied Angie. 'The only trouble is.' She pointed to the rack of suits and dresses. 'The bus isn't all that big. And if we put all our stuff in there with us, our dancing gear's going to get crushed to a pulp.'

'And the Wagga Wagga dancing queens don't want to come out looking like eight frumps,' said Les.

'Right on,' nodded Angie.

'Righto. Suits me I suppose. But bloody hell! I wouldn't be hanging around here too long when you get back. Just grab your stuff and split. Pronto.'

'For sure, for sure Les,' said Angie. The others all nodded in agreeance.

'Okay.' Les turned to Rinh. 'You got all the instructions and passes and that Dogs?'

Rinh nodded. 'Everything's in my bag.'

'Okay then,' said Les. 'Let's rock 'n' roll. We got a grand final to win.'

'Yeah. Let's boogie,' said Angie.

'Before we go though,' said Felix. 'I just got to say one thing, the Varns.'

'What's that, Cats?'

'You're looking good, Reg. That's the filthiest outfit I ever seen. Especially the tie.'

Les adjusted his collar. 'Why thank you Catman,' he smiled. 'I never thought you'd notice.'

The boys got their travel bags, the girls got all their stuff and they filed out of the garage. Les locked it, got his own bag from the back seat of the Datty and they all piled into the bus.

Not much was said as they headed into town towards Central and Parramatta Road. The boys were naturally more than a little apprehensive with the big game in front of them. The girls seemed to be worried, though they still managed to maintain the cocksure attitude they had in the garage. This attitude disappeared when they stopped for a red light at Randwick Junction and a police car pulled up alongside. The driver had his eye on the traffic lights, but the young cop on the passenger side started giving the bus a bit of a once over for something to do.

'Don't take any notice of them,' said Les. 'Just keep looking straight ahead. Straight ahead.'

The lights changed, the police car pulled away and Les slowly moved in with the other traffic.

'Shit! That was close,' said Rinh.

'Yeah,' agreed Les. 'I guess it's just our lucky day.'

The conversation dropped right off after that. Which suited Les, because the traffic going up Parramatta Road was horrendous. One non-stop, procession of cars, trucks and buses that seemed to inch its way from one exhaust fume shrouded set of lights to the next. Les glanced at the faces in the rear vision mirror and knew exactly what everyone was thinking. They'd be glad when this whole thing was all over and they could get out of the city and back home. So will I, thought Les. He glanced at his watch. And just a few more hours and it will be. Then I'll have my money and life will return to normal. He stepped on the brakes for another set of lights burning through the clouds of carbon monoxide. Or as normal as my life seems to get these days.

If the traffic was bad along Parramatta Road, when they got to the Homebush Bay turn-off at Australia Avenue it seemed to multiply by ten and looked as if everybody in the Wetern suburbs with a car had descended on Homebush for the day. On top of this, the state government was digging the whole place up in preparation for the Olympic Games. Half the roads were closed or barricaded off with red, plastic strips and around all the confusion swarmed hordes of workmen along with their accompanying rumble of cranes, bulldozers, prime movers, trucks and just about every other type of monstrous earthmoving equipment there was. Les didn't have a clue where he was going, the only thing that seemed to save them was a traffic warden in a broad-brimmed hat, sunglasses and a fluorescent green vest at every cordoned-off roundabout waving them along. Up on the left, Les noticed a massive building of tubular metal scaffolding and cables jutting up from a hill of dry grass and a bit further on a sign pointing towards it saying Aquatic Centre. This has got to be it, thought Les. Another traffic warden waved them on, Les swung the bus up to the left and went behind the building towards the car park then swung the bus right when he saw another sign saying Bus Parking Area and pulled up alongside a row of empty buses as the rest of the traffic surged past.

'Okay gang,' he said, switching off the engine. 'Looks like we're here.'

'Yeah. This is it all right,' said Rinh.

'God. It's big,' said Angie. 'I've never seen anything like it. And what about that traffic.'

'Yeah. I hope it's not as bad driving out,' said Norton.

Les picked up his overnight bag and helped a couple of the girls off with their gear while Rinh carried the flag; then after locking the bus they all started trooping around to the main entrance.

It wasn't all that far from the parking area and in an odd sort of way the building reminded Les a little of an atomic bomb shelter, the way the arched entrance was set into the side of the hill surrounded by thousands of roughly hewn, stone and granite slabs. A shiny, black obelisk sat out the front, and across the arch in blue was a sign saying SYDNEY INTERNATIONAL AQUATIC CENTRE, while along the walls inside the entrance were bronze plaques with the names of famous Australian olympic swimmers: Harold Hardwick, Sandra Morgan, Terry Gathercole, Beverly Whitfield, John Devitt, Lyn McClement, Mark Tonelli, and dozens of others. The boys and the girls looked at them in admiration, then they all squeezed through the crowds of people and went inside.

On the right was a counter, then a sports shop, in the middle sat a row of turnstiles and on the left against the wall, a glass showcase full of different brand trainers. A tall, fair-haired man in blue trousers and a white shirt saw them milling around and walked over from the turnstiles.

'Can I help you?' he asked.

'Yeah,' answered Les. 'We're the Murrumbidgee Mud Crabs. We're here for the grand final.'

'No problems,' said the attendant. 'Go straight through that turnstile. Go left under that archway then take the stairs on your left down to the pool. They're expecting you.'

'Thanks mate,' said Les. 'Righto gang. This way.'

They trooped through the turnstiles then, before they headed downstairs, stopped on the walkway in from the entrance to take a look around. Les had never seen the Aquatic Centre before and when people said it was about the best in the world, it seemed they weren't far wrong. Below on the right was a huge pool roped off into lanes, another pool for waders, a giant water slide, and several open showers spraying water into another shallow pool. Pastel-coloured, tubular scaffolding ran everywhere and one wall was built almost entirely of huge windows, letting the sun in on a small forest of indoor palms. The noise rising up from the thousands of people either swimming, wading or walking around was incredible, and for some reason the sheer height and size of the place reminded Les of a biosphere. Below them on the left side of the walkway were another two huge pools surrounded by seats leading nearly up to the ceiling that were already almost filled with spectators. The closest pool was roped off and divided from the other by a tiled walkway. In the distance Les could see a diving tower and an electronic scoreboard above the second pool along with several TV cameras. There was a bandstand in the right hand corner and going by the hubbub of the crowd in the stands and the people milling around Les surmised this was where they were holding the grand final. He was about to say something when a four piece band in T-shirts and jeans materialised on stage and started belting out 'Whole Lotta Shakin'. Les couldn't tell who the three blokes and the girl were, but they weren't bad at just playing good time, boogie woogie, rock 'n' roll. In next to no time the band had the punters in the stands clapping and singing and doing everything but dancing in the aisles, giving the whole scene a boogie down, carnival atmosphere.

'Shit! What about all this,' said Les.

'Unreal,' agreed Rinh.

Angie was wide-eyed. 'I've never seen anything like it.'

'Me either,' said Les. 'Anyway, let's go. The fans are waiting.' They picked up their bags and headed for the stairs.

Down in the pool area it was slightly chaotic with staff, officials and TV crews everywhere. A slight ripple went through the stands, which soon turned into cheering and clapping when the fans saw who it was coming round the side of the pool. A tall woman with short, brown hair carrying a clipboard and wearing a blue dress and matching Channel 7 jacket approached them.

'Hello,' she smiled.'You must be the Mud Crabs.'

'That's us,' said Les. 'We're running a bit late.'

'Yes, we were starting to wonder where you were,' said the woman. 'If you'll follow me I'll show you your change room.'

'Thanks.'

Les felt a little more relaxed now. He was hoping someone would find them and tell them what to do, because despite the coat and tie, he was playing the manager bit totally by ear. They followed the woman across the walkway to the bandstand side of the second pool. A sign above a double doorway said Change Rooms and hanging off a railing in the stands above the doorway was a banner in red and silver saying Go Mud Crabs. Between the change rooms and the bandstand was a roped-off dining area swarming with more people and TV crews sipping coffee from polystyrene cups, while they all ran around playing hurry up and wait. Les glanced across to the opposite side of the pool where another banner hanging from a railing said Go Sea Snakes. Les looked up at all the Sea Snakes fans for a moment, then a familiar face near the diving tower caught his eye. It was Neil Brooks. They'd taken out the diving boards and he and two other blokes from the Channel 7 sports section had their commentary table up there. He saw Les, smiled and waved. Les smiled and waved back.

'So we're defending this side of the pool,' Les said to the woman.

'That's right,' she replied.

'Where do the Sea Snakes get changed?'

She pointed to a doorway in front of the other pool. 'In the members change room.'

'Uh huh.'

She stopped when they got to their change room and gestured. 'There you go. Let me know when you're ready.'

'Righto. Thanks,' said Les. Two security men in blue uniforms stepped aside to let them enter. The boys filed into the change room on the left and the girls took the one on the right.

A slatted, wooden seat ran round the wall of the change room with a wider, square one in the middle opposite the mirrors and washbasins. Les was about to toss his overnight bag amongst the others, then changed his mind.

'Hey fellahs, while you're getting changed I might duck outside and see if I can find Nizegy. He should be here somewhere.'

'Yeah righto,' said Raymond, amidst a chorus of nods and okays from the rest of the team.

Les humped his bag over his shoulder and walked out to the pool area. The band was now twanging out their version of 'Green River' while the fans sang along in the stands, lights skimmed over the pool and people and TV camera crews seemed to be swarming everywhere. Les peered around the stands and up at Neil Brooks on the diving tower but there was no sign of Neville Nixon. Les was starting to think it was a bit strange. You'd imagine on the big day Nizegy would be there with open arms to both greet the teams and bask in the limelight; after all, the whole concept of Extreme Polo was his idea. With a little help from Norton of course. But it didn't appear to be that way. Les gave his chin a thoughtful stroke and was starting to think it was a bit strange that he'd only seen Nizegy once during the whole time, when he felt a tap on his shoulder. He turned round and it was Coyne in a pair of grey slacks and a bright blue Hawaiian shirt.

'Hello Les,' he beamed. 'How are you mate?'

Les beamed right back at him. 'Coyne. Hello. How's things?'

'Good mate. You got here all right?'

'Yeah,' nodded Les. 'The boys are inside getting changed. The big Russian should've arrived safely into your hands. I kept my side of the bargain.'

'You sure did, mate,' agreed Coyne. 'And so have we.' The big man was carrying a small, green overnight bag which he handed to Les. 'There's your two hundred grand.'

'Thank you.' Les took the money from Coyne and whipped it into his overnight bag that fast the zipper clanged when he slammed it shut.

'Not a bad little earn for less than a week's work,' said Coyne.

'No,' admitted Les. 'Not bad at all.' He offered Coyne his hand. 'And if I seemed a bit out of order round my place last night – what I said about you and Neville, I didn't really mean it.'

'Hey. No worries, mate,' replied Coyne, giving Norton's hand a quick shake. 'I know how you feel.

They're a terrific bunch of young blokes. But, business is business.' A smile spread across the big man's, lived-in face. 'But you never know. They might still get up.'

'Yeah. I don't think I'd put the rent on it though,' said Les. 'Hey, where's Nizegy? Shouldn't he be here?'

Coyne looked genuinely puzzled. 'I was starting to wonder that myself. Maybe he's got stuck in the traffic.'

'Yeah. It's a nice shit fight out there,' said Les. 'We were late getting here ourselves.'

'Well, I'd better get back with the lads,' said Coyne. 'And keep an eye on things.'

'Righto. Hey Coyne, before you go . . . Say there is an upset and the boys do win. Where do they pick up their money?'

'Off me or Neville.' Coyne stared at Les. 'Why? What makes you say that?'

'I don't know,' shrugged Les. 'The thought just crossed my mind, that's all.'

'See you later, Les.'

'Yeah. See you, Coyne.'

Norton's eyes followed Coyne as he walked back round behind the dive tower then climbed up into the stands and sat down in a front row seat with two other casually but smartly dressed men wearing sunglasses. Les watched them for a moment or two then, with his overnight bag slung securely over his shoulder, went back inside the change room.

The boys had their red, silver, yellow and black lycra crab outfits on now and apart from one, small individual photo it was the first time Les had ever seen the boys wearing them. They looked sensational. The way the plating design on the lycra front melded in with the shell effect on the back, plus the pincers and claws running down their arms and the eyes on their helmets, they looked like seven Mud Crabs. Seven very fit, very well-built Mud Crabs.

'Well, I'll be buggered,' said Les. 'Don't you guys look the goods?'

'You think so?' said Felix.

'I'm sure so.' Les looked at the team standing around him carrying their webbs and fins and suddenly it seemed very quiet. Outside was madness. But in the dressing room you could just about hear the proverbial pin drop. 'Well boys,' said Les. I guess this is it. The big one.'

'Yeah. This is it,' nodded Clarence.

Les made a gesture with his hands. 'What can I say?'

Rinh lightly tapped his fins together. 'Not much I suppose.'

'You're right, Dogs,' said Les. 'I just wish I could though.'

'But we'd like to say something Les.'

'Yeah? What's that Dogs?'

'Just thanks.'

'Yeah. Thanks Les.'

'Thanks Les.'

As one, the entire team came up, shook hands with Les and thanked him. Norton didn't quite know what to do or say. It was a great feeling though, he knew that. He was about to try and say something when the woman with the clipboard walked in.

'Are you ready, Mud Crabs?' she said.

'Yeah. We're ready,' answered Garrick.

'I'll see you out at the pool.'

Norton looked at the Mud Crabs grouped around him and a strange, slightly sinister smile lit up his face. 'Come on, fellahs,' he said, slamming a huge right fist into his left hand. 'Let's get out there and boot those Sea Snakes right up the arse.'

'Yeah, let's.' Rinh picked up the Rainbow Serpent flag and they all followed Les out of the dressing room.

Around the pool the previous chaos now seemed to have formed itself into some sort of organised confusion. The band had finished their last song, the TV crews were at the ready, and an MC in a tuxedo and holding a roving microphone was standing on the walkway between the two pools revving up the crowd. Around him, the beautiful Sea Snakes dancing girls in their snake skin vests and shorts were getting ready with their red, blue and dark green pom-poms. Up in the commentary box, Neil Brooks was going live to air while the punters whistled and screamed from the stands. The Mud Crabs stood just outside the door to the change room, Rinh had the flag unfurled while Norton stood proudly alongside them, his overnight bag between his feet where he could keep an eagle eye on it.

The MC's voice boomed around the aquatic centre. 'And now ladies and gentlemen, as we approach this historic event – the first grand final of the wildest game on water, Extreme Polo – will you give a big welcome to the game's fiercest competitors ... the Sydney Sea Snaaakkkeeesssss.'

The MC no sooner spoke than the Sea Snakes theme song 'Tearing Us Apart' started thundering through the speakers. Seconds later, the team came out of their change room waving to the screaming crowds in the stands and strode between the Snakettes standing on either side of the walkway and now ripping energetically into their dance routine in a razzle-dazzle of coloured pom-poms, high kicks and frilly blue knickers. More coloured lights flashed everywhere and the Sea Snakes fans went crazy as their team walked around then stood confidently at their end of the pool flexing their muscles and looking awfully strong and mean under their padded caps. Their theme song ended, the dancing girls finished their Sea Snake shuffle and the MC got on the microphone again.

'Thank you. Thank you, ladies and gentlemen. And now, let's hear it for their worthy opponents. All the way from Wagga Wagga, way down in the Riverina. The dream team. The Murrumbidgee Mud Craaaabbbbsssss.'

There was another deafening roar from the crowd up in the stands and Rinh stepped forward waving the Rainbow Serpent flag, as the Mud Crabs behind him waved to the fans and their song 'All Mamas Children' began bopping through the speakers. Les noticed a movement to his right and the Crabettes cartwheeled from out of dining area to over in front of the bandstand. Four of them were wearing purple, zoot suits, complete with key chains, French seams and twelve inch pegs. The other four were wearing loose black skirts, wide black belts, white socks and sneakers and yellow cowboy shirts. As soon as they landed on their feet, they split into pairs and started rockin' and rollin' every jive step imaginable; the pretzel, wrapper, hatchback, American spin, neckbreak and more. The punters in the stands went mad again as the girls from Wagga gave it everything they had and then some. The song finally cut out and they finished with one huge leap of swirling dresses and swivelling shoulder pads to a thunderous, standing ovation from the stands. One of the Crabettes in a zoot suit took the flag from Rinh then they vanished back into the dining area as the boys got ready by the pool.

The crowd settled down and it was time for the national anthem. Les propped next to the Mud Crabs as everybody stood up to the strains of 'Advance Australia Fair'. Up in the stands above the Sea Snakes, he noticed a flash of blue Hawaiian shirt and got a smile and slight wave. Les smiled and gave a slight wave back. Then from amongst the Sea Snakes, Les thought he saw a half wave from the biggest Sea Snake; their number 6. Les gave him a half wave also. So, thought Les, while the anthem played, looks like they got Vadim playing in the front row. You don't wonder why. The national anthem finished and that was about it. There was nothing else Les could do now. He wished the boys good luck for the last time then found a seat and sat back from the pool with his overnight bag between his legs to watch the proceedings.

A whistle blew and both teams slipped into the pool to take up their positions; the way they effortlessly sliced through the crystal clear water in their multicoloured outfits it almost looked as if they were floating on air. Rinh dropped back in front of the goalmouth and adjusted the strap on his helmet as the Sea Snakes number one did the same thing, while Clarence dropped back to give Rinh extra support. The clock ticked around for the time and the electronic scoreboard hung patiently on zero. Another whistle blew, then an official in white with a red baseball cap tossed the grenade into the pool to a wild roar from the crowd and it was on.

The Sea Snakes charged straight into the Mud Crabs taking advantage of their size and strength and using Vadim up front as a human battering ram. With the water churning around them players were going everywhere as the grenade seemed to fly from one end and one side of the pool to the other. The Mud Crabs were fast all right, just as Felix said, but the size and strength of the Sea Snakes, especially with Vadim in the team, certainly made the difference. The game was barely five minutes old when Vadim tore up the middle, got the grenade to another forward who swam straight over Raymond and got it back to Vadim, who slammed it in for a goal. Rinh tried desperately but the rubber grenade came at him like a cannonball. With their confidence high, the Sea Snakes swam back to take up their positions. It wasn't long before they had the grenade; using much the same tactic, Vadim charged up the middle, then got the grenade to a back who slammed it in for a quick one pointer – a zip.

Norton didn't have a clue about the rules or the tactics. But from what he could see, the Sea Snakes game plan was to just smash the Mud Crabs using any methods they could get away with. They punched, elbowed, kneed and did things in the water Les had never seen before. They'd dive in front of an opposing player then kick out and try to catch him in the face with a heel. Another trick was to swim level with an opponent then move away slightly and slam in a side kick to the ribs. The fins slowed the blow a little, but even under water, a kick under the heart from someone twice your size hurt. They incurred a number of penalties. But this didn't seem to worry them, just as long as they could smash their smaller opponents. Les also soon got the feeling this was a grudge match. The Sea Snakes did have it in for the Mud Crabs. They were the pretty boys. The dream team. The Sea Snakes had probably thrown their last game against them as well. So now was the chance to show who the real men were, and if a couple of pretty boys from Wagga Wagga got carried off, even better. However, the Mud Crabs never looked like flinching. They were fast and they never stopped moving, swarming all over their bigger opponents when they could, tackling their hearts out and performing some amazing manoeuvres in the water. They even managed to score a goal and two zips; the Sea Snakes goalkeeper was big, but he wasn't anywhere near as fast as Rinh. Which was another of the Sea Snakes tactics: for every shot they took at the goal area they'd also try to knock Rinh's head off. Felix covered for him as much as possible, but Rinh copped a number of grenades in the face which rattled him; face guard or no face guard. The hooter rang to end the first third with the Sea Snakes leading 12–5. Three goals and three zips to one goal and two zips. The boys climbed out of the pool and headed for the change room with Les as the band started up again with a hot version of 'Burning Love' while both teams of dancing girls got into another routine.

When the boys got their caps off in the dressing room they were a pretty battered-looking lot. Garrick and Rodney were holding their ribs, Felix's nose was bleeding, Raymond had a split lip and Rinh had the makings of sensational black eye coming up.

'I see what you mean when you said they play rough,' said Les.

Jamieson lay back with his fins under his head and rubbed his jaw. 'Tell me about it.'

'But you're going all right,' said Les. 'There's only seven points in it.'

'Yeah. We're going terrific,' said Felix, mopping his nose with a towel.

'Who's that fuckin' number six?' said Raymond. 'I don't remember playing him last time.'

'Me either,' added Garrick. 'He's a nice monster.'

'Yeah. You're gonna have to watch him,' said Les. 'But one thing I noticed, their goalie is a bit slow. Try and run him off his feet. Or swim him off his flippers with those zips.'

'You reckon coach?' said Rodney.

'Yeah,' nodded Les. 'That. And keep your defence up. And I reckon you're right in this.'

'You think so?' said Rinh.

'I'm fuckin' sure so, Dogs. You're going good.' Les knew he was lying; they were on the verge of a hiding. But what could he say? A siren sounded in the background. 'Anyway, there's the hooter, men. Let's go get 'em.'

Rinh dragged himself to his feet. 'Yeah. Let's go get 'em.'

The Sea Snakes played the second third same as the first: rough, hard and mean. The Mud Crabs were giving it their best. But Vadim was the difference; he was just too big, too fast and too strong. Time and again he'd charge up the centre of the pool, draw two or three Mud Crabs, then slip the grenade away to the backs or another forward before the Mud Crabs could get it off him. If Vadim's team mate couldn't score he'd at least try to knock Rinh's head off, then they'd try and foul one of the Mud Crabs while the officials attention was concentrated on the goalmouth. The Mud Crabs kept defending though; and they also took notice of what Les said about the Sea Snakes' goalkeeper, managing to land six long-distance zips. But at the end of the second third the Sea Snakes had scored another two goals and four zips. When the boys got out of the pool for the break, the score was 22–11, with what looked like worse to come.

'You're going well, boys,' said Les, walking round the change room from player to player, his overnight bag slung securely over his shoulder. 'Eleven points is nothing. We're still in this.'

'Ohh, piss off,' groaned Felix, before rolling over and vomiting up about a litre of water.

'Now don't be like that Cat Man,' said Les. 'Remember, winners make it happen; losers let it happen.'

'Well, I'll tell you what's happening out there, Les,' said Garrick. 'We're getting the shit kicked out of us.'

'Bullshit Harry. You've just had a couple of plays go against you and they've had all the grenade. That's all.'

Garrick was right though. The Mud Crabs were getting an awful battering. If they looked bad before, now they looked like they'd been pulled out of a train wreck. They were all carrying pains around their rib cages, their arms and legs were covered in bruises, their faces were a mess, and Rinh's right eye was almost closed now while his left one was turning black.

'All right,' said Les, gesturing round the change room. 'I admit it doesn't look good. But I just got a feeling the tide's going to change in this last third.'

'Tide?' said Clarry. 'How the fuck's the tide going to change? We're in a swimming pool.'

'I meant it metaphorically, Clarry,' replied Les. 'I just reckon they'll slow up and you'll get a second wind. Or third, or whatever.'

'Slow up?' said Rodney. 'If you ask me they're getting faster.'

'Yeah. Especially that fuckin' number six,' said Raymond, feeling inside his mouth for a couple of loose teeth.

'Okay. He's bad news,' admitted Les. 'But you can't give up now. You've got two hundred grand riding on this. It's a lot of money.'

'Yeah, you're right,' said Rinh, squinting through the swelling round his eyes. 'It is a lot of money.'

'You trained your rings off all year in that freezing cold river to get here. Don't give up now,' said Les.

'We're not giving up, Les,' said Rinh. 'Our condition's still good. We could swim all day. But we're just getting belted. And we're not big enough or mean enough to play dirty.'

'Okay. Fair enough, I suppose.' Les looked around the dressing room at the battered Mud Crabs. They'd be flat out getting through the final third, let alone win it. 'But fellahs, if you've got anything left in the tank, go for it now and give it your best shot. I still reckon you can come from behind.'

'Well, I'm glad you do,' said Rodney, through swollen lips.

'Of course you can,' continued Les. 'And always remember, fellahs. If you walk towards the light, the shadows are always behind you.'

Rinh squinted at Les through his one good eye. 'What the fuck's that got to do with us getting our heads punched in?'

'I don't know, Dogs,' replied Les. 'But it sounds good.' The hooter wailed outside for the final third. 'Well, this is it fellahs. What do you want to do? Win or lose?'

'Yeah, why not,' said Jamieson. 'We may as well be completely rooted as the way we are.'

'That's the spirit Jam Tin,' said Les. 'And remember that other old saying fellahs: every time a child says I don't believe in fairies, somewhere out there a little fairy falls down dead.'

Rinh squinted at Les again as he adjusted his helmet. 'Are you sure one of those grenades didn't hit you in the head?'

'Just get out there, Dogs,' said Les. 'And oogie, oogie, oogie. Do the Mud Crab boogie.'

The band finished, the dancing girls ended their routine and the MC gave the crowd its last rev-up before the final third. The teams got in the pool, a whistle blew, the grenade hit the water to another deafening roar from the crowd and it was on again for the last time.

There was a great flurry in centre pool as the fourteen players churned the water to foam like a mob of giant piranhas in their mad scramble for the grenade. From out of nowhere Vadim grabbed it, elbowed Raymond aside, swam straight through Rodney then in a one-man rampage surged down the pool and belted the grenade straight at Rinh. Rinh just managed to deflect it from the goal area, but the grenade still flipped in behind him for a one pointer. It was now 23–11 as the Sea Snakes swam confidently back to take up their positions. Up in the commentary box Neil Brooks was sadly shaking his head.

'Well viewers,' he said into the microphone on the side of his face, 'I think that's about it for the Mud Crabs. They're seven tired boys out there. They've taken a dreadful battering from a much bigger team and I can't see them coming back from twelve points down. In fact, it's not so much a matter of the Sea Snakes winning, it's what they're going to win by.' Brooksie was about to turn to his fellow commentator when he stopped. 'Just a minute. There's something going on down there in the pool.'

The players had just about swum back to their positions when suddenly Vadim started throwing what looked like some sort of a fit. He thrashed round and round in the water, screwed up his face then clutched at his ribs and howled with pain. He rolled over a few more times then swam to the edge of the pool with this wild, horrible look of fear on his face and with his back to the tiles screamed at everyone to keep away from him. The crowd was stunned, the officials were aghast; a couple of Vadim's team mates swam over to him to see what was wrong. Vadim screamed something at them again in Russian then lashed out with a straight right that caught number three flush in the face, breaking his nose and knocking him out cold in the water. The Sea Snakes number two wasn't quite quick enough to get out of the way and he copped a backhand left that almost broke his jaw and had him seeing stars all over the Aquatic Centre. The burly team manager ran across to see what was happening just as Vadim rolled over in the water, gave another agonised howl and shit himself. He didn't just shit himself. The big Russian's bowels opened up like a thunderclap, filling his snake outfit from head to toe with shit. The lycra jump suit was tight, but it still couldn't contain it there was that much. A few tiny turds appeared in the water around Vadim's face and a greasy, brown cloud started spreading in the water behind him.

Norton jumped to his feet and began waving madly. 'Foul! Foul!' he screamed at the top of his voice. 'It's a foul. Forfeit! Forfeit!' Les turned to the Sea Snakes manager and pointed to Vadim doubled up in the pool. 'You've forfeited the game. Your number six just shit in the pool. Foul! Foul! Get the rule book.' Somebody get the rule book. If that's not a foul, nothing is. Foul! Foul! Forfeit! Forfeit!'

While the officials were getting the rule book the attendants got a vacuum hose and started sucking the shit out of the water. Although Vadim was completely stuffed now, his team mates were still a bit cautious about going near him. Somehow the attendants managed to get a rope around his leg and drag him from the pool onto a stretcher with two extra blankets over and under it to soak up the shit. It stunk too. There was stuff coming out of Vadim that he must have eaten when he was a kid learning to swim in Vladivostok. While they carried Vadim off, a doctor attended the Sea Snakes number three, still out cold on another stretcher. But there wasn't much they could do: his nose wasn't just broken, it was pulverised. So he was off for the rest of the game and their number two wasn't in much better shape.

Up in the commentary box Neil Brooks was still trying to work out what had happened. 'Well, this is unbelievable, viewers. It looks like the Sydney Sea Snakes have started fighting amongst themselves. Twelve points in front and the Sydney Sea Snakes have started brawling amongst themselves at one side of the pool. Now two have been carried off with injuries.' He turned to his dark-haired, co-commentator. 'Have you seen anything like that before Gavin?'

Gavin shook his head. 'Never Brooksie. And their number two doesn't look real good either.'

'Unbelievable. Absolutely unbelievable.'

'Do you think the Mud Crabs might get up in this last third, Neil? With a two man advantage?'

Brooksie shook his head. 'It's a big ask, Gavin. A big ask.'

While they sucked the shit and blood from the water, an official called time-out and consulted the rule book. There was nothing in the book about anybody shitting in the water and punching out his team mates. So the Sea Snakes couldn't forfeit the game. However, the game had to continue to the final siren and they would have to play two men short. They were the rules and the Sea Snakes were informed. While all this was happening, the Mud

267

Crabs were in a huddle treading water near their goalmouth. Les walked over and knelt down.

'Hey Les,' said Rinh. 'What's going on?'

'I don't know, Dogs. But they're down to four men. Two are off for good and their number two's a passenger. So . . .'

Before Les could finish, an all-girl chorus screamed out from near the dining area. 'Oogie, oogie, oogie. Do the Mud Crab Boogie. Goooooo Mud Crabs.'

'You heard the ladies,' said Les. 'Now's your big chance. Go get 'em boys.'

Felix banged his hands together. 'Yeah, come on. Let's have a go. I'm sick of getting my head punched in.'

Les left them and walked back to his seat. He looked up in the stands above the Sea Snakes end of the pool at a blue Hawaiian shirt that seemed to have suddenly wilted. Yes Coyne, mused Les, I guess you could say the Shatkov's just hit the fan. What Les would loved to have told Coyne and the Mud Crabs was that, when he picked Vadim up and took him down to the Gull's Toriyoshi for a snack, he slipped a handful of Bahloo Berries into Vadim's Yakitori. Les wasn't sure which ones the big Russian would choose or how much he'd need, so he spread the lot in all four. George Brennan was going to miss out, but Vadim had enough laxatives going through his system to clean out the engines on a nuclear submarine. Oh well, thought Les, taking a quick glance towards the Sea Snakes' dressing room – you're not the only one feeling crook, Vadim. Right now I'll bet there's a skinny black dog dragging its ring over every patch of grass in Bondi between Lamrock Avenue and Hastings Parade too.

The crowd quietened down in their seats as a strange hush of excitement suddenly settled over the stands. The Mud Crabs had taken an awful hammering from their bigger opponents in the first two thirds. Now with a two-man advantage, could they come from twelve points behind and possibly snatch victory from the Sea Snakes in the final third? The clock ticked over again, an official blew time, and away they went for the remaining twenty-two minutes of the final third.

The grenade hit the water and there was another frantic surge in mid pool as the players fought for possession. Only this time Raymond came up with it for the Mud Crabs. With the grenade against his chest, Raymond swam straight around his opposite number then slipped it to Clarence who swam right over the top of the Sea Snakes number four. Clarence then speared the grenade across to Jamieson who took off up the pool like a barracuda and when he was about two metres in front of the Sea Snakes goalkeeper leapt up out of the water past his knees and slammed the grenade into the net for a three-pointer. The Mud Crabs fans went wild in the stands, Les punched the air and cheered with them while the Crabettes danced and did their thing in front of the band stand. After that, the demoralised Sea Snakes didn't know what hit them. Not only were they two men down, including their best player, but one of their backs still didn't know where he was and they were all too tired as well as too disorganised to carry him. The Mud Crabs on the other hand seemed to have got a second wind and were playing the game the way they liked to. Fast.

Before the Sea Snakes knew it, the Mud Crabs had slammed in two more goals to make it 23–20. The Sea Snakes hit back using every dirty trick they could. Somehow they managed to elbow and kick their way in for two zips; but they were lucky to get them. The Mud Crabs threw the grenade from one side of the pool to the other like it was a live hand grenade and surged through the water like dolphins; flipping themselves into the air, swimming under their opponents legs, spinning round in the water like alligators to keep the grenade from the Sea Snakes. They slammed in another goal while the Sea Snakes managed to punch their way to the line for a zip. The Mud Crabs hit back with a quick zip; then the Sea Snakes had a quick huddle and changed their tactics.

There was only two points the difference, but with five minutes to go time was on the Sea Snakes side. They decided to stack the goalmouth and not bother scoring. If they could just keep the Mud Crabs out for five minutes they'd win. Their number two was starting to come back to life so they propped him alongside the goalkeeper right in front while the others spread themselves across the outer goal area and stayed there. They were all big men and though the Mud Crabs peppered the goal area, it was like trying to get the grenade through a brick wall. Although the Sea Snakes were tired, the Mud Crabs were tiring as well from the non-stop attacking; all the Sea Snakes had to do was tread water in front of their goalmouth and defend. With less than a minute on the clock the crowd in the stands fell silent as the battered Mud Crabs took the grenade up for one more roll of the dice; the Sea Snakes, facing them across the goalmouth shoulder to shoulder like a human barricade; were determined nothing would get through. Felix got it across to Clarence, he got it to Rodney who then speared it to Raymond, the grenade razzle-dazzling across the water in an effort to confuse the Sea Snakes. The grenade spun over to Garrick, back to Rodney then across to Jamieson. But the Sea Snakes were watching it like hawks. What they didn't see in all the confusion and white water was Rinh leave the goalmouth, catch up to his team mates then dive under them. With Felix holding the grenade, the Mud Crabs charged through the pool at the Sea Snakes goal line. The Sea Snakes were waiting. Three metres out, Jamieson swam to the left a little and propped. Felix still had the grenade. He sent it in a short pass right to Rodney, then Rodney flicked it to Jamieson still floating in the water. The Sea Snakes waited for him to pass it, only he bobbed down in the water; then, as he rose, Rinh came flying out of the water behind him and quick as an eel slid up onto Jamieson's shoulders. Jamieson kicked up and gave Rinh the ball, while Rinh bent his knees then dived off Jamieson's shoulders, the momentum taking him almost two metres into the air. He dived down towards the Sea Snakes goalmouth like a rocket, hurling the rubber grenade at the same time. And that was all the Sea Snakes number two saw. The grenade slammed down behind him into the net for a goal as Rinh tucked himself into a ball and bombed into the pool a metre away from the goalmouth. A second later the hooter rang and the Mud Crabs had won the grand final 27–26. It was only by one point, but that was all they needed.

The Mud Crabs fans went beserk in the stands; even the Sea Snakes supporters begrudgingly clapped the winners. The cheering all round was deafening. Les punched the air and hollered at the top of his voice, then started tap-dancing round the edge of the pool before going over and hugging all the Crabettes and getting into their high kicking dance routine with them. The TV crews had zoomed in on the exhausted Mud Crabs floating in the pool, too battered and tired to even congratulate each other. Up on the diving tower Neil Brooks seemed more excited than anybody.

'Well Gavin,' he said, still shaking his head with disbelief, 'that has to be the best finish to any grand final of any sport I've ever seen.'

'I have to agree, Brooksie,' replied his co-commentator. 'It was simply sensational. Controversial maybe. But definitely sensational.'

'The hammering those kids took in the first two thirds. Then to come back like that, even with a two-man advantage, was almost unbelievable.'

'I still can't believe that last goal, Neil.'

'Neither can I.' Brooksie peered into the crowd. 'There's no sign of Neville Nixon, Gavin. But I see one of the Mud Crabs' trainers over there. Les Norton. I'll go down and have a word with him before the presentations.'

'Okay Neil.'

Down in the dining area Les was still dancing around with the Crabettes. They finished their last high kick and went over to the boys, who had drifted painfully across to the edge of the pool and the waiting media scrum. Les looked up in the stands.

Nizegy was still nowhere to be seen, but Coyne had his face buried in a mobile phone his jaw almost on his chest. He stood up and beckoned to his two well-dressed friends.

'There's still no sign of Nizegy,' Les said to Angie.

'No,' she replied. 'It's a bit of a funny one.'

'Coyne's up there though.' Les pointed to the Hawaiian shirt in the stands. 'I think I'd better have a word with him.'

Les was about to leave when Brooksie appeared with his TV crew. 'Les,' he said. 'Do you mind if I have a word with you?'

'No. Go for your life,' replied Les, keeping one eye on the Hawaiian shirt in the stands.

'A great finish to a great game, Les. They don't come closer than that.'

'No, you're right, Neil,' said Les. 'That was something else all right. I'm still flat out believing it myself.'

'I think everybody else feels the same.'

'Yeah,' laughed Les. 'But I'm only the part-time manager, Neil. This is the man you should talk to. Him and the team deserve all the credit.' Les reached down and helped Rinh from the pool. 'This is the team captain, Rinh Tin Trinh. Dogs, to all his mates. He'll fill you in Neil.'

'Okay. Thanks Les.'

Up in the stands, Coyne and his two mates had a quick huddle and with worried looks on their faces started making a move. Les left a dazed Rinh and his team mates behind him dripping water all over the place, while he headed over to the walkway to cut Coyne off as he came down from the stands.

'Coyne. What's doing mate?' Les grinned and made an expansive gesture with his hands. 'You're not staying for the presentations?'

Coyne stopped. His two friends gave Les a quick once up and down before Coyne walked over. 'Hello Les,' he said. 'How's things?' The usual cheery banter was noticeably missing and his voice sounded quite flat.

'Couldn't be creamier, Coyne,' replied Les. 'Great finish. And you were right. They could still get up. You never told me Vadim was an epileptic though.'

Coyne came right up to Les and looked him in the eye. 'I'll tell you something, Les. Only because you're not a bad bloke. Nizegy just got busted.'

'He what?' Les couldn't believe what he just heard.

'Nizegy's been busted on his yacht. And I'm out of here. So have a nice day, Les.'

'Hang on. What about the boys' two hundred grand?'

A hint of a sardonic smile creased the corners of Coyne's eyes. 'Tell them it'll be round the garage at . . . seven o'clock.'

Les was about to say something like 'don't give me that bullshit,' when Angie appeared next to him.

'Hello Coyne,' she said. 'Top game.'

'Yeah. Sensational,' replied the big man.

'So what's happening?' said Angie. 'Where's the boy's money?'

'I was just telling Les, Angie,' replied Coyne, 'Neville's been in a car accident. And it'll be at the garage at seven o'clock, so wait there. Isn't that right, Les?' Before Les had a chance to even nod or mumble a disbelieving reply, Coyne said, 'I have to go to the

274

hospital. See you.' He disappeared into the crowd with his two shifty friends.

Les turned to Angie. 'You heard him,' he shrugged. 'They're going to drop the money off at the garage. We're all going back there anyway.'

Angie stared moodily after Coyne. 'Yeah. I just hope he's fair dinkum and this isn't some sort of scam. I've never really trusted that dropkick. Or his bloody mate.'

'Well, I don't know them all that well,' said Les. 'But I can't see any reason why they wouldn't pay up.'

'Yeah.' Angie gave Les a quick once up and down as if she suddenly didn't trust him either.

'So how are the boys?'

'Rooted. Half of them should be in hospital. They all need to see a doctor.'

'The presentations and all that rattle finished?'

'Yeah.'

'Well, why don't we all get changed and get out of here? We haven't got all that much time if we're going to be at the garage by seven. And don't forget, the cops are still looking for you and your girlfriends.'

'Yeah. Good idea,' said Angie. 'Let's not be here. In fact, the sooner I get out of Sydney, the better I'll like it.'

'I know just how you feel, Angie,' sympathised Les.

Back in the dressing room, Angie wasn't joking when she said the boys were rooted. They looked more like they'd just taken Pork Chop Hill for the fifth time rather than won a grand final. They were all slumped around with their headgear off, moaning and bleeding, holding their heads and ribs, and too tired and in too much pain to talk let alone move.

Sitting on the wooden slats in the middle of the room was the trophy. A bronze torpedo mounted on a wooden base. Les looked at it, then looked round the room again and thought, there has to be an easier way of earning two hundred grand than that. Then you have to whack it up seven ways plus the girls would have to get something too. And pay tax as well. Another even worse thought struck Norton – that's *if* you get paid.

'What can I say, fellahs,' said Les, trying to sound uplifting. I told you, you were a big chance in the last third and I was right. You won.'

There was a deafening silence then Raymond mumbled through swollen lips. 'Yeah. Terrific.'

'I've never felt so fucked in my life,' said Felix.

'I never saw Nizegy at the presentation,' said Rinh. 'Do you know what's happening with our prize money?'

Les had to look twice to make sure it was Rinh, his face was that swollen. 'I was just talking to Coyne a few minutes ago. Nizegy's been in a car accident and they're delivering the money to the garage at seven o'clock. Angie was there. She'll tell you.'

'Nizegy's been in a car accident?' said Rodney. 'I feel like I've been in one.' He finished talking then put his head between his knees and dry retched.

'Anyway fellahs,' said Les, clapping his hands together. 'That's the story. We have to get out of here.' He had another look round the dressing room. 'I might get the girls to give you a hand to get changed.' Les walked to the entrance to the girls change room and called out. 'Hey Angie!' She appeared a few seconds later. 'Angie, can you give the boys a hand to put their tracksuits on? Don't bother taking their lycra gear off. Put them straight on over the top.'

'Righto. I'll get the girls.'

Angie went back inside the Ladies dressing room. Les returned to the Mens and looked around at the battered Mud Crabs again. There wasn't much he could say, or wanted to say. Although there should have been jubilation, Les felt awful. How could he tell the boys that after training and playing all year, then finally winning the grand final and getting their heads bashed in for their trouble, Nizegy had just got busted, Coyne was on the toe to parts unknown, and they'd been given a use. He looked up as Angie and the Crabettes came in.

'Listen, while you're doing this,' he said to Angie, 'I might see if I can find that sheila with the clipboard and get her to sneak us out a back way or something to the bus.'

'Yeah, good idea,' said Angie. 'I doubt if the boys'd be able to get up the stairs.'

With his overnight bag slung securely over his shoulder, Les went back outside to the pool area. There was now a crush of people leaving, with a knot of groupies and autograph hunters hanging round the door, TV camera crews packing up and the Aquatic Centre staff trying to sort out all the mess. He found the woman he was looking for sipping coffee from a polystyrene cup in the dining area next to Brooksie and some other staffers from Channel 7. Les explained the situation and the woman was only too happy to oblige. She took Les round the back, unlocked one of the double glass doors and pointed out the way to the bus parking area. Les thanked her and walked back to the dressing room. The boys had their tracksuits on and were on their feet, but they were still a very sad, very sore team of swimmers.

'So how are you feeling now, boys?' asked Les.

'Terrific,' replied Felix, trying to focus. 'Real good.'

'Did Angie tell you what's happening with your money?'

'Yeah,' answered Rinh. 'It'll be round the garage at seven o'clock.'

'That's what Coyne told us,' said Les.

'Yeah. That's what Coyne told us,' repeated Angie, her voice dripping with sarcasm.

'Anyway, if you girls want to get your stuff,' said Les, 'we'll meet you outside. I'll carry the flag and the trophy if you like.'

'See you outside,' said Angie.

Les watched the Crabettes leave, then turned to the Mud Crabs. 'This way, boys,' he said, pointing towards the opposite entrance. 'Unless of course you want to go out the other way. There's about twenty young groupies waiting outside the door. You might like to have another bun on the bus going back to Coogee?'

Rodney spat a gob of congealed blood into one of the washbasins. 'You got to be fuckin' kidding.'

'That's the spirit,' said Les. 'I'm glad to see you finally got sex and filth off your young minds.'

Les led the boys round to where the girls were waiting outside and they walked down to the glass door. Les pushed it open and they were outside and on their way to the bus before anyone knew. It was a slow painful walk back to the bus; the girls had to help the boys along, then help them on board when they got there. Les regretted now that he'd made that flippant remark in the dressing room, because they were in a lot worse shape than he'd thought and Angie was right when she said they needed hospital treatment. The way Clarence was moving and trying to hold his back, Les was certain he had badly bruised kidneys. They got seated and stowed their gear, Les kicked the engine over and began reversing out of the parking area. As they left the Aquatic Centre, Les started to feel a bit down himself; if his young friends from Wagga felt bad now, the trip home with no money would be a lot worse.

The drive out of the parking area wasn't anywhere near as bad as coming in. It was a much shorter distance going out to the expressways and before Les knew it, they were bumping steadily along down Parramatta Road. Les deliberately left the radio off. You could bet Nizegy getting busted would be on the news and if the others found out that would be the end of it. Nobody said anything, however. The girls were too busy playing nurse and the boys were in too much pain. So the only sounds coming from the back of the bus were moans and groans, interrupted now and again by bouts of painful coughing. They continued on in silence. Les stopped for a set of lights outside an old, boarded up picture theatre on the left called The Midnight Star. As he stared at its sad, deteriorating appearance he tried to mull over what was going on. Nizegy busted on his yacht? With what? Coke, heroin, pot? And how long had he been dealing? It was news to him. Was all this money drug money? It sure looked that way. Norton's eyes moved down to the radio still switched off in the dashboard. He would have loved to have known what was going on? Yes, it was like he'd said earlier all right. This Extreme Polo thing was turning out to be a nice shit fight. A giant one. Oh well, thought Les, as the lights turned green and he eased his foot off the brake pedal, at least I got my money. That's the main thing.

Alone with his thoughts in the painful silence of the minibus, the trip back to town went faster than he expected and in what seemed like no time they were through Broadway and approaching Randwick Junction. Les came down behind Coogee Oval, drove alongside it and turned right into the street where the garage faced the oval. As the bus approached the garage, Les stared out the windscreen and couldn't believe his luck; or his bad timing. A police car was cruising past the garage in their direction flashing a torchlight over the buildings. The light washed across Norton's old Datsun parked in the driveway, before moving along to the units on the corner.

'Hey Angie,' he called out. 'Have a look at this.'

Angie came and sat down in the seat opposite. 'Shit!' she said.

'Yeah. Shit!' echoed Les.

Les drove the bus straight past the garage and the police car to the next roundabout. In the rear vision mirror he could see the police car move off up the street and by the time he slowly took the roundabout and parked the bus against the oval as usual, it was gone.

'Righto,' he said, switching off the motor. 'Leave everything on the bus. We'll wait in the garage and bring the rest out when you leave.'

Les picked up his overnight bag and they all got off and walked over to the garage. He locked his overnight bag in the boot of the Datty, then when they got inside handed Angie the keys to the minibus.

'There you go, the Varns,' he said. 'You're the new driver. In the meantime, I suggest we sit here very quietly – no radio, no TV – and wait for the money.'

'Yeah. Wait for the money,' repeated Angie.

'There's not much else we can do,' said Les, through a thin smile.

While they were waiting the girls tended to the boys as best they could; making them comfortable on their bunks, wiping away the blood, getting them glasses of water. As he was watching them, Les couldn't help feeling more sorry for them than ever. They were a mess all right. He also couldn't help wondering what he was doing there. No one was coming round with any money, and if the cops came back and sprung him with that two hundred grand in the boot, as soon as they connected it to Nizegy, he was off tap. He gazed around the room and saw Angie looking at her watch.

'They're not coming,' she said. 'This is bullshit.'

'It wouldn't surprise me,' said one of the Crabettes, holding a glass of water up to Felix's lips. 'I'd trust Neville Nixon about as far as I could punt kick a beached whale.'

Rinh sat up a little on his bunk. 'Well, I trust him. I reckon the money'll be here.'

'Good for you, Dogs,' said Angie.

'What do you reckon, Les?' asked Rodney.

Les shrugged. 'I don't know. I reckon it'll probably turn up.'

'Well, that's a definite maybe if ever I heard one.'

Angie gave a scornful little laugh and gave Les that same look as if she suspected he was part of it.

Les shrugged again. 'You asked me.'

The minutes silently ticked by. The only sound in the garage was every now and again one of the boys would groan or cough with pain. Nothing was happening. Nothing was going to happen. The only thing happening was time going to waste. And from the way the Crabettes were looking at him, Les started to get the impression they'd put their heads together in the back of the bus and decided he was in with Neville and Coyne too.

Les stood up and moved across to the door. 'I might go outside and have a look around. See if anybody's out there.'

'Yeah, whatever,' said one of the Crabettes.

Les stood in the driveway and shook his head. Apart from the odd car and the people further down the beachfront there was nobody. And there wasn't going to be anybody. At least there was no sign of the cops. But you could bet they'd be back before long. Les shook his head again. What am I doing here? I think I might say my goodbyes and split. This is not a good place to be.

Back inside the garage it seemed gloomier than ever. 'I couldn't see anybody,' said Les. He had a quick look around him then went back to leaning against the wall.

'Isn't that a surprise,' said Angie.

'We're stuck between a rock and a hard place in here,' said one of the Crabettes. 'No one's gonna show with the money. And the longer we wait here the more chance there is of the cops coming back.'

'Yeah,' agreed Angie. 'I think we should cut our losses and split.' She stared at Les. 'Just put it down to experience.'

'Wait another ten minutes,' said Garrick.

Angie looked at her watch. 'It's nearly half past seven now Harry. Another ten minutes and we could all end up in gaol.'

Les raised himself off the wall again. 'I might have another look around outside. At least there was no sign of the cops last time.'

'Yeah. Go out and have another look around, Les,' said Angie. 'Tell us what you see.'

Before he closed the door behind him Les heard one of the girls say, 'I reckon that's the last we've seen of him. He won't be back.'

A voice came from one of the bunks. 'Hey, don't say that.' It sounded like Felix.

Les stood at the end of the driveway and gazed absently over at the bus. Well, that's that. I'm out of here. This is just a giant waste of time. They don't need me to help them onto the bus. And knowing my luck, you can bet the cops'll come back and nick the lot of us. Besides, that sheila inside said I wasn't coming back. Let's not prove her wrong. Adios Mud Crabs. Better luck next time. Les turned around and walked towards the car. Suddenly it was if some strange, invisible beam came down from the stars gripping him with an unexplainable force that took over his mind and body, stopping him in his tracks. Les looked up at the night sky, his face a portrait of abject misery and a tiny tear rolled down his cheek. Why do you do this to me, he silently asked? Why? What have I done? I'm going to hate myself for the rest of my life for this. And into the next life as well. But tell me why you make me do these things? Why? Please?

'Well, look who's back,' said one of the Crabettes, when Les stepped inside the garage.

Despite the gloomy atmosphere and his tear or two outside, Les was all smiles when he closed the door behind him. 'Yeah, it's me again.'

'We're about to leave,' said Angie. 'This is fucked.'

'Okay,' said Les. 'But don't go without this.' He handed her the green bag Coyne had given him at the Aquatic Centre.

'What's this?'

'It's your money. Count it. It's all there. Two hundred thousand dollars.'

Angie opened the overnight bag and quickly rifled through it. 'Shit! It is too. Hey look at this everyone! The money's here!'

The garage suddenly seemed to come to life as Angie flashed the bag of money at every one. 'Hey, look at that,' said Clarence.

Jamieson smiled through his loose teeth. 'Unreal.'

'Who brought it over?' asked Rinh. 'Coyne?'

Les shook his head. 'No. It was couriered by taxi.' He turned to Angie. 'So you can stop bagging Nizegy and everybody else now, misery guts. And have a bit of faith in people for once. Christ! Talk about a whinger.'

A self-conscious smile spread over Angie's face. 'I wasn't whingeing Les. I was just . . .'

'Yeah, I know. Whingeing.' Les clapped his hands together. 'Anyway, there's no need to hang around here any longer. The sooner you get on the bus and get going the better.'

'Sounds good to me,' said one of the Crabettes.

Les would have loved to have shaken hands with all the boys and kissed all the Crabettes goodbye. But the boys were all too sore and there wasn't much point in hanging about with the cops cruising around somewhere. They got their stuff from the garage, Angie climbed behind the wheel and the last person to get on the bus was Rinh.

'Well, we did it, Les,' he said.

'Yeah. You sure did, Dogs,' smiled Les. 'You won the grand final and you got the money. Good on you. I'm proud of you.'

'But I don't think we'd have done it without you, Reg.'

'Ohh bullshit! I did nothing. It was fun.'

'Maybe. But we had a talk earlier. And you can have a thousand dollars if you want it.'

'What!?'

'We decided to kick in and give you a thousand dollars.'

'Dogs, get on the bus before I give you another black eye to go with the two you've already got. Go on. Piss off.'

Les put his arms around Rinh before he climbed aboard, then Angie hit the starter and the door closed behind him. She turned the bus around expertly, Les waved everyone off and the last he saw of them was someone waving from the back window as the bus disappeared into the night. Les watched for a moment, then went over to the Datty and got behind the wheel. Oh well, no good hanging around here, he sighed to himself. Goodbye Coogee, goodbye Mud Crabs, goodbye two hundred thousand dollars. He started the engine and reversed back down the driveway. I need my fuckin' head read.

Les flogged the mighty Datty up the hill towards home, still wondering about Neville Nixon and wishing the car radio worked. Anyway Warren should be home. He's a news and current affairs perv. He would have seen something on TV or heard something on the radio for sure. Nizegy busted on his yacht? The one he didn't tell me about . . . Les stared through the windscreen. I'd love to know what's going on. Les was still immersed in thought as he neared the Burnie Street turn off to Clovelly Beach, when his headlights picked up a not bad sort on his side of the road in a pair of cut down jeans and a dark blue T-shirt. It was Houston trying in vain to catch a taxi. Les stopped a metre or two in front of her and wound down the window.

'Hey, Spare One,' he called out. 'What are you doing?'

Houston came over and looked in the window. 'Tooties. What's your story?'

'I'm just on my way home. You want a lift to Bondi?'

'Oh, do I what. You going near Sir Thomas Mitchell Road?'

'I go right past it. Jump in.'

'Unreal.' Houston climbed in the front and did up her seat belt. 'So where have you been, Tooties?'

'A wedding,' answered Les.

Houston gave Les a quick once up and down. 'In that outfit? Whose was it? Rock Hudson's?'

'Very funny.' Les gave Houston a quick once up and down as they continued up Arden Street. 'So what are you doing out in the middle of nowhere anyway, Spare One?'

'Ohh Tooties. Would you believe, I've gone down the Clovelly for a Sunday cool one. And I meet this really cool guy. So we're off back to his place in his BMW for a bit of whatever there is. When his totally spare, fucking girlfriend tries to run him off the road in a four wheel drive. They start having this giant blue in the middle of the street. So Tooties got out and left them to it. I mean, you can do without that, thanks very much.'

'How long have you been waiting for a taxi?'

'Too long.'

'Lucky Uncle Les came along.'

'Yeah.' Houston ran her eyes over the crappy upholstery. 'I like your car, too. I didn't know they still allowed these on the road.'

'Only on Sundays. Between six and ten.'

Suddenly Houston got all excited and slapped Les on the knee. 'Oh Patooties, did you hear the news about Neville Nixon?'

'Neville Nixon?' Les looked thoughtful. 'Isn't he the rock promoter? Didn't I see you working on his yacht or something early in the week.'

'That's right,' said Houston. 'Down at Rushcutters Bay. Well the cops busted him on his yacht.'

'Fair dinkum? What happened?'

'Me and Jinny were working on it this morning. We finished what we had to do and wandered up to the club for a feed and a cool one before we went home. Jinny left her jacket behind so we started walking back to the yacht to get it. Next thing there were cops everywhere. The feds, the DEA, the state cops. So Jinny and Tooties just kept on walking.'

'Bloody hell! So what did they get him with?'

'Thai Buddha.'

'What? On the yacht?'

'No. Evidently he'd been bringing shipments in on the yacht, but all the stuff was somewhere in Coogee.'

'Coogee?'

'Yeah. Twenty million dollars in cash. A tonne of dope. I only heard bits and pieces on the news. But fucking how about that, Tooties.'

'Yeah. How about that.' Les started coming down behind Bronte and Tamarama towards Bondi. 'Well, I don't know Houston. I never thought Neville Nixon was in the dope business.'

'Neither did anyone,' said Houston. 'Though I had an idea something was going on.'

'Yeah? Why's that?'

'The cash, Tooties. He seemed to have buckets of it.'

'Nizegy liked the readies eh?'

'Did he what, Tooties. But have a look at this.' Houston opened her handbag. 'He paid me this morning. A thousand dollars. Check it out though.' Houston flashed a roll of fifties with a thick, black rubber band round them. 'Have a look at that. It's all paper money. You can bet this has been buried somewhere.'

Les looked at Houston's roll of money and recognised the rubber band. It was the thousand dollars he'd given Nizegy for the supposed bet. Make that two hundred and one thousand dollars I'm down on the week, Les cursed to himself. The night just gets better.

'Yeah,' said Les. 'I wouldn't be surprised if that was drug money.'

'Not that Tooties gives a stuff what sort of money it is,' said Houston. 'It's all the same in the bank.'

'Yes. I have to agree, Spare One.' Bronte School went past and then Tamarama Beach.

'Did you ever meet Nizegy, Les?'

Les shook his head. 'No. But I heard he wasn't a bad bloke.'

'He sure wasn't. I'd like a dollar for every favour he's done me.'

'You reckon you'd be rich, Spare One.'

Houston gave her handbag with the money in it a pat. 'I'd have a few more of these, Tooties.'

Shortly after, Les pulled up outside the Trattoria on the corner of Campbell Parade and Sir Thomas Mitchell Road. 'Well, here you are, Spare One. Don't say I've never done you a favour.'

'Thanks Les.' Houston started climbing out of her seat belt. 'I'm going in here to meet a girlfriend. She knocks off soon. Why don't you come and have a drink with us? I'll shout.'

'No, I've got to get home. I got other plans. Thanks anyway.'

'Okay. See you, Tooties.'

'Yeah. See you later, Houston.'

Les turned up Lamrock Avenue and a few minutes later he was outside Chez Norton. Parked in front of Warren's Celica was Debbie's purple Mustang. Les switched off the engine and closed his eyes. I think I might just sit here for a little while before I go in and face that. Quiet time.

Feeling a bit weary all of a sudden, Norton rested his head on the steering wheel and had a think. So what's the end result? I just wasted the best part of a week and blew two hundred and one thousand fuckin' dollars. Great. On top of that, Nizegy's been bringing in shipments without telling me and I've been driving all over the place with a boot full of drug money. The cunt. Why did he pick me though? Probably because he genuinely thought he owed me a favour and he knew he could trust me. And why not? I'm a nice mug. Still, I can't really knock him. He made certain I got my money. It's my own silly fuckin' fault if I'm dopey enough to give it all away. And I'm positive he would have paid the boys if he hadn't got busted. No, Nizegy's all right I suppose. But what a genius. He brings in millions of dollars worth of pot, washes it somehow by getting that Extreme Polo thing going on TV, then him and Coyne almost pull off the betting scam of the century. If everything had fallen into place they would have finished up with squillions. All kosher too. Bad luck the wallopers arrived on the scene and stuffed things up. Anyway, I'm home safe and sound. That's the main thing. And did I have a bit of fun? I finally got it together with Kathy – not to mention Evelyn with the giant, humungous boobs. Les chuckled to himself. I even got my photo in the paper again. And bugger it, those kids deserved that money more than I did. I can't really complain. He rubbed his eyes and took in a deep breath. Anyway, let's go inside and see what Croden and Zanna have got to say. Les got his bag from the boot and walked up the front steps.

He dropped his bag in his room first then changed out of his coat and tie into the same blue tracksuit, even if it was getting on the nose. He splashed some water over his face in the bathroom then walked out into the

290

lounge room. Warren was seated on the lounge in a pair of white cotton pants and a black T-shirt. Debbie was sprawled alongside him in a green and white tracksuit and fluffy socks. The TV was on with no sound coming through and they were listening to some FM station on the stereo down low. Two glasses of Vodka and Ruby's Red grapefruit juice were sitting on the coffee table next to the bong and neither of them appeared to be feeling any pain.

'So what's doing, gang?' said Les, spreading himself into the nearest lounge chair. 'I suppose you watched the grand final?'

'Did we ever,' answered Warren. 'What a game! Sen-fucking-sational.'

'Yeah. It was unreal,' said Debbie. 'Especially that last third after the fight.'

'Tell me about it,' said Les. 'I was there. Poolside.'

'Yeah. We saw you on TV. You looked great. I've taped it.'

'Thanks Woz. I did my best.'

'How did the boys finish up after the game?' asked Debbie. 'I heard Brooksie say they weren't real good.'

'They were buggered. I just put them all on the bus back to Wagga. Poor bastards.' Les looked at Debbie. 'Bad luck you never got to meet them before they left. What happened?'

Warren stroked Debbie's leg. 'The poor girl was sick.'

'Sick? Yeah? What was wrong, Zanna?' said Les. 'Space bugs get you?'

'I had a migraine,' replied Debbie. 'So I took a sleeping pill and didn't get up.'

'Oh well. Bad luck, Zanna,' said Les. 'You would have liked them; they were nice blokes.'

'Hey! Talking about nice blokes,' said Warren. 'Have you seen the news?'

'No, I've been flat out with all this other rattle. Why? What's happened?'

'Nizegy got busted.'

'Busted? What do you mean busted?' Les thought he'd compare Warren's version of events with Spare One's before he said anything.

'The cops arrested him on his yacht in Rushcutters Bay, then charged him with all this stuff in a garage in Coogee?'

'A garage in Coogee?' Les gave Warren a double blink. 'Not the one the Mud Crabs were staying in?'

'No, another one. It was on TV. Hang on, I taped that too.' Warren picked up the remote and found the rewind button.

'The cops called the garage Aladdin's Cave,' said Debbie. 'Because of all the loot that was in there.'

'Yeah,' said Warren. 'There was two hundred kilograms of pot. Six million dollars in cash. And a million dollars worth of Krugerrands.'

'Krugerrands?' said Les. 'What are bloody Krugerrands? Klingon hot dogs?'

'South African gold coins. Ounces.' Warren pressed a button on the remote without adjusting the sound. 'There was a bit on Channel 7. And a bigger blurb on the ABC.'

Les stared at the silent TV screen. There was a photo of Neville Nixon in a suit taken a few years ago; film of the yacht bobbing at its moorings in Rushcutters Bay; then film of him getting out of a police car surrounded by big, beefy cops. The screen went fuzzy for a moment, then the ABC coverage came on.

'This is the garage,' said Warren.

Les continued to stare at the TV. There was another shot of Nizegy in a sports coat; more film of him getting out of a police car surrounded by cops; then the camera panned onto a garage in a suburban street. Something about the garage looked familiar. The camera zoomed in on the number, then back over the garage. Les edged forward a little as the newsreader came back on, then the news cut to a flash flood in Europe.

'So what do you think of that?' said Warren.

'Unh,' replied Les, still staring intently at the TV.

'Neville Nixon. Millionaire dope dealer.'

'Unh.'

'And you're working for him. Or were.'

'Unh.'

'Yeah. I can see you're real interested,' said Warren.

'I have to go to the bathroom,' said Debbie.

Warren moved to let Debbie up then turned back to Les. 'So what are you doing now?' Les shook his head and didn't reply. 'Well, I was just going to watch this show on SBS. Vox Populi. It's a TV expression, Les, you naturally wouldn't know about. Catching people on camera when they're not quite ready.'

Les left Warren's words hanging in the air and went to his room. He switched on the light and started rummaging through his dirty clothes basket till he found the pair of white jeans he was wearing that Kathy splattered with Ovaltine on Friday night. The page out of Nizegy's notebook Kathy had handed him at Sunderlands was still in the fob pocket, the page where he got Nizegy to write down the address of the garage that the Mud Crabs were staying in so he could check it out. Les opened it up. It was the same number as the garage on TV. 171. Despite all the passive smoking Les had to endure from Warren's bong, Norton's memory wasn't going on him. Even though it was the wrong one, he'd gone to the right garage all right. Neville Nizegy, or Neville Vague Guy, had written down the wrong address. His dope garage. The one that was on TV. The Aladdin's Cave. The Mud Crabs garage was probably a decoy. Or more than likely Nizegy would use it for another shipment when the boys moved out. Norton's eyes narrowed for a moment. So if the garage on the piece of paper Nizegy gave him was the garage that was on TV ... and if that was the garage he went to in the early hours of Wednesday morning ... Then ...

Norton's feet were moving that fast when he flew out the back door and across the backyard, he didn't notice he'd ripped the flyscreen off its hinges. He was in the toolshed for a couple of minutes, then he flew back inside, slamming the door behind him; he scuttled to his room for a couple more minutes, then came back out to the lounge room and sat down again as if nothing had happened.

Warren stared at him in disbelief. So did Debbie, settled next to Warren after coming back from the bathroom. 'Are you all right?' asked Warren.

'Me?' replied Les. 'Yeah. I'm okay. Good as gold, actually. Why?'

'Didn't you see what you just did?'

'No.'

Debbie kept staring at Les. 'You ran outside and ripped the back door off its hinges. Then ran back inside again like your feet were on fire and your arse was catching.'

'What was that all about?'

'I just went outside to check something, Woz.'

'Like what?'

Les looked at Warren for a second. 'The rock pool.'

Warren waved his hands around and rolled his eyes. Debbie did much the same thing. 'Oh no, not the dreaded rock pool again,' said Warren. 'What's wrong now?'

'It appears I'm still a few tiles short, Woz,' replied Les.

Warren shook his head. 'Stop the fight.'

'Shit!' said Debbie. 'What a bummer. You're still a few tiles short of your rock pool. How many Kahless? Did you count them while you were out there?'

'Yeah,' nodded Les. 'Exactly fifty.' Norton rubbed his big hands together and smiled at Debbie. 'Anyway. Forget the silly bloody rock pool, Zanna. Let's watch the vox popping thing Warren's picked for us on SBS. I got a feeling this could turn out to be a bit of all right.'